The Darkening Hills

ALSO BY KERRY BUCHANAN

HARVEY & BIRCH SERIES
Book 1: Knife Edge
Book 2: Small Bones
Book 3: Deadly Shores
Book 4: The Darkening Hills

THE
DARKENING
HILLS

KERRY
BUCHANAN

Harvey & Birch Book 4

Joffe Books, London
www.joffebooks.com

First published in Great Britain in 2024

© Kerry Buchanan 2024

Cover art by Nebojša Zorić

ISBN: 978-1-83526-786-8

To Jane, Brian and Kirsty, whose tales of life in Africa inspired me to write this book, and to Eddie Matchett, a real-life adventurer who is sadly missed.

PROLOGUE

County Antrim, Northern Ireland

Outside, the dog howled its grief and confusion to the rising sun. Inside the cottage, the heavy, metallic scent of its master reached even Caro's less sensitive nostrils, as the last of his lifeblood pooled on the stone floor.

It had taken many years and all her skill to follow each tenuous lead. Most had petered out as dead ends, or false clues he'd scattered as he'd run, but she had him now. He'd anticipated a hunter on his trail; he'd changed both his name and his appearance, turned his back on his profession, and gone to ground in a most unlikely part of the island.

She'd been able to take her time with him — he'd chosen such a remote place to make his den that there'd be no one nearby to hear his screams — and she had so very many years of grief and hatred to release.

Awareness still flickered in the depths of those pale eyes. Soon, they'd glaze over in death, and then she'd be free of him. Free of the hatred that had driven her to dedicate the best years of her life to this relentless quest.

The final breath left his body in a low gurgle, frothing from his lips. His chest fell, and didn't rise again.

She waited until the eyes took on that flat, membranous look of death. The moment passed, but the release she'd been promised didn't come. Bitterness still poisoned her mind, churning in her belly. Would she never be free?

With a feral scream, she raised her hands to the sky. They were red to the elbow with her victim's blood, but that wasn't enough. She fell to her knees, stooping until her lips touched his cooling flesh, and drank. As she drank, she made a vow. No other woman would suffer what she had suffered if she could prevent it.

CHAPTER 1

Gerren Penrose staggered as cold morning air collided with the beery fumes rising from his over-full belly. Maybe he should have gone a little easier on the beer last night. He remembered May Dunlop laughing like a girl as she pushed yet another bottle of the local brew across the table to him.

His battered Series III Land Rover sat alongside the wall of the old surgery, as she had since he bought her almost new more than thirty years before, when he came to Northern Ireland as a young vet. She was probably worth a fortune by now, especially since the company, bought out by some big foreign group, had stopped making proper workhorses and was instead pandering to the Chelsea Tractor set. But he wouldn't part with Poppy for all the real ale in the glens.

He tried to put the key in the lock, but the damn thing wouldn't stay still, and the key slid across the pale blue paintwork, leaving a metallic scrape behind. Blast!

He bent down to peer at the lock, but it looked as it always did. Maybe he had the wrong key.

After two more attempts, he managed to get the key in, turned it, and opened the door. The familiar smell of farm manure and old diesel oil hit him, and he smiled. The driver's

3

seat had worn through, allowing the foam stuffing to peek out in places. The leather was stiff from years of him climbing in with coveralls soaked in blood, urine, faeces, or a combination of all three.

He eased himself behind the wheel. It seemed to have moved out a bit over the years; he didn't remember it pressing so hard against his belly in the past. He made himself as comfortable as he could for the drive out to Rob's wee farm in the hills. At least there was little traffic at this time in the morning, with the sun barely risen above the heather-covered slopes.

On the main roads, Poppy annoyed other drivers with her slow speed, and by wandering wherever the hell she wanted across the wide, level surface. Only when Gerren turned into the first of a web of winding lanes, each narrower than the one before, did the old Landy begin to shine. The last mile was along a rough track that barely deserved the name. Two parallel furrows wound between steep banks and outcrops of rock with barely enough width even for Poppy in places.

Deep pools of standing water sat in the tracks, but the old Landy splashed through them, her engine growling happily, rocking her driver from side to side in his seat.

He'd told Rob often enough that he should drop some rubble into the biggest holes to make it more passable, but his friend just laughed and said it was his best security measure.

At last, the roof of the cottage came into view over the top of a clump of whin. Odd that there was no smoke from the chimney. Rob usually kept the solid fuel range burning day and night even in summer because it heated his tiny home against the Antrim chill, heated his water, and was his only way to cook food.

He parked Poppy at the front of the cottage. "Hovel" would be a better name, perhaps. It had once been thatched, but now it had a rusted tin roof, and the walls had been built more than a hundred years ago of mud and rubble. Two small paned windows stared out like eyes, one either side of the low door, green paint peeling from the woodwork to reveal layers of faded colours beneath.

Gerren climbed out, his hangover forgotten. The back of his neck itched as though someone was watching him.

Rob's dog, Jack, usually ran out barking at the sound of Poppy's engine, tail wagging so hard it shook the old collie's back end with it. He'd take a lump out of anyone else who visited, but he and Gerren were old friends, despite the smell of the surgery that lingered on the vet's clothes.

Rob must have taken the dog up into the hills for a long walk, maybe with his easel and charcoal. The old man liked to sit and paint when the light was right, although he'd never shown his work to anyone but Gerren. That's where he'd be. On a low tussock, skinny arse perched on his waxed jacket to keep the damp from his worn corduroys, lost in contemplation of nature's beauty spread out before him. He often painted sunrises, the shades of blood red and purple suiting his style.

Gerren turned slowly, scanning the surrounding hills. The cottage was in a little glen of its own, surrounded by higher ground. Rob wouldn't have expected him this morning — he usually went up in the evening, but he'd been distracted last night — so his friend could be anywhere. There was no point trying to guess which way the man had gone, but it seemed a pity to have come up all this way for nothing.

And he really needed a cup of tay.

He'd go inside and put the kettle on the stove, that's what he'd do. When Rob got back, he'd find the tea stewed to perfection and he'd be glad to sit with his feet up, drying his socks in front of the hot oven door.

Happy with his decision, Gerren walked across to the cottage and went inside.

* * *

The slaughterhouse stench — blood and faeces and fear — knocked him back on his heels. Gerren stood in the doorway and blinked, willing his eyes to adjust from the brightness outside to the dim interior of the cottage. All the hairs on the back of his neck were standing up, but he told himself to wise up. There'd be an explanation for it. There had to be.

A rectangle of sunlight stretched away from him across the floor, broken up by his shadow. Something lay there, just at the very edge of the light. He leaned forward, bending at the waist, trying to see what it was. A glove? His eyes adjusted a little more to the darkness. Gloves didn't have blood-encrusted fingernails.

The fingers, thick and callused from hard labour, were half-bent, raised towards the ceiling as if in supplication, but where the wrist should have been, Gerren could see only the pattern of the rug.

He didn't throw up — decades of treating horrific wounds in animals had hardened him. Instead, he stepped closer so he could see around the door frame into the living space of the two-roomed cottage.

Other body parts were scattered across the sanded floor. A foot lay by the cold range, with a woollen sock still on it. There was a hole in the knitted end and a big toe stuck through. The nail of the toe was thickened and ingrowing.

Rob — what was left of him — was propped up against the small two-seater sofa by the far wall. He wore a faded checked shirt and a dark green moleskin waistcoat, but the waistcoat had been torn open, the buttons popped so they'd fallen around it on the floor like confetti, and the shirt beneath was so blackened by blood that it took Gerren a moment to realise that there was a ragged, gaping hole where his chest wall should be.

He didn't remember getting outside, opening Poppy's door, reaching across for his mobile phone, and dialling 999, but he must have done all those things, because a professionally detached female voice was asking him questions and sounding slightly impatient because he wasn't answering.

"Which service do you require?"

She may have said it more than once.

"Police," he said. No point in asking for an ambulance. "Someone's died."

6

The operator's interest sharpened. "Just police, sir? No other service?"

"Just police."

There was a click on the line and a pause, then another professional voice answered. "Police emergency. Please give me your name, the address you're calling from, and the nature of the emergency."

"I'm Gerren Penrose," he said. "I'm at Rob Harris's place, up in the hills above Ballygroggan. I've found a body."

"Could you repeat that please, sir? You've found a body?"

"Yes. A dead body. Only it's not in one piece. I think it's Rob, but I can't be certain."

The operator's voice remained calm and professional. "Can you describe precisely where you are, please, sir? I'm sending a team out to you now, but they need to know exactly where to go."

Gerren did his best to describe the location of the remote farmstead, but he'd driven this way too many times over the years to be able to remember landmarks. He just *knew* the route. It didn't take conscious thought.

"But they won't be able to drive up here, not in a police car. They'll need a Landy or something."

"If you stay on the line, sir, we'll triangulate your position and then they can get straight to you."

The bright young man on the other end of the phone didn't seem to have heard what he'd said about the track not being passable. Well, they'd find out soon enough.

He couldn't bring himself to go back inside, so he leaned against Poppy's warm bonnet. Despite the August sunshine, a deep chill had entered his bones.

His mind still shied away from replaying in detail what he'd seen inside the cottage. Maybe it had been some sort of sick joke? A children's guy or a clothes shop dummy staged to look like a dead body. He wondered what his punishment would be for wasting police time. Probably double what it normally was, after they'd dragged themselves all the way up here.

Maybe he should go back inside to make sure he hadn't been seeing things. He'd drunk a fair bit last night.

That raised another concern. What if they breathalysed him? Would he be over the limit for driving? Beads of sweat broke out all over his skin.

He swallowed and forced himself away from the comfort of the car. One more look. It couldn't do any harm, surely?

He was halfway across the yard when a new sound caught his attention. A faint squeak, like a door with rusted hinges blowing in the breeze. But there was no breeze.

He turned slowly, trying to work out where the sound had come from.

There was only one place it could be. The big, open-fronted shed where Rob kept his tractor and his winter store of hay for the handful of sheep he grazed on the hill. There'd be wooden hurdles stacked there, ready to be used to build lambing pens come winter, but there were no doors to creak.

Gerren walked towards it. Only as he moved into the deeper shadow cast by the high roof did it dawn on him that there could be a murderer lurking nearby.

He hesitated, undecided, then the sound came again. It wasn't so much a squeak as a whimper, and it had come from underneath the little grey Ferguson tractor.

Heart pounding, Gerren dropped to his knees in the dry dirt and lowered his head. The ground beneath the tractor was covered in wind-blown straw and spider webs, but there was a puddle of darkness there too, deeper than the shadows.

"Jack?"

Another whine and a rustle as a feebly beating tail stirred the straw. He reached out to the dog and his hand met the thick ruff of hair around its neck. He took a handful and tugged. "Come on, lad. Let's have a look at you."

The dog yelped as he pulled it out into the light, but it didn't try to bite him. Its tail was clamped tight between its back legs as it cowered at his feet with flattened ears, licking its lips nervously.

"It's all right, Jack," Gerren said, but his voice broke on the words, because fresh blood stained his hands where he'd hauled the dog out by its scruff. Whether the dog's blood or that of its master, nothing was ever going to be all right again for either of them.

CHAPTER 2

The police finally arrived on foot, a man and a woman, both in uniform and wearing deep scowls. Mud splattered their dark trousers all the way to the hips, and in the case of the woman, who wasn't tall, almost to waist height.

"Mr Penrose?" the male officer asked, but it came out more like an accusation than a question.

"Yes, that's me."

He'd placed the injured dog in the back of his Landy. He still had enough supplies back there to give Jack an injection of long-acting antibiotic, and he'd managed to clean up and decontaminate some of the dog's wounds. The rest would have to wait until he got back to the surgery, where he could clip the blood-matted hair away and maybe suture—

Except he couldn't, because the surgery didn't belong to him anymore, did it? The building and its contents now belonged to a big chain of vets that planned to turn it into a "Centre of Excellence".

"I understand you think you've seen a dead body?" the man said. His tone made his doubts clear. "Could you show us where?"

Gerren nodded wordlessly towards the cottage, hands still in his pockets.

The older officer tramped to the entrance, snapping on a pair of gloves but he didn't do more than peer around the doorway, the same as Gerren had.

Bile rose in his throat. Now the police were here, he was beginning to think he'd imagined the whole thing. If it hadn't been for Jack's blood staining his hands, he might have.

There was silence from the cottage for perhaps the length of five heartbeats, then he heard retching noises and the officer stumbled away from the door, his hand to his mouth. It was useless. Vomit seeped from between his gloved fingers, splashing his uniform, his hand, and the door post he leaned against to keep himself upright.

The woman asked him a question, to which he nodded, then she was straight on the radio, presumably confirming that the call had not been a hoax and there really was a body.

"And tell them they'll need at least a four-wheel drive, maybe a tractor to get up here. We had to abandon our car over half a mile from the place." Then she turned to Gerren, ignoring her colleague, who was pale and sweaty but vaguely vertical again. "When did you arrive here, Mr Penrose?"

Gerren pulled a hand out of his pocket and checked his watch. "An hour? Maybe a little less. I didn't check the time when I got here."

The two officers were staring at him, open-mouthed. The man had his hand on the black plastic grip of the gun in his belt, and he looked as if he was about to draw it.

Gerren glanced nervously over his shoulder, thinking the murderer must have appeared, but there was no one there. When he turned back, both had their guns drawn and the barrels pointing steadily at him.

"Put your hands behind your head, sir," said the woman. "Turn around slowly and drop to your knees."

"What's going on?" he asked. This couldn't be happening. He tried to obey. He got his hands up, and as he did, realised what they'd seen. His right hand was gloved in dried blood where he'd pulled Jack out from under the tractor. The

11

relief was overwhelming. "This isn't human blood," he began, holding out the offending arm. "It's—"

"Get down!" The two officers stepped away from each other, their faces cold and calculating as they bracketed him with their weapons. "Now!"

He tried, but his old knees wouldn't bend. He got so far, then without the support of his hands, which he still had raised, his body collapsed and he landed face down in the mud. He must have let out a groan, because the next thing he knew, a growling, snarling hairy shape was between him and the two police officers.

"Down, Jack!" he managed, then, "Don't shoot! It's Rob's dog. He was attacked too. Please don't hurt him!"

The stand-off might have gone on for some time if the dog hadn't turned to lick Gerren's face, whining. He was on three legs, one foreleg dangling uselessly, but the aggression had gone out of him.

"Please don't shoot him," he said. "The blood's his. Whoever did . . . that . . . in the cottage, they hurt him too. I'm a vet. I was trying to help him."

He got through to them at last. The woman was first to put her gun away, and the man not far behind, but they still kept a wary distance, and Gerren didn't think it was just because of the dog.

"Can I get up, please?"

The woman nodded. He tried to rise, but his feet slipped in the stinking mud, and Jack didn't help by fussing around him, whining and licking. On the third attempt, he managed to turn himself so he was sitting up instead of face down, and massaged his left knee. "Maybe I'll stay as I am. Not as young as I used to be."

The woman made an impatient noise and came over to him, side-eyeing the dog. When Jack made no aggressive move, she held out a gloved hand to Gerren and he allowed her to help him to his feet.

His tweed jacket was ruined, caked with mud and shit. He'd treasured it over the decades, removing it and laying it carefully on a clean gate or wall before he'd done anything dirty. It was a symbol of his profession, a badge of honour. The tweed jacket with the leather patches on the elbows. Gone, with all the rest of his professional pride. He was reduced to a tramp with beery breath.

The sound of an engine drifted to him on the breeze: a Range Rover, set in low ratio, no doubt, churning its way through mud and over the rocks until it pulled up in the yard behind Poppy. A uniformed copper sat behind the wheel, but the low sun hid the identity of the passenger until the door opened and a young man climbed out. Tall and thin with a mop of unruly dark hair that flopped over his forehead, he wore an open-necked shirt beneath a black jacket — and he'd had the forethought to put wellies on, sensible lad.

"Mr Penrose?" The newcomer couldn't have failed to notice the blood and mud, but he remained respectful. "I'm Detective Sergeant Aaron Birch." He raised an eyebrow, letting his eyes wander over Gerren's dishevelled state. "Are you all right, sir?"

"Yes, Sergeant. I fell, that's all." Gerren didn't look at the other two officers, but he could feel the slight unwinding of tension as he spoke. He wasn't going to make a fuss, and that was a relief to them, he was sure.

He found a length of baling twine in his pocket and fashioned it into a makeshift lead for Jack, but the old dog had run out of steam. He lay by Gerren's feet, panting, occasionally licking at any wounds he could reach.

"Will you be okay for a bit longer if I go inside and take a look? I have scene of crime officers on their way up here, but they might be a while. I'd like a chat with you in a moment, once I've got the lie of the land."

Gerren immediately took to this confident young detective. "I'm going nowhere, lad. You do what you need to do."

CHAPTER 3

When the four-wheel drive had finally sucked itself out of the quagmire that led up to the cottage, the sight that met Aaron's eyes sent his heart plummeting. The cottage sat in a hollow, dwarfed by the scrubby hills around it and shaded by conifers on one side that grew almost to the back wall. A corrugated tin roof that might have once been green was now more rust than paint. A chimney stood up from the centre of the roofline, and the walls were green with slime. Against one side, a low lean-to shed held chopped logs ready for the winter.

But it was the ancient Land Rover standing outside the cottage that had first caught his attention, and the elderly man leaning against it with a scruffy black-and-white collie at his feet. Both man and dog were filthy, caked in mud; the man's hand was dark with blood, and the responding police officers looked hostile. Even now, as he stepped away from Gerren Penrose and made for the cottage, Aaron wasn't too pleased with the way the two PCs had handled things. He'd have to have a word with his new team about their bedside manner, that was for sure.

This would be Aaron's first major crime scene on his own, without a more senior officer telling him what to do. He needed to do everything by the book here. No contaminating the scene, but he had to see for himself what had happened.

The smell was bad even from outside the cottage. He didn't go inside, just peered around the partition that protected the rooms from the wind when the front door opened. Flies rose in a lazy cloud and settled again on a shape over near the far wall. Aaron waited for his eyes to adjust, and gradually the shape resolved itself into the upper part of a body.

His old DI and good friend Asha Harvey had taught him to compartmentalise his mind at times like this. *'Don't think of a body as a person who's been walking and talking until recently. Think of it as a science project. Analyse it. Focus on details at first until your head's in the right place. We can't afford to have empathy when we first walk the scene; that comes later, and it's what drives us to bring the killer to justice.'*

So he was able to mentally catalogue what he saw in that room, speculating on what might have happened, without becoming too involved in the person whose body parts these were. He peered into the second room. This was a small bedroom, with a single bed against the far wall, neatly made, and a wardrobe against the wall at the front of the house. The room was dim and shadowed, lit only by the single small window to the front of the building.

Moving away from the cottage, he drew in clean, fresh air with relief.

"What do you think, sir?" asked PC Gordon. "Is he lying?"

Aaron looked down at her. "What makes you ask that, Nic?"

She shrugged. "I thought he looked a bit shifty, that's all."

"What really happened up here before I arrived?" he asked. "The mud on Penrose's coat is fresh."

She flushed and didn't quite meet his eye. "We saw the blood on his hands, and thought—"

"I hope you didn't manhandle him? He must be seventy if he's a day."

15

"Didn't lay a hand on him," she said stiffly. "But he's lucky one of us didn't shoot the dog. I thought it was going to go for us."

The collie was flaked out on its side, chest rising and falling quickly. The old man was bending over it, worried. Blood matted the pale fur on its belly. A lot of blood.

"Is he okay?" Aaron asked, walking over.

"I should be getting him down to the village," Penrose said. "Need to clip away the fur and see how much damage he's taken. He's not a young dog, are you, Jack?"

The dog wagged its tail, but it was still panting, eyes closed.

Aaron stooped to fondle the dog's ears, and the creature leaned into the contact. "Do you need me to call an ambulance?" he asked the old man. "So the paramedics can check you over. You must have had quite a shock this morning."

"I'm fine, thank you. I'm fit to answer any questions you have."

"I'll need to get a formal statement later," Birch said, "but for now, could you run through the basic facts while my colleague makes notes?"

"Ask away, lad."

"When did you last see Mr Harris?"

Penrose hesitated. "We usually meet up a couple of times a week," he said at last. "I think the last time was a couple of nights ago. Usually I come up here, bring some beer with me, and we sit and chat and play dominoes."

Birch nodded. "Was it always evenings, then?"

"Nearly always. Rob was an artist. Oils. He liked to walk the hills with Jack during the day." Penrose gestured to the dog at his feet. A tail wagged at the sound of his name. "He'd stop and sketch whenever the mood took him, then finish the painting when he got home."

"So, what brought you up here this morning?"

"I was supposed to come up here last night, but I . . . I got an invitation to dinner, so I didn't. I meant to, but I'd

16

had a couple of beers, and I decided driving wasn't a good idea." He swallowed, looking shifty. "That's why I came up this morning."

"What's the name of this friend?" Birch asked. "And how long were you there?"

Penrose looked as if he was struggling within himself, but he quickly seemed to give up the fight. "May Dunlop. She and her son have the butcher's shop on Hill Street. I was there until, I dunno, maybe nine?"

Aaron made a decision. "If you've given PC Gordon here your address and phone number, you can go and sort out this fella. But I'll still need you to come to the station as soon as you can to sign your statement and answer a few more questions."

"Thank you," Penrose said. "I'm right grateful to you, and so would the dog be, if he understood."

He lifted the injured collie carefully and carried it over to the old Land Rover, placing it in the back. Then he climbed in and started the car. A puff of black smoke shot out of the exhaust, and the roar of the engine might have woken the dead, but the vehicle moved away smoothly enough, bumping over the rough ground until it disappeared down the track towards the main road.

"There was alcohol on his breath," said the male officer, whose name Aaron was struggling to remember. Aaron had only been posted in Ballymena police station a little over a week, and he still hadn't met all the other officers yet. Stanley, that was his name, but was it his first name or his surname?

"Quite probably," he said. "He admitted to having a beer too many last night, and that's why he didn't drive up here then."

"Not that we know of," Stanley muttered darkly. "Maybe he did drive up here. Fell out with his old mucker, Rob. Lost his temper, and Bob's your uncle. Realised what he'd done, so he drove back down to the town to establish an alibi, and then came up here this morning to 'discover' the terrible crime and report it."

Aaron regarded the older man coldly. "You really think an old man who can hardly bend his knees could cut up a human body? You've been watching too many American cop shows. We follow the evidence."

Nic Gordon turned away. Aaron thought it was to hide a smile, but he couldn't be sure.

"I think he's coming back, sir," Nic said. "Listen."

The engine noise that had been receding into the distance was growing louder. Aaron listened, then he smiled. "Nope. I think that might be our SOCOs."

He was proved right when a small van bumped into the clearing. How Marley had managed to get it through the potholes in that lane without ripping out the sump, Aaron couldn't even begin to imagine, but the mud splattering its sides gave evidence of its struggle.

The driver was a big man who struggled to squeeze his paunch into a white forensic suit, but the passenger was a petite redhead with a scattering of freckles across her nose.

"Hello, Jana, Marley. Glad to see you two."

"Yeah, thanks so much for dragging us out all this way to the rear end of nowhere," Jana said in her clipped Polish accent. "Where's the body?"

She was never as friendly to Aaron as she was to Asha, but he was still relieved to see her. She was the best, and they'd worked together many times.

"In the house," he said.

"And how many people have been tramping over our crime scene with their big PC Plod feet?" she asked.

"No one's been all the way in," he said. "Just stood in the entrance hall and peered into both rooms." He glanced at PC Gordon and she nodded agreement.

"I'm afraid there's some vomit near the door." She flashed a look at her partner, but he said nothing, arms folded as if it had nothing to do with him. "The man who found the body said he'd only gone in as far as the entrance too."

"Hey, Nic!" Jana said, raising a hand for a high-five that PC Gordon returned with a grin. "The grapevine whispered that you had gone to the dark side and sold your soul."

Nic glanced at Aaron a little warily. "More rented out my soul for now, Jana. Still a probationer."

"Oh, you will have no trouble," the little redhead said scornfully. "Okay. Leave us to it, then. We will tell you when you can come in."

* * *

When in doubt, Aaron always asked DI Asha Harvey's opinion. In this case, he was in more doubt than he liked. The old man, Gerren Penrose, had seemed an innocent soul, but he knew better than most that outward appearances didn't always give away what went on inside someone's head.

He walked up to the top of the hill behind the cottage, and found an outcrop of granite that would serve well enough as a seat. Before he sat down, he turned slowly, taking in the low hills covered in heather and bracken in all directions. The only sign of habitation for as far as he could see on this clear day was the tin-roofed cottage he'd just come from. Apart from birds and a few grubby specks that probably represented sheep, there wasn't a living soul to be seen. Not a wisp of smoke from a chimney, not the dark ribbon of a road. The only sound, apart from the occasional rumble of voices from the yard below, was an eerie *cur-lee* sound from an undistinguished brown bird with a long beak, and the rippling, musical song of a skylark far above in the leaden grey sky.

Asha picked up on the third ring. "Hello, stranger. How's it going in the back of beyond?"

He laughed. "If you only knew. I'm currently freezing my butt off sitting on a rock in the middle of nowhere."

"That sounds like fun," she said. "Are they giving the new boy all the shitty jobs?"

"No. They've been very supportive. In fact, I'm on a murder case right now."

19

"Oh?"

"Yes. Not nice. Dismembered corpse of an elderly white male found in his cottage by his equally elderly friend this morning."

Asha made a sympathetic noise. "How's the friend coping?"

Typical of her to go straight for the human angle. "Pretty shaken, I think. Didn't help that when our first responders appeared, he was covered in blood. They leaped to conclusions, and he ended up in the mud, poor old sod."

"Not surprised. How come he had blood on him?"

"The victim's dog was injured in the attack, and the old man is a vet. Says he was tending to the dog's wounds, and that's how he got all the blood on him."

"But you're not sure?"

He sighed. "I'm ninety-nine per cent sure." He stared down at the scene below. A windowless van was struggling through the mud, followed by a small SUV he hoped belonged to the duty pathologist. The van would be here to take the remains away for post-mortem, although they'd have to kick their heels until the pathologist had examined the body. "But I've just realised that I let him leave with the injured dog and I should have sent him to the forensics medical officer first."

The silence that followed went on a little too long. "I suggest you get after him pronto and get the clothes bagged up. It might not matter, but then it might be vital if he turns out to be your prime suspect."

"I'll go now." He felt sick. It was a rookie error. He should never have let Penrose leave the scene. Not for the first time, he wondered why the hell he'd ever taken his sergeant's exams. He wasn't cut out to be in charge of a case.

"Aaron?"

"What?" His voice sounded leaden even to him.

"Don't regret mistakes, just learn from them. Does the old man have an alibi for the time of the murder?"

"We don't have a time of death yet. But Asha, there are body parts scattered all over that cottage — it must have been a frenzied attack. This old retired vet isn't exactly spry."

"Maybe so, but a vet knows his way about with a surgical saw, so wait for the forensic evidence, huh?" she reminded him. "You should go after him and get his consent to being swabbed and all the rest. The sooner, the better."

"Yes, boss."

"Not your boss this time," she said.

"The sooner Sergeant McBride gets back from maternity leave and I can get back into civilisation, the happier I'll be," he grumbled.

Despite his sinking feeling at his error in letting Penrose go early, his mood had lifted after the call. Asha always had that effect on him.

He strode down the hill, grateful for the new boots he'd bought for this short-term placement. Jana and Marley were taking a break by their van, Jana chatting away in her usual fashion and Marley looking grumpy.

"Anything I need to know?" he asked.

Jana shrugged. "It's a bloody abattoir in there. Someone has tramped through the blood, knelt in the blood, dipped their hands in the blood—" Aaron thought of Penrose with his arm covered in gore to the elbow —"and apparently there are traces of saliva around some of the wounds. You will be keeping the pathologist busy, my friend." She flashed him a smile so brief he wasn't sure he hadn't imagined it.

It was a while before the pathologist emerged from the cottage with a clipboard tucked under her arm. This was a young woman Aaron hadn't met before, and she was frowning as she stripped off her protective clothing. When she saw Aaron, she gave a brittle smile and held out a chunky hand. "Doctor Shaw. Are you the SIO?"

He shook the hand, trying not to wince at her grip. "Yes. DS Aaron Birch from Ballymena."

She held his hand a little longer than he considered strictly necessary. "New there?"

"Temporary post to cover maternity leave," he said.

"Oh yes. Sheenagh McBride. She'll be back as soon as she can, if I know her."

Aaron tugged his hand out of her grip, not in the mood for small talk. "Is the saliva canine?" he asked, thinking of the injured collie.

She shrugged. "We won't know until we get the lab results back, but I don't expect so. Any paw marks in the blood were overlaid by more blood, and by the handprints and footprints. I'd guess human."

A jolt of revulsion passed through him, but he forced himself to ask the question. "Any toothmarks, or just saliva?"

"Clever boy," Dr Shaw said, as if he was the dog in question. "Yes. Definitely not a dog."

"Do you have an estimate for time of death yet?"

She grimaced. "Recent." She consulted her notes. "I won't bore you with detail, but I'd estimate between four thirty and six o'clock this morning."

He mulled over her words as Constable O'Neill drove him back down the track to the road and all the way into the village of Ballygroggan. Judging by the time of the 999 call Penrose had made, he must have arrived up there not much after six in the morning. It could put him in the frame for the murder.

Penrose's faded-blue Land Rover was parked down a side street in front of a terraced cottage. The paint on the front door had been a brave blue at some time, but now it was bleached and beginning to peel. Hollyhocks and roses surrounded the entrance, and the tiny front garden was green, filled with herbs that scented the air.

Aaron pressed the doorbell, but there was no sound, so he knocked for good measure.

Gerren Penrose opened the door, wiping his hands on a towel. "Looking for me?"

"Mr Penrose," Aaron's heart sank at the clean arms and scrubbed hands. He should have taken a sample of the blood from the old man's arms as well, he realised belatedly. Still, he could scrape under the nails and hopefully find something to work with. They'd need to know if it was animal or human, and he'd better get a set of fingerprints while he was at it, for elimination purposes if nothing else. "How's the dog getting on?"

The black-and-white collie stood in the hall, a little wobbly and lopsided where his long fur had been shaved in patches. It wagged its tail and staggered, almost falling over. The shaved areas showed the severity of the old dog's injuries, and neat lines of stitches made a ragged pattern across its flank and shoulder. It looked to Aaron's uneducated eye as if the dog had been lucky to walk away from the attack.

"He'll be all right," the vet said gruffly. "Won't you, Jack?" His face hardened. "But if I could get my hands on the man that did this, to Rob and to him, I couldn't answer for my actions."

"Hmm. Can you spare me a few minutes, please, Mr Penrose?"

CHAPTER 4

Caro watched the tall, slim man making a phone call not thirty metres from her hiding place. She'd plastered herself with cold mud and stuck heather and marsh grass all over to break up her outline. If she stayed still, a searcher might walk within feet of her and never suspect her presence. And she was good at staying still.

But all their focus seemed to be on the old man in the beaten-up jeep. She allowed herself a small smile. She couldn't have ordered it better. Her hand throbbed where the old collie had bitten her, but she bore it no ill will. It was just defending its own. Still, she should have killed it. She was getting soft.

With infinite patience, she watched as the local police worked, searching for the weapon — which they'd never find — and filling plastic bags with evidence. The remains of her victim were carried out in a black body bag on a stretcher. That answered a question that had been amusing her for the last hour or two: would they carry out each body part in a separate evidence bag, or shove everything in the same bag? Now she knew.

Finally, the SOCOs drove off in their white van, and the farm was calm again. Blue-and-white tape fluttered in the breeze, warning away sightseers, but this place was so remote that the chance of anyone making it this far to satisfy their voyeuristic impulses was slight. Maybe once it made the news programmes, but not until then.

She waited until the sun was setting behind the heather-topped hills, before easing herself to her feet. Even then, she stayed low, moving slowly and keeping below the skyline in case the police had left anyone on guard down there.

The place was empty. She strolled around, making sure to walk only on the stones and clumps of grass so she left no trace of her presence.

Inside the cottage, she trailed her gloved fingers along the wall. His dried blood, sprayed across the whitewashed wall, made an impressionist image that reminded her of a wolf, howling to the moon.

She had time, this evening, to explore his world. To try to understand how so dangerous a man had been able to live in this little rural idyll. How could a man like him have found peace here? How could his conscience allow it?

A framed painting on the wall made her pause. It depicted a wild ocean scene with waves rising almost to the height of the towering cliffs that dominated the left-hand side of the picture. Dark and frowning, these masses of black stone seemed to suck the eye into their depths.

But moonlight leaked between dark clouds, casting a silvery hue on the peaks of the waves, giving them a life of their own. If she inhaled, she could almost smell the salt and seaweed, almost hear the seagulls' wailing cries.

She shook herself and tore her eyes away from the picture. Now she knew how he'd coped. He'd let the darkness within him seep into his art.

The knife slid down her sleeve and into her hand without any conscious thought. She might have killed him in the flesh, but his evil lived on in his work. She slashed, almost expecting the canvas to scream, but all she got was ripping fabric. Another slash, and another. Strips of canvas flapped like ribbons with the wind of her frenzied attack.

Finally, she stood with heaving chest, a snarl curling her lips, spittle in white flecks across her chin. There would be more paintings, and she needed to destroy each one if she was to wipe his taint from the earth.

It was full dark before she'd finished. She took his ruined creations outside into the yard, under the overhang of the hay barn, and poured petrol on the pile of splintered wood and torn canvas. A flick of her lighter and flames shot up, reaching for the ceiling. The floor was thick with scattered hay and straw, and before long she had to step smartly back to avoid little fires started by flying sparks.

As she walked away across the hill, she didn't bother to glance back over her shoulder. The fire might spread to the cottage, or it might not, but it didn't matter. His spirit wasn't there anymore. It was burning in hell, where it should have been decades ago, twisting and snapping in the night breeze.

It took her an hour to walk to where she'd left her car, hidden in a dry ditch and covered with old wet straw she'd stolen from a field shelter that stank of cattle. It wouldn't have stood up to a close examination, but she'd broken up its outlines and hard edges enough to trick the eye of a casual observer. She used the ten-litre canister of water she'd stored in the boot to wash any traces of blood and mud from her skin, then changed into clean clothes, bundling the filthy ones into a black bag to be dealt with later.

The drive into Belfast passed in a blur. Her mind raced, thinking back over the years since her mother had confessed, finally, to who her real father was.

There'd been a moment of relief when she'd learned that she wasn't the daughter of the monster who'd made her childhood a misery and driven her mother to suicide, but that feeling had rapidly been overtaken by fury.

She'd been a bastard all her life and never known it.

She could have lived a comfortable life, the daughter of an army officer, but instead, she'd been the unwanted and unloved adopted child of a mean industrialist who cared more for his shipments than he'd ever care for any human being, a man who'd beaten her each time she'd met his eye or spoken when she hadn't been told to. At least she knew why now.

At the age of seventeen, even before she knew the truth about her parentage, Caro had started martial arts classes, joined a gun club, built on her natural fitness and stamina. At first, she'd kept it secret from Pieter, but when he'd found out, he'd encouraged her, recommending a former Olympic marksman as a coach and taking an interest in her progress. Later, when she learned the truth about her blood father, she wondered if he'd set her on this track on purpose.

She was so angry, and had been looking for someone she could punish, make suffer as she had suffered. She'd promised herself that once she'd punished her father for abandoning her and her mother to a life of pain, she'd find peace of a sort — but the promised release still hadn't come.

She pulled up outside the hostel, intending to run in and grab her bag before returning the hire car. The hostel and car booking were both in the name of one of her alter egos, but she didn't want to hang around this godforsaken place any longer than she had to.

The foyer buzzed with raised voices as she strode through, but she kept her head down and didn't break her stride. Within minutes, she was in the lift and along the corridor to the room she'd rented for two nights.

There was another woman, sitting on the window ledge in the six-bed dorm with her knees pulled up to her chin, but Caro paid her no attention. Her bag lay ready-packed, so she retrieved it and her belt-purse from her locker at the foot of her bunk bed. It contained a choice of passports, and cards in names to match as well as cash in euros, sterling and dollars. She checked it all, shielding her actions with her body.

As she turned to leave, a tiny sound drew her eye to the figure on the windowsill. The woman, barely bigger than a child, had tried to pull her black hijab across her face, but it wasn't enough to disguise eyes reddened from crying.

27

Caro hesitated. She didn't have time for this. Two steps and she'd be away, out of this room and on the move again like a shadow, impossible to pin down. And she had a phone call to make, as soon as she could. But not now, not in the middle of the night.

Then another sob escaped from the frightened figure. The eyes looked young, childlike in the dark-skinned face.

In a flash, Caro was back in South Africa, cowering at the end of her own bed while her father — stepfather — drew back his arm to take another swing at her.

She lowered her bag to the ground slowly, not making any sudden moves, then crouched down, not getting any closer to the woman.

"Do you need help?" she asked. It was the question she'd prayed someone would ask her, but no one ever had.

A little head shake, eyes wide and frightened.

Caro sighed and sank down to a sitting position. "Well, if you don't need help, that's fine. I'll just sit here for a while and keep you company. If you need to talk, I'll listen."

CHAPTER 5

With Jack laid down on a blanket and sleeping off the dregs of his sedation, Gerren could allow himself to think. He wasn't stupid, the young policeman had taken away his clothes and scraped his nails for a reason. He wasn't out of the woods, not by a long way, and he still hadn't been asked for a proper statement yet. What had happened up there at the cottage?

He could see the scene in his imagination: Rob would have been waiting for Gerren in his sitting room, the range groaning and popping as wood burned in its belly.

There'd have been a sound from outside. An engine? No, probably not. He hadn't seen any fresh tracks in the mud of the yard. The intruder must have arrived on foot. Rob's first warning would have been Jack.

Or maybe not. The old dog was a little deaf now, and so was Rob. Maybe it had been the shadow of a figure entering the cottage that alerted them both. Jack would have leaped up, barking, and run at the man. A knife would have slashed and the dog would have dropped, whimpering, and crawled away.

No! There was something wrong with this scenario. Jack would never have left his master while Rob had breath in his body.

29

He tried again and again, but each time the memory of his friend lying dismembered pushed its way into the picture, and the scene fragmented and spun away.

Rob was nearly as old as Gerren, but he'd been fit and wiry, and he knew how to handle himself. He kept a gun too. Not just the shotgun he used to shoot rabbits for the pot, but a businesslike pistol of some sort.

Gerren wasn't supposed to know about the handgun, but he'd found it one evening when Rob had gone outside to the privy, and he'd gone in search of some pipe tobacco when his own ran out. He'd been opening drawers in the sideboard when his eyes fell on the dull metallic gleam of a gun.

He'd still been staring at it when Rob appeared silently at his side, reached past him and closed the drawer. Nothing had been said between them then, but a year or so later, when Rob had taken too much whiskey, he'd tried to explain.

"Used to be in the army," he'd slurred. "Years ago. Young and stupid." Then his chin had come up with some remnant of pride. "Crack shot in those days. Went all over the world." He belched. "Kept the gun." Tapped his nose with a forefinger. "Can't be too careful."

And that had been it. But Gerren had witnessed Rob's skill with the shotgun. The man had never missed anything he'd aimed at. He wondered what had happened to the pistol.

So how had someone sneaked up on him and not only got past Jack, but past Rob's own defences?

Perhaps it had been someone they both knew? Someone Jack allowed in, and Rob trusted enough to turn his back on?

He swallowed painfully. There was only one person Gerren knew of who fitted that bill. Himself.

What if he was going senile? Could he have driven up to Rob's place last night, still drunk, and attacked his friend with such savagery? A band seemed to be tightening around his chest and he had to brace himself against the wall to stay upright.

Then Jack whined and tried to stand, tail wagging tentatively. No. If he'd attacked Rob, and Jack, the dog would never have trusted him again, he was sure of it.

Almost sure.

"You awake now, Jack? I'll get you a drink."

He'd never imagined that he'd still be living in this cottage after all these years, but he'd never had time to look for anywhere better, so here he was. The only difference was that he owned the place now. His landlady, Mrs McKee, had left it to him when she died.

Lucky, really, because the old dear would have been black affronted at the sight of a dirty farm collie sprawled out on the rug in her sitting room with one of her fine china bowls on the floor for drinking water.

"You stay here, Jack," he said as if the dog could understand. "I need to go and buy you some dog food. I won't be long."

A bushy tail wagged. Maybe the dog did understand, after all. Collies were intelligent beasts.

He bought a bag of dry dog food and a few tins, realising he had no idea what Rob had fed his companion. As an afterthought, he stopped in at the butcher's shop for a half-pound of mince. If the dog didn't want it, he could make mince and tatties with it, so it wouldn't go to waste.

He'd hoped May Dunlop might be in the shop, but her son, Walter, was alone behind the counter.

"Hello, Mr Penrose. Had a good night last night, did you?"

The young man's face was open and friendly, and there wasn't even a hint of innuendo in his voice. Gerren smiled. "Your ma's a great cook. I had a lovely evening, thank you."

Walter nodded. "Ma was a bit disappointed you couldn't stay. Was your friend all right?" When Gerren stared at him blankly, the boy's expression shifted to puzzlement. "She said you had a text from old Mr Harris and that you needed to go up there. Worried about you, she was, driving all the way up there in the dark."

He'd said that? Another memory crept back in like a bedraggled cat who'd been in a fight. Damn that local brew. He'd been looking for an excuse to leave so he'd whipped his mobile out of his pocket and squinted at the screen.

31

"I'll have to go, Mrs Dunlop," he'd said. "I promised Rob I'd run up to his place this evening to help him rehang that barn door of his. He's wondering where I am, I expect."

It hadn't been quite a lie. He'd only implied that Rob had texted him.

May Dunlop had sagged a little, then she'd straightened again and given him a bright smile. "You're far too good to that old layabout, Gerren, but I suppose promises are promises, and it's not as if anyone else around here will even give the poor man the time of day. I'll fetch your coat and hat."

It was all perfectly innocent, but if that peeler, the one who'd vomited all over the crime scene, got hold of the information, he'd definitely leap to the wrong conclusion.

But was it the wrong conclusion? Doubt still gnawed at him. He could remember little after he'd staggered out of May Dunlop's back door into the chill night air.

* * *

Gerren had another shock when he saw the young police sergeant standing outside his front door for the second time that day.

This time he gestured for Sergeant Birch to go all the way through into the sitting room. He thought with misgiving about the mild chaos that always existed there. He'd left his work boots in the middle of the floor and tossed his green coveralls across the back of one of the armchairs, and a handful of odd socks decorated various other surfaces around the room.

Living on his own, he realised, had led to sloppy habits. His old pa would have been disappointed.

He scrabbled around, kicking the boots under the coffee table and snatching up socks. The coveralls were stiff on the upper surface and slimy in the folds where various bodily fluids hadn't had enough air to dry out. As he lifted them, the room filled with the warm, bovine smell of his last farm call-out, to the difficult calving of a Jersey heifer who'd been accidentally bred with a Belgian Blue bull. He'd ended up having to deliver a dead bull calf by caesarean.

The detective didn't even glance around. He found a space on the couch and lowered himself down before Gerren could warn him. He continued to sink until his knees were on a level almost with his shoulders.

"Sorry," Gerren said, trying not to laugh at the lad's expression. "Springs are a bit shot on the old girl. Want a hand up?" He reached out and hauled the tall young man to his feet. They stood facing each other, a pair of laughing brown eyes looking down into his from a height. He decided he liked this youngster. "Try the armchair," he said, pointing to one that wasn't covered in clothes. "I'll put the kettle on, shall I?"

Gerren listened for the kettle's piercing shriek while he washed up a couple of mugs in his tiny kitchen, and found some teabags in a canister left over from Mrs McKee's time. They smelled faintly of tea and nothing else, so he shoved them in and hoped for the best. By the time he'd poured hot water in and stirred it, the stains in the mugs would be barely visible.

When Gerren carried the drinks back into the sitting room, the detective sergeant was writing in a notebook. He put one mug on the floor next to his visitor's feet and nursed the other between cupped hands.

He realised how it must look to the police. There was no doubt he'd be a suspect, maybe their only suspect. Despite this lad's good manners and easy ways, Gerren wasn't reassured. They'd be coming for him sooner or later, to "help them with their enquiries", so he'd need to do what he could before that happened to find out who had really killed his old friend.

Maybe he'd made an involuntary sound, because the policeman looked up sharply, his eyebrows raised in query.

"Haven't any biscuits," Gerren said to cover his confusion. "I can pop out to the corner shop and buy some if you like?"

DS Birch grinned and patted his belly. "No thanks. Got to watch the waistline."

Gerren nodded, thinking sour thoughts about the lad's flat stomach compared to his own barrel-like shape. "All right. Tea's near your foot there, on the floor. Don't spill it."

"Can we go over your movements last night again, please?"

Gerren perched nervously on the edge of the couch, the only way to avoid being sucked down into its sagging depths. "Of course."

Young Birch flipped back a few pages in his notebook. "You mentioned that you usually went up to visit Mr Harris in the evenings, and that you'd planned to go last night. Is that right?"

Here it came. Straight to the tricky part. "Yes, Sergeant. I planned to go up to visit him, but then I bumped into Mrs Dunlop, and she invited me to take a meal with her." He looked up from under his brows. "At my age, the offer of a meal isn't to be sniffed at, like, and Rob's always been pretty easy-going. We never had no schedules or nothing. I reckoned I could just as easily go up the next day."

"At what time did you leave Mrs Dunlop?"

"I already said," Gerren muttered. "Sometime around nine, I reckon. Not sure exactly when."

"At that time, it would still have been light. Did you not think about going up there afterwards?"

Gerren was pretty sure he'd answered that one earlier too. "Had too much to drink," he said shortly. "Decided driving was a bad idea."

"How often would you have visited Mr Harris in the mornings?"

"Hardly ever," Gerren said before he'd thought it through. His head was starting to throb with a dull ache behind the eyes from the strain of trying to give the right answers. And probably from the beer too.

"So why did you decide to go up there this morning?"

And there it was. Why had he gone up this morning? He remembered waking fully dressed, with a dry mouth and the nagging feeling that there was something he'd forgotten to do, then he'd got up and gone straight out to Poppy, with the intention of driving her up to see Rob.

He'd taken too long to answer. The young sergeant didn't prompt him or make any impatient noises, but the silence hung between them like an accusing finger. He licked his lips. "Not really sure. Maybe I felt guilty that I hadn't been up there last night. Rob leads a solitary life out there in the hills." He thought about it. "Led."

That's when it really hit him for the first time. Maybe it had been shock at first, but the sight of Rob's body, dismembered and defiled, had been like watching a TV show. It hadn't felt real. Now, it occurred to him that he'd never see his friend again, and the loss was a yawning chasm in his soul. Then he was back in the cottage, the image of such butchery sharp and clear, along with the stench of death.

He didn't remember standing up, and he definitely didn't remember falling, but the next thing he knew was the pale oval of a worried face looking down into his, and cool fingers unbuttoning his shirt collar.

He tried to speak, but the words wouldn't come.

"Don't try to talk," the lad said. "You fainted. Take a moment or two to recover before you try to sit up."

Gerren realised he was lying on his back with his feet resting on the couch, raised above his body. The detective had put something behind his head as a pillow. Basic first aid, but his respect for the lad increased a little more. Cool under pressure.

After a while, the rushing in his ears subsided and his skin ceased to feel as if it was too tight for his body. He swallowed. "I think I'm all right to sit up now, but maybe you could give me a hand, just in case?"

He felt much better upright, even though he didn't try to lift himself back onto the couch. The floor felt just fine for now. "Sorry about that," he said. "It just came over me, all sudden-like, that I wouldn't be seeing Rob again."

"It's okay. You've been friends a long time, I suppose. This sort of thing would hit anyone hard."

Gerren nodded. "I reckon I was so busy up till now I hadn't had the chance to dwell on it." He glanced up at the pale face. "Sorry," he said again.

"The best thing you can do for your friend now," the detective said, "is to help us find whoever did this to him. Is there anyone I can call to sit with you? Mrs Dunlop, maybe?"

"No!" It came out explosively. "No," he repeated. "I don't really know May Dunlop that well. She's just one of the ladies in the village who're hanging out for a husband." He regretted the words immediately. "I don't mean—" he stammered.

A boyish grin lit up the sergeant's face. "It's okay, Mr Penrose. I understand. I don't suppose there are that many eligible bachelors available in a place like this."

"That's it," Gerren agreed. "I spend half my time avoiding them, but Mrs Dunlop's son said she'd cooked a nice leg of lamb. A leg of lamb is hard to turn down, but even then . . ." Walter had made it sound as if it was a family meal, with him and his wife there as well as his mum, but when Gerren had walked into the little back room behind the butcher's shop, Walter had been putting on his coat and leaving. It'd ended up as a tête-à-tête with May Dunlop, and far too much beer. "I hadn't realised it'd be just her and me, see?"

From the understanding in those brown eyes, he reckoned the lad did understand. He'd probably been in similar positions, a well-set-up chap like that.

"You're not a local man, are you?" Birch asked. "What's that accent? Somewhere in England?"

Gerren raised his chin, national pride coming to his support. "Not England. I'm a Cornishman. Generations of Penroses lived and farmed and fished and squired down Helston way." He shook his head. "Not so many left there these days, leastways not of my lot. Scattered all over the world, we are. Only my cousin left in the old place now."

The confusion on the young detective's face made him laugh, despite the grief that lay heavily on him. "We Cornishmen don't think of ourselves as English," he explained.

"We're a separate people, we are, and have been ever since young Arthur was born at Tintagel after Merlin magicked his mother into thinking King Uther was her husband."

He could see that he'd lost the lad again.

"Never mind, lad. It's all a load of nonsense now anyway. Hardly any Cornish left in Cornwall. Place has been taken over by emmets."

CHAPTER 6

Just what the hell were emmets? Aaron's confusion must have been clear in his expression, because the old man laughed.

"Emmets be tourists," he explained. "It means ants, and that's what they're like. Locals can't buy a house now because they're all snapped up as holiday homes for prices locals could never afford." He scratched his nose with a stained fingertip. "Been like that for years now. The reason I came here after I qualified was because it was the one place my family wouldn't visit. No tourists here in those days, so it was peaceful enough."

"I see." Penrose would have qualified in the 1970s, when the Troubles were in full swing, before Aaron had even been born; from all he'd heard, he'd hardly have called it peaceful. "Talk me through your impressions when you arrived at the farm this morning, would you? What time did you get there?"

Penrose sagged. "I don't know, lad. Sun was up, but only just. I should have known there was something wrong when there was no smoke coming from the chimney, but I thought he'd banked the stove and gone up the hill with his easel and the dog, to paint the sunrise."

"You mentioned before that Mr Harris was an artist?"

Penrose snorted. "Hard to imagine, isn't it? I'm not saying he was a great artist, because I'd be no judge myself, but

I liked what he painted. Reckon he had an eye for colour, like." He gestured to a framed picture on his wall, above the fireplace. "That's one of his."

It was a landscape, Aaron supposed, possibly the village of Ballygroggan, nestled between frowning hills beneath a pewter sky. He shivered. The lines and shapes bore little resemblance to reality, yet he swore he could feel the icy wind coursing through him and the soft patter of rain on his skin. He dragged his eyes away.

"I see what you mean."

"He doesn't paint for the tourist market," Penrose remarked. Then his face twitched. "Didn't."

"So, you arrived and thought he was out with the dog. When did you decide to go inside the cottage?"

"Thought I'd put a pot of tay on. I needed one — best hangover cure, a pot of strong tay — and I knew Rob would be ready for one when he came back down. He wouldn't have minded me going in," he added, a touch defensively.

"I'm sure he'd have been glad of it," Aaron said. "How far inside did you go?"

Penrose swallowed. "Far enough to smell it," he said in a low voice. Aaron had to lean closer to hear. "Then my eyes got used to the dark and I saw his hand. And then the rest of him. At first I thought there'd been a terrible accident, and he might have been lying there, hurt and helpless." He shook his head. "But I reckon I knew in my heart he was dead. It wasn't just the smell, but the feel of the place. I've worked alongside Death in my job often enough to recognise his signature."

Aaron supressed a shudder. There was something about this little sitting room with its small windows and dreary interior that sucked joy away. And that painting didn't help.

"Did you touch anything?"

Penrose shot him a scathing look. "I did not. I backed away outside, fetched my mobile phone from the Landy, and called 999."

"And he was definitely dead when you saw him? Did you go close enough to make sure?"

"Lad, there was no doubt in my mind that he was dead. His eyes were glazed, and there was too much blood around for him to still be alive." His voice rose in anger, and Aaron made a soothing gesture.

"I'm sorry. The reason I had to ask was because the pathologist mentioned that she thought the time of death was very recent. We're waiting for the doctor's report, but it seems you may have been lucky. The killer may have left not long before you arrived. Did you see any evidence of anyone on the track on your way up?"

Penrose's chin raised. "No. Did you?"

Aaron remembered that hellish journey, being bounced around on the deep ruts and rocks, one moment thrust hard against his seatbelt, the next trying not to smack his head on the window. He'd not taken in any of the surrounding countryside, being too busy holding onto the grab handle above his head — and he'd only been the passenger; Penrose had driven himself up there.

He scratched the back of his neck. "I see what you mean. But no sign that another vehicle had been up there before you?"

This time, the old man closed his eyes in concentration. "No," he answered slowly. "I'd swear nothing had been up there since the last time I drove Poppy up — she's my old Landy. That was a couple of days ago, like I said. We had heavy rain over the weekend, and it'd even washed my tracks away." He rubbed the bristle on his chin reflectively. "Not like where I grew up, where all the grass would have died in the summer, and we had hosepipe bans and all. Different world."

Aaron wrote it down, frowning. "So, there were no fresh tyre tracks, and you didn't see anyone coming down. The killer must have gone up on foot, then?"

Penrose shook his head vigorously. "You'd be mad to try it. There are bogs both sides of that track, deep enough to swallow a cow. You'd need good local knowledge to go up there on foot, and the only man I know who could have done it is lying dead, butchered like an animal."

40

"Yet someone did," Aaron said quietly. The possibility that Penrose himself had been the only one to go up there was hard to ignore. Shouldn't be ignored.

Then the old man sighed and reached down with a shaky hand to stroke the dog's head. "I want to find this man as much as you," he said. "Rob and I, we weren't best pals like the kids these days talk about, but neither of us had anyone else, really, so we grew used to one another."

Aaron wanted to ask if they ever fell out, but that was too inflammatory a question for this informal chat, so he saved it for another time.

"Did no one else ever go up there to see him?"

"No. I already said. I was the only one."

"I mean utilities, like someone to read his electric meter, or to fill up his oil. What about a postman?"

"No." He must have realised how awkward he'd sounded because he softened a little. "He was self-sufficient, was Rob, growing his own vegetables and shooting rabbits or pheasants for the pot if he wanted a bit of meat. No electric, no oil, no gas. He chopped wood from the forest and dried it to burn in the range. That gave him heat and he cooked on it. Used the well for his water, got dressed and undressed by the light of a paraffin lamp. Went to bed when it was dark, got up when it was light. Simple life."

Hard to imagine so harsh an existence. "Didn't he ever get letters?"

"None that I've ever known of. Wouldn't get no postie going up that track. I'd buy his lamp oil for him and he'd pay me back in cash. He'd tell me what he needed and I'd fetch it for him from the village, but he didn't need much. Just the occasional form signing for the Ministry, for the sheep. I helped him with that."

"A solitary man," Aaron said neutrally. What did Rob Harris have to hide? Or maybe he'd been afraid of something — or someone. "Was he always like that?"

"Not so much in the early days. He'd come down to the village from time to time then, maybe bring a few sheep to market. He had a prize ram once, won at the local show, but he got funnier as he got older. Bit of a recluse. Didn't like people much. I always reckoned he'd had a hard time of it when he was in the army. Said his nickname was 'Trigger', so maybe he'd seen some action. Scars a man, that sort of thing."

"How long had he lived there? Was he there when you came here or did he arrive later than that?"

"That I can't tell you, lad. He's been here a good while, that's all I know, maybe as long as me, maybe not."

Fat lot of use that was, Aaron thought.

* * *

"I need to know everything about Rob Harris," Aaron said when he returned to Ballymena police station. "Where was he born, where did he grow up, what did he do, was he retired? Driving licence? Passport? He might have lived a solitary life for the last few decades, but he was young once, and he must have left a trail behind him somewhere."

Nic turned immediately to her computer keyboard and began typing. PC Stanley — *Dave*, that was his name, Aaron remembered at last — shot Nic an irritated glance.

"There's nothing on him, Sarge," Stanley said. "I already looked. No criminal record."

Aaron sighed. That wasn't what he'd meant. "I'd like to find out where he came from before he settled here. It seems unlikely his killer just stumbled over him by accident, and there's something personal about the severity of this attack. Something created a lot of hatred, and I need to know what. The answer might be in his past."

Stanley was pushing sixty and he was still a PC. He had a belligerent attitude that put Aaron's back up, but the difference between being a constable and a sergeant was the need to hide your feelings and manage people. He'd had a great teacher, but he wondered again how the hell Asha had managed it.

Nic's fingers flew across the keyboard, her tongue sticking out at the corner of her mouth in a gesture that was as immature as it was unconscious.

She'd always been a good kid, but the last thing he'd expected was to see her in the service. He hoped she'd learned to be a little less reckless with age or he'd have to watch her like a hawk to keep her out of trouble.

She made a satisfied noise.

"Got something, Nic?"

"It's more what I *haven't* got, sir. He's not on the electoral register, no evidence of a driver's licence or passport. The cottage and the land around it are owned outright, freehold, and the name on the land registry entry is his, but otherwise he's a ghost." She tapped a few more keys.

Aaron looked over her shoulder. She had about a dozen tabs open and was flicking between them. "According to Gerren Penrose, Harris had been living at the cottage for maybe thirty years. Follow the trail and see where it leads, but don't get ahead of yourself.

"Dave, I need you to look into Gerren Penrose's movements in the days before the murder. Check out his alibi, but don't put the scarers on him. He's cooperating at the moment, and I'd like to keep it that way. And don't go letting anyone in the village think we're looking at him for the murder. You know what these wee villages are like. They'll have made up an entire story about him and be sure it's true if you give them any encouragement. I need all our witnesses to keep open minds as much as possible, so don't go putting thoughts in their heads."

He'd said too much. Stanley's expression darkened as he spoke, resentment kindling. He needed to backtrack, and fast. "That's why I'm giving you the job, Dave. You have the experience to get the balance just right, and this is important."

He wasn't sure if he'd gone too far the other way and over-egged the pudding. Stanley was a prickly one, and he took careful handling. Aaron tried not to sigh in frustration.

43

Asha had always made this stuff look so easy, but it really wasn't.

"At present, I don't think news of this murder has leaked out, but a place like this runs on gossip, so it won't be long. Once we have the press sniffing around, it'll become far harder for witnesses to keep a clear head, so move swiftly if you can."

He looked around the tiny incident room. Maybe a Major Investigation Team would arrive to take over this case? A brutal murder like this would be big news, and there'd be pressure on the PSNI to get it solved as quickly as possible.

Well, whoever took over, he'd make sure the ground was prepared for them so they could get on with solving the crime. He hoped they'd let him stay involved, in however minor a role. This case was beyond anything he'd worked with Asha.

The door opened and O'Neill walked in. The older man always made Aaron feel a bit better. His unflappable calm and his apparent trust in the new sergeant's judgement settled Aaron in some undefinable way.

"Scene of Crime have finished, sir," O'Neill said. "Jana said to tell you she'll have everything logged by lunchtime tomorrow."

Aaron shot him a questioning look.

"Apparently there was a lot of material to collect," O'Neill said stolidly. "Took them a while."

Stanley sniggered. "Took the pathologist a while just to gather up and bag all the bits of Harris, I expect, never mind anything else."

"A bit of respect, please, Dave," Aaron said. His fists had curled into balls, but he'd managed to keep his voice level. The constable glanced at him with resentment, but he must have seen the anger in Aaron's eyes, because he muttered an apology.

There was no window in this room, but the sounds of a shift change penetrated through the open door where Chris O'Neill still hovered. Aaron glanced at his watch. Nearly seven already. Where had the day gone?

"All right, folks. Let's call it a day for now. Hopefully we'll have the PM results tomorrow and we can have a look at anything the SOCOs collected too. Briefing at eight thirty."

Dave Stanley was out of his chair and halfway across the room before Aaron had finished speaking, shrugging himself into a leather jacket, but Nic just typed a little faster, not meeting his eye. He exchanged a look with O'Neill, who shrugged.

* * *

He wasn't looking forward to shuttling between the village of Ballygroggan and the police station in Ballymena, never mind the drive to and from the flat in Belfast that he'd shared with Faith. It seemed pointless, now, to drive all this way at the end of a long and tiring day, and if it hadn't been for Marmaduke, Faith's cat, he wouldn't have bothered, but the ginger colossus needed company, at least at night. Being fed by the neighbour wasn't really enough.

As he unlocked the door, he could already hear piteous miaows and scratching. He pushed the door inwards, foot in the gap as a reflex to prevent the cat from slipping past him and out onto the busy road.

"Sorry I'm late," he murmured. "We've got to find a better system, haven't we, old fella?"

Marmaduke — stupid name for a cat — twined between his legs as he made his way into the kitchen, flicking on light switches as he went. There was a note on the table in Marjory's spidery hand. The old lady had been in and fed the cat, but she'd also left him a pie in the warming oven, as she called it, and some new potatoes and peas to go with it.

He tucked in, fending off the cat with his elbows as it tried to sneak in and steal a lick of gravy. The pie was home-made, the pastry crisp and flaky on top and thick and heavy beneath, just the way he loved it. If Marjory had been a few decades younger, he'd have been proposing marriage.

"Okay, chum. You can be the prewash cycle again," he said, pushing the plate away from him. Marmaduke purred like a diesel engine as his rough tongue mopped up all the bits Aaron had failed to capture with his fork.

While he waited for the kettle to boil for coffee, he washed up. A bottle of Longrow single malt sat on the shelf, trying to seduce him into opening it, but he resisted. It was getting harder each night, but he'd promised himself he'd never drink alone. That way lay the slippery slope.

There'd be nothing worth watching on the telly, so he sat on the sofa with his feet on the coffee table and woke up his iPad. It wouldn't hurt to find out a bit about the history of Ballygroggan village and more specifically the outlying farms.

The village had an active history society, albeit with a pretty basic and old-fashioned website. He skimmed through the photos, seeing if any of the faces looked familiar, but most of them predated the period he was interested in. They were more focused on the late 1800s and early 1900s.

He moved on to a more general search, and found what he was looking for on a site about the annual agricultural show. Held on a farm a couple of miles outside the village, it seemed everyone from miles around tried to attend each year, bringing their cattle and sheep and pigs. Kids with pigtails and bright-eyed ponies competed for rosettes and the wee wifies entered their homemade jam and cakes with fierce determination to win the prize.

It was in a photo of a prizewinning ram that he spotted Gerren Penrose. Apparently that ram had been such a fine specimen that it featured on the cover page, despite the fact that it had probably been mutton for at least two decades. In the background was a younger Gerren Penrose, chatting to a tall, heavy-shouldered man with a slim waist and dark hair. The photographer had caught the man in the act of turning away, so his image was slightly blurred, but Aaron was fairly sure it was Harris. His face had been covered in blood in the crime scene photos, so he couldn't be certain.

The date at the bottom of the photo was June 1995. So if it was him, Harris had been living in or near the village by then. That was getting on for thirty years, and the two seemed to already be friendly.

When Harris had been killed, he'd been a thin, wizened man, maybe a little bent with age. The tall, confident man in this photo had the same features, though.

He took a screenshot of the image. He'd ask Stanley to show it to some of the older villagers, see if the sight of Harris at the show sparked any memories about his background.

A yawn caught him unawares. Marmaduke had curled up heavily on his lap, a dead weight that bent his knees backwards. He shed the big cat with a sideways shrug of his legs and hauled himself to his feet, stretching the creases in his spine from sitting slouched for so long.

His bed was cold and too big. The sheets felt damp against his bare legs, and it was too quiet without the little snuffly noises Faith made when she breathed, but he'd have to get used to it. She wasn't going to be back anytime soon.

CHAPTER 7

Caro's fists clenched. The young woman she'd befriended, Hadhira, sat limp and exhausted, her head on Caro's shoulder. "You're safe now," Caro said. "Your father won't touch you again, I promise."

The girl had cried herself out, but she shook her weary head. "He'll find me, and this time I've run away, so it'll be even worse next time."

"He won't hurt you anymore."

The thin shoulders tensed. "I have to keep running. A friend said there is a place where girls can go, where they'll be safe."

"You can't run forever, child. I should know." Her mind raced, analysing the fragments of detail she'd picked up from the girl's story. Her father had beaten her, and now he wanted to marry her to her first cousin. When she'd cried, he'd beaten her again. It hadn't been hard to tease enough clues from the girl to work out where the man lived.

She persuaded Hadhira to get into bed, gently smoothing the damp hair back from her forehead where it had broken free from the scarf. Long, dark eyelashes curled on cheeks that had paled to dull amber from exhaustion, and her lips were parted to show small, even white teeth. She looked so young.

By that age, Caro had already lost hope, self-respect, and any faith in her mother's ability to protect her. But if she could save just one girl from suffering as she had suffered, maybe that sense of completion would finally come to free her.

Once Hadhira was asleep, she retrieved her laptop from the car. Satellite view and then street view of the target property showed her this should be a straightforward operation. The house Hadhira's father occupied was one in a rabbit warren of terraced houses on the outskirts of Newry. It was the sort of place where a stranger wouldn't stand out, and you could probably burgle a house in broad daylight without anyone calling the police.

A glance at her watch showed it to be just before 3 a.m. Allow an hour and a half to drive there, using minor roads to avoid cameras, and she could be finished and back home before breakfast. By then it would almost be a civilised time to make her phone call too, reporting success.

The car was a powerful one with headlights that lit up the fields either side of the road as she sped cross-country towards Newry. Once there, she used the map in her memory to find her way to the house, just as she had done to find her father's farm. She knew all about saved destinations in satnavs and wasn't about to make such a rookie mistake.

The sky was just brightening towards dawn as she parked up a few streets away. Gloves were a habit, but she also slipped on a scene of crime suit. She'd dyed a few of them in patchy dark colours so she could keep herself from contaminating a scene but still be hard to spot at night, and now she was glad of her forethought.

Her planned access route took her down the side of the end house in the terrace, across its back garden, over the wooden fence at the back and into the target garden. A cat hissed and puffed itself out as she ghosted past.

The houses either side of the target were in darkness, but one solitary upstairs light suggested someone at home in the middle house. She examined the drainpipe. Cheap plastic, not up to her weight. It would have to be a ground-floor entry, then.

The windows were modern, recently replaced, but the lock was no challenge to her, and she had the barrel out and the door open in half a dozen heartbeats.

The house was an old one, maybe 1960s, and it creaked as the temperature changed. Caro moved silently to the bottom of the stairs. The upper hallway was dark except for a thin line of light at the foot of one door. She checked the downstairs rooms, but they were empty, stinking of stale food and greasy, unwashed human.

She removed the light bulb on the upper landing, setting it aside so she wouldn't crush it with her foot if she had to flee later. There was no sound on the other side of the door, so she checked the bedroom with the light beneath the door first.

Two single beds. One was empty and unmade, the second had a dark head on the pillow. This would be Hadhira's little sister, Nadira, eight years old. Apparently she had frequent nightmares, hence the night light. Caro closed the door quietly.

The mother would probably be in the main bedroom. Taking out the father without alerting her would be difficult, so she'd hatched a plan. A quick check revealed two heads sleeping in a small double bed, the one closest to her with a dark beard. Perfect.

She ran lightly down the stairs, took out the lower light bulb, then hammered on the front door from the inside.

It took a couple of repeats before sleepy voices protested and the bed springs creaked. The door opened and a shadowy figure appeared, only visible because of his pale pyjamas. A hand reached for the light switch, and a hoarse voice cursed when nothing happened.

She counted the steps as he descended the stairs, then when he was within range, his arm raised to reach out for the light switch by the front door, she struck.

The knife went home with a sucking noise as she twisted it. Instead of the chest, she'd chosen the brachial plexus, the network of nerves and arteries in his armpit. It was a weakening blow, not a killing one, not immediately.

With the knife still embedded, she leaned close enough to inhale his stale breath. "This is for Hadhira," she hissed, then withdrew the knife and drove it deep into his chest. "And this is for Nadira." Another blow. "For my mother." Her voice was coming as a sob now. He wasn't fighting back. Maybe it was shock at the sudden attack, but he sagged against her as if he was already dead. The last blow sliced rather than stabbed as he fell to the ground. "And that one is for me," she finished.

She lost her grip on the slippery hilt, his bodyweight tugging it out of her grasp as he slumped. She tried to feel for the knife, but everything was sticky wetness, and she couldn't find it. Afraid of cutting herself on the blade, and leaving DNA on the scene, she felt around cautiously. It had to be here somewhere. She couldn't leave it to be found; it was too distinctive.

Then an upstairs door opened and a tiny voice said, "Babi?"

Shit! Her breaths were coming in short gasps. Bedsprings creaked and a woman's voice called the child's name. Time to cut her losses.

He was alive as she left, she was fairly sure, but there wasn't time to check. She was certain he wouldn't stay that way for long, even if they got an ambulance to him straight away.

As she darted through the kitchen to the back door, a high-pitched scream split the night. The wife must have followed him down, stupid woman. Well, it would make no difference now. She was too late to save him, but he might die in her arms. That would serve her right for not protecting her daughter better.

As she ran to her car, she stripped off the suit, turning it inside out in a practised manner to keep the blood from escaping, then bundled it into a plastic bag she'd brought for the purpose. Now she was in dark jeans and a roll-neck sweater, hair inside a beanie. Anyone seeing her would have trouble describing what they'd seen, and she knew she ran like a man, not like a woman. It was another skill she'd taught herself.

51

On the drive back to Dublin, she kept to the speed limit, but her fingers danced a beat on the steering wheel and adrenaline surged through her veins.

Was she complete? No, not yet, but like a jigsaw puzzle with the edges finished, she was starting to see her way at last. Maybe helping others was more rewarding than helping oneself or following orders?

She drove on, her borrowed car's headlights piercing the foggy night on the A1. No point in going back to the hostel. Hadhira would wake up and wonder where her new friend had gone, and she'd no doubt panic when she realised she'd been abandoned, but the newspapers would soon be reporting the sad death of a certain Jibreel Khan in Newry, and then she'd know her friend hadn't let her down.

A couple of hours later, she was threading her way through the backstreets of Dublin, following a route that avoided CCTV cameras. She returned the borrowed car to her colleague's driveway. He was away on holiday in New York for a week, and he rarely cleaned it, so a bit of extra dirt would go undetected. Most people didn't notice what their mileometer said either, and she'd made sure to leave the car with the same amount of fuel it had when she stole it. He'd never know it had been taken.

Her own car was where she'd left it, two streets across. Someone had shoved a load of flyers under her wiper blade, so she ripped them out and threw them in the gutter. They were half-dissolved anyway. Must have been raining heavily here over the weekend.

* * *

The next morning, she turned up to work as usual, dressed in smart casual and carrying her trademark designer handbag. Heads turned as she passed, and colleagues called out greetings. Her partner, Geoff, looked up as she reached his end of the room.

"Hey, Carol. Had a good weekend off? Nice and rested?"

"Why?" she asked suspiciously.

"We've a new case. Some bastard's hacked into a corporate banking mainframe and the shit's really hitting the fan. Right up your street."

Her pulse quickened, as it always did when the prospect of tracking down a ransomware designer was dangled in front of her. This was her skill, this tracing of digital clues to bring a hacker down and free his victims.

"Unusual they're involving us and not one of the private companies."

Geoff laughed. "Word's spreading that we've one of the best cyber detectives in the world on our team, and now everyone's coming to the Garda when they need help."

CHAPTER 8

Nic waited until the noises in the station had settled down before she relaxed. With all the budget cuts, Ballymena station was only open from 11 a.m. to 7 p.m., so the only other inhabitants would be cleaners and maybe the odd neighbourhood policing team member still writing up statements.

She turned off the overhead light and worked on by the dull glow of her desk lamp's low-energy bulb. She was excited to be involved in this case, however menial her role. When she'd been sent to this outpost as a probationer, she hadn't expected to see any action at all, and as a city girl at heart, she'd been unenthusiastic about the largely rural area she'd be covering.

She'd run out of places to look for more about Rob Harris's past until she remembered something Gerren had said about Rob being ex-army. What was it? He'd had a nickname, hadn't he? She scrolled back through Aaron's report. Trigger, that was it. That nickname led her to one mention of him in the online newspaper archives, a name listed among other combatants from the Gulf War, but she couldn't find any photos of him from that time. Apparently he'd been part of a small, elite force that had carried out covert missions, but the details were swathed in secrecy, which probably explained the lack of detail. All she had was a copy of his driving licence issued in Swansea from the 1980s, so no photo, and a passport from the same era. The photo on that was terrible quality: a white man with a square chin and thick dark hair growing low over beetling brows.

There was definitely something off about Rob "Trigger" Harris. The need to impress Aaron was eating away at her, driving her to find links where perhaps there were none. She puffed out an exasperated breath.

Aaron Birch had been one of the investigating officers in the case that had ripped her family apart a few years ago, and she still carried a burden of guilt for the injuries he'd received that time. Everyone had told her it hadn't been her fault, that she'd saved his life with her quick reactions, but that wasn't how it felt. When he'd turned up here, covering Sergeant McBride's maternity leave, she hadn't known how to react, but Aaron had slid effortlessly into his role as her superior as if there'd been no history between them, and she'd followed his lead. Perhaps it was better that way.

Rob Harris must have come to live here once he left the army, but she couldn't pin down a date for that. Army records were notoriously difficult to access, but she found a tiny paragraph in a newspaper from Zimbabwe about a local boy made good, someone called Harold Cavendish, a major in the British Army, and mentioning that he'd fought in the Gulf War. It listed the names of the rest of his team: Beecher, Roy; Bailey, George; and Harris, Robert, which is why it had come up on her search. Maybe it was worth looking up his old army pals; one of them might have been carrying a grudge around and finally taken revenge on Harris.

She began with Cavendish, the Zimbabwean. That gave her a new avenue to explore. Her uncle and aunt had once lived in Zimbabwe. It was too late to call them, but her cousin, on the other hand . . . She picked up her mobile and found his number.

"Nic? Do you know what time it is?" The sleepy voice still retained a trace of a Zimbabwean accent even though Paul hadn't lived there since he was ten years old. "Some of us have work to go to in the morning."

She glanced guiltily at the clock. It was getting on for midnight. "I'm sorry, Paul. Did I wake you?"

"Don't be stupid; I'm in the bar. What can I do for you?" That's when she noticed the background hum of conversation.

She snorted. "You're terrible! I'm trying to track down a man who used to live in Zimbabwe, back in the seventies. Apparently, he joined the British Army at some stage because he fought in the Gulf War in some sort of elite squad, but that's all I've got. Any idea where I should start searching on the Zimbabwe side?"

"Nineteen seventies and a military type, huh? He might have been in the Rhodesian army, or even in the BSAP."

"BSAP?"

"British South African Police — the Rhodesian police force. Nothing to do with South Africa, despite the name."

"But probably better to start with the army?"

"Maybe. But the BSAP was also military. How much do you know about Zimbabwean history?"

"Only that it used to be called Rhodesia and that Robert Mugabe was the leader at one time. That's about it, I'm afraid."

Paul snorted. "Okay. Well, back in the sixties, Rhodesia declared itself independent from the UK. But most of the farmland belonged to us white folk, and we wanted to keep power. The old boys used to moan about the Mau Mau uprising and say Africa was heading the same way. Unfortunately for them, the British government and most of the world refused to recognise the new republic, and it ended up with civil war between the white-minority government and a couple of different black nationalist groups. The BSAP fought for the government in a sort of guerrilla warfare."

"So it was an all-white force?"

"No, it was mostly black, actually. But it supported the white-minority government. Officially keeping the peace, upholding law and order and so on, but there was a lot of bloodshed. You should know all about that, living in Northern Ireland, right?"

Nic pulled a face, not that he could see her. "So when did the war end?"

"Around 1978, but the fighting went on a couple more years until the elections in 1980, around the time it changed its name to Zimbabwe." He paused for a moment and went on in a different voice, "You coming to the *braai* this weekend?"

"Can't. We have a big case going on here, and I expect we'll all be doing overtime for the foreseeable. Give my love to Auntie Jean and everyone."

"Will do."

She typed *Rhodesian army* into the search engine but the results stretched back into the Victorian era, so she tried *BSAP* and found her way to a clunky website, probably run by old people. There, she found a link to a mounted division with photos of men galloping horses across African landscapes.

Then she tried searching for *Harold Cavendish BSAP*, and finally found a page listing obituaries for ex-members of the force. There was Cavendish, Harold Arthur, then a date of death in 1992 and a list of his medals, including a PCG, which turned out to be a Police Cross for Conspicuous Gallantry, an old-fashioned term that made her think of knights in shining armour. She rubbed at eyes itchy with tiredness, but she'd caught the scent now, and she wasn't about to walk away just yet.

The obituary gave his date of birth as October 1952 in Fort Victoria, Rhodesia, so he'd have been forty in 1992, just after the Gulf War, but if he'd died in 1992 he couldn't have been the one to kill Rob Harris in the present day.

She went back to the next man on her list: Beecher, R., followed by Bailey, G. Neither added to her picture of Rob Harris, and lethargy was creeping over her. She'd made a beginner's mistake and crawled down a rabbit hole of research that was barely related to the case in hand.

But one of the references to Bailey also mentioned Harris again. It was a very short article in a military newsletter, only part of which was available as a jpeg on the internet.

Her head was spinning with ideas, but she couldn't seem to grasp a single one. A yawn caught her unawares and she realised it was now well past midnight. Strong tea was what she needed.

The soles of her boots clicked on the lino in the corridor as she walked. The lights came on automatically, proving no one had been along here before her, at least for a while. Nic often wondered why she wasn't more afraid of the dark, and put it down to the fact that nothing the darkness held could be as frightening as the events she'd survived a few years ago. Maybe she'd been desensitised to fear.

The station machine dispended horrible, weak tea that usually tasted of soup, but she knew where Sergeant McBride hid her fancy stuff, the sort that came in little pyramidal tea-bags with strings attached to them. She didn't think the sarge would mind Nic borrowing the odd teabag now again. Except when she opened the tin, she discovered there were barely any left. Shit. Had she taken so many? She'd need to replace them before the sergeant came back from maternity leave — if she came back. Some women didn't.

She put the teabag back and decided instead to call it a night. Tomorrow, she could have another run at both Harris and Cavendish.

* * *

Her alarm clock woke her at seven. Someone had grated pepper into her eyes, and her mouth tasted like a French public toilet, but she managed to sit up, head throbbing. Rain beat against her window, turning the view of the buildings opposite into a grey kaleidoscope, and her bedroom door creaked in the wind. The one-bedroom rented flat had been all she could afford, even in Ballymena, and it wasn't exactly luxury. More of a bedsit, really, on the top floor of a dilapidated terrace house, but at least it was handy for the station.

She showered quickly, washing hair that she'd cropped short only a few days ago for convenience, because the shower head only managed a thin trickle of water. Her skin pimpled as she towelled herself dry. Even at this time of year, this place seemed cold and damp. Just time to shove a Pop-Tart in the toaster to nibble on as she walked. If she was quick, she might even be able to grab a cup of tea from the machine on her way from the locker room.

Nic pulled her hood up and ran the short distance to the police station, head down to avoid the driving rain. Bloody Irish climate. You never knew from one day to the next what you'd get, but you could usually be pretty sure it wouldn't be sunshine, even in midsummer. The rain should at least have the decency to be warm, but it never was. Her boots slid on the wet lino inside the door, and for a moment she thought she was about to do the splits, but she regained her balance and managed not to fall.

"Dramatic entry," said a familiar voice.

Nic pulled her hood back, swiping her dripping fringe out of her face, and met a pair of warm brown eyes smiling down at her. The sight of the tall, slim figure gave Nic a lift that wasn't purely professional. Detective Inspector Asha Harvey had also worked on Nic's case when she'd been abducted, and Nic had nursed a slight crush for the charismatic Indian woman ever since.

"Asha! I mean, Inspector Harvey." She tried to control her breathing. "What are you doing here?"

"I've been sent over to advise on your case. Briefing at half eight, is that right? Maybe you could show me the way, Nic."

Nic led the way up the stairs to the backroom they were using as an incident room, aware of those dark eyes on her back. In the cold light of day, the station seemed dingy and tired, and with Asha's tall, confident figure dwarfing her, it also looked very small.

Aaron, of course, was already there, and he exchanged a nod with Asha from his perch on the corner of a desk. He'd been looking at the whiteboard Nic had pulled together the night before. She'd intended to tidy that up first thing this morning and chase the PM results, but it was too late now. No sign of Dave Stanley yet, or O'Neill, so it was just her and Aaron and Asha, the way it had been the last time she'd seen Asha.

Aaron flashed her a grin. "You've been busy. Did you get any sleep at all last night?"

"A bit. I sort of ran out of people to chase, although I've a list of calls to make this morning, once all the offices open."

"You did all this, Nic?" Asha asked. She walked over and took a closer look at the photos stuck to the plastic board and the lines drawn between with Nic's scrawled notes scattered throughout.

No one had ever shown her how to pull together an investigation board, but she'd watched enough TV shows to know what it should look like. Now she wondered if real detectives even used the things at all. "It was just a way to get my ideas down in one place," she said defensively.

"You do realise we have a computer programme for all this, don't you?" Aaron was laughing, but he didn't seem angry with her. Not yet, anyway. "Have you been introduced to HOLMES yet?"

Nic felt the cool air of the room against her reddening cheeks. "Yes, sir, and I submitted all the details I was certain of to HOLMES, but there's a lot here that's still speculation at the moment."

The door opened and a very senior-looking officer entered, straight-backed and proud. She might be in plain clothes, but there was no mistaking that air of authority. Asha straightened up, eyebrows raised in surprise that didn't seem much mixed with pleasure. "Ma'am?"

"Oh, relax," said the newcomer in a crisp voice that matched the crisp make-up and neat, expensive hairstyle. "I'm not staying. I just wanted to say a few words of encouragement, then I'll be away."

That didn't seem to reassure Asha much.

CHAPTER 9

The appearance of Aunt Harriet knocked Asha off balance. Superintendent Sewell hadn't mentioned the ACC would be here when he'd told her he was sending her to Ballymena. "It's been quiet here since last year," he'd said the night before. "And our new DS in Ballymena needs a bit of support, apparently. I'd like you to go up there in an advisory capacity, but there's no need for you to take over as SIO — unless you feel Birch isn't quite ready for it, of course."

He hadn't needed to ask twice. Ever since Aaron's phone call, the horrific murder of the old man in that lonely cottage had been on her mind. It seemed so unnecessary, all the violence.

"Don't try to pretend you haven't been interested. If that lad has any sense, and I think he does, he'll already have been on the blower to you. There's not much support for him over there. Two inspectors from community policing and a clutch of uniformed constables but no one with experience of this sort of crime."

Asha had been thinking about this case as she drove over from Bangor, and spent some time on HOLMES yesterday, familiarising herself with the basic facts to pad out what Aaron had told her on the phone. Her gut told her there was something fishy about Rob Harris's past, but facts were what solved cases, not hunches. She'd had that drummed into her from an early age by her mother's best friend, Aunt Harriet, or Assistant Chief Constable Miller as she was in her working life.

She hoped she'd managed to hide her surprise when she saw the tall, slim figure waltzing into the tiny incident room.

"Delighted to see you, ma'am," Asha said, and almost meant it. Harriet Miller had been a great support in the last case she'd worked with Aaron, but Asha still couldn't help herself. She was scared of this woman who'd drifted in and out of her life for as long as she could remember. Her mother's best friend, the ACC, was only an honorary aunt, and her gimlet eyes had kept young Asha on her best behaviour even without the whipcrack of her voice.

The ACC halted, staring at the whiteboard. "Who did this?"

Nic's misery was palpable. She raised a hand as if she was still at school. "I did, ma'am, but I can soon take it down."

Harriet's eyes flashed. "Why on earth would you want to do that? There's a place for a physical investigation board like this, despite what the *techies*—" she poured contempt into the word —"say. I think it can help to use both visual and tactile aids when working out the timelines. Good work."

Nic flushed, unable to meet anyone's eye. Asha felt for her. The ACC, a force of nature, could be terrifying even when she was doling out praise.

"Now, DS Birch — congratulations on your promotion, by the way — will you bring me up to speed, please?"

Aaron took them all through the known facts, even admitting his own error in not bagging Gerren Penrose's clothes immediately. He was quite right to, because if it came out later, especially in court, the defence would use it to their advantage. Better to cough up and take the punishment than try to hide a mistake.

But the ACC didn't blink or question it; she just nodded for him to go on.

While he was speaking, two other officers shuffled in. One was a middle-aged man with a paunch, greasy dark hair, and food stains on his uniform jacket, as if he'd been eating a McDonald's on the way in and accidentally squeezed out the brown sauce. He didn't meet anyone's eye as he slid furtively into a chair. His manner set Asha's teeth on edge.

The other was a similar age, but well turned out and serious-faced. He reminded her a little of PC Jim Christie from Bangor: steady, reliable, but not the sharpest knife in the drawer. He nodded an apology to ACC Miller and dragged a chair out from behind a desk so he could sit facing the whiteboard.

"Now that we're all here," Aunt Harriet said pointedly, "I'd like to introduce DI Asha Harvey. She's here in an advisory capacity, at least for now, as this case promises to be a tricky one. DS Birch is still SIO. Birch, what are your proposed courses of action for today?"

"We need to check Gerren Penrose's alibi. I've asked PC Stanley to follow that up, as well as canvassing the neighbours about our victim and Mr Penrose."

"Is Penrose a suspect, then?"

"We can't rule him out, ma'am, but I can't see much in the way of motive, not if they've been friends all these years. This was a brutal murder, committed by someone with a lot of bitterness inside them, and Penrose just doesn't come across as the type."

Harriet nodded. "Who else is in the frame, then?"

Aaron shrugged. "No one else at this stage. I hope we'll find a clue to motive by investigating the victim's past. There must be a reason why he was attacked with such ferocity and violence. We have reason to think the murderer may even have used his teeth, like an animal. And it would have taken considerable strength and skill to disable and then dismember a full-grown man."

64

"Very good. Who is looking into the victim's past?"

Nic raised her hand again, and the corner of Aunt Harriet's lips twitched. "Yes, you may go to the toilet." The hand was snatched down. Nic looked as if she wanted to disappear inside her voluminous jacket. The older constable sniggered, which reinforced Asha's dislike of the man.

"Probationary Constable Gordon has already made a good start on that task," Aaron said quietly.

"What have you discovered so far?"

Nic cast a troubled look at Aaron. He gave her an encouraging nod.

"Ma'am, I've been trying to find out where he came from before he moved into the cottage where he was killed. He's lived there since at least 1991 or 1992, but before that there's very little about him. I've a feeling he was in some sort of hush-hush squad in the army, but there's not much detail available without security clearance. I tried following up his known contacts in the army, but that also didn't shed much light, except to suggest that he might have been a bit of a hero."

"Where are the members of his old squad now?"

Nic consulted the sheaf of papers, then frowned as she flicked back and forth between pages. She raised her eyes to the ACC and swallowed.

"They're all dead."

The ACC raised her eyebrows. "Excellent work." Asha tried not to smile at Nic's expression. "Continue investigating. The motive for this man's murder may lie in his past, so the more you can find out about Harris's earlier life the better."

"But, ma'am?" Nic seemed to almost raise her hand again, but thought better of it.

"Yes?" Frostiness in the voice this time. Aunt Harriet might have encouraged the youngest member of the team, but she had limits.

"They're *all* dead, ma'am."

"Yes, you just said that."

65

"According to this article I found, Rob Harris is also dead. He died in Delhi in 1990."

Asha was standing, but didn't remember getting up. "Are you sure it's the right Rob Harris, Nic?"

"Not a hundred per cent yet, ma'am, until I can find a photo of the Rob Harris who died in 1990 for comparison. I'm not having a lot of luck with military records — just don't have the clearance." She glanced at the ACC hopefully, but met Aunt Harriet's poker face.

The ACC turned to Aaron. "We've asked for a media blackout, but it was refused. Has there been any interest from the vultures yet?"

He shook his head. "Not so far, but it won't be long. As soon as we start canvassing the locals, word will get out. Only the remote location of the scene and Penrose's reticence has kept it quiet so far. It can't possibly last."

He'd barely finished speaking when the phone rang. The greasy-haired constable picked it up, then put his hand over the microphone. "Local rag," he mouthed.

Aaron took the phone from him. "DS Birch."

A voice at the other end talked for a while, but Aaron only made neutral noises, then he said, "If there's anything that needs to be in the public domain, a statement will be released in due course. In the meantime, you'd be doing yourself no favours by inventing details of a crime that may or may not have taken place."

He ended the call and looked up sheepishly at the ACC. "Just trawling for now, I think. I was spotted yesterday when I visited Penrose to take his statement and of course the word got around. The journalist was just clutching at straws, asking about an accident on a farm or something."

Aunt Harriet sighed. "It was going to happen. You handled that well enough, but we'll have to release something soon for the press, if only to keep the wolves at bay." She looked around, letting her eyes rest for a moment on each face. Asha held her gaze steadily, but then she'd had years of practice. "I'll leave you to get on with it, then."

When the door closed behind the ACC, the whole room seemed to take a deep breath. Aaron rubbed his hands together. "Right, you heard the ACC. Let's get on with it. Dave, you're canvassing today, both trying to pin down Penrose's alibi and flashing the sheep photo to see if anyone recognises a younger Rob Harris from it, so hop to it. Go a bit easy on the old fella; he had a funny turn when I was with him yesterday, and he's not young, but the clock's ticking."

The constable got to his feet and shrugged himself into a coat, pocketing his phone and notebook. He scowled as he left, but maybe that was because rain had begun to pound down on the roof above them.

"Nic. Go on with what you're doing, but remember to keep it objective. Chris, if you could check in with the SOCOs to see if they turned up anything useful, and liaise with the pathologist about the PM, that would be really helpful. I'd like to attend if I can, so give me a shout when you hear what time it's on." He frowned. "Where do they do PMs for this area? Antrim Area Hospital?"

The constable he'd called Chris cleared his throat. "They all go to Belfast, sir."

Asha smiled. "We can renew our acquaintance with our old friend, the Prof. What do you want me to do, DS Birch?"

This time Aaron blushed. He'd forgotten about her! She probably should have been offended, but it gave her a warm feeling, seeing him take control of a case like this with such assurance. She'd never felt as at ease during the difficult early phase of a new case as he seemed to be.

She took pity on him. "I'd like to attend the PM with you."

He gave an embarrassed grin. "Of course, but would you mind going with PC O'Neill first to speak to CSI? It's Jana and Marley. Jana will give you more information than she would anyone else."

Bravo, she thought ruefully. He really was learning to manage people. "Delighted," she said through clenched teeth.

O'Neill, or Chris, as he shyly introduced himself once they were in the corridor, was reticent but not unfriendly.

They walked in companionable silence down to the basement, where evidence was being logged in to the storage facility by SOCOs. Although the detail would end up on HOLMES 2 eventually, it was quicker to talk to the scene of crime officers.

Marley was at a computer, sorting through digital photographs and entering them into the system, but Jana, knee-deep in boxes filled with plastic bags, was muttering to herself in Polish, probably cursing.

Asha stopped just inside the door. Jana was bent double with her back to them, digging around in one of the boxes. She wore bright pink laddered tights and a short tartan skirt in shades of brown and orange that clashed horribly with the tights and the lime-green hoodie that only partially hid her bright lilac hair. She'd always had her own unique sense of style.

A face appeared upside-down between the pink-clad legs, split in a grin. "Asha! You admire my rear end, no?" She wiggled her hips provocatively, causing the sturdy PC O'Neill to choke.

"Oh, is that you, Jana? I thought someone had vomited a rainbow all over the evidence."

The little CSI straightened and turned to face them, eyes twinkling. "Now my cup is filled. I have the gory murder, with so much blood spatter, and here you are to make my day perfect."

"PC O'Neill," Asha said gravely, "meet Jolanta Wiśniewska, known as Jana, and Marley, known as, well, Marley." She realised she'd never known his full name. "What do you have for us?"

Marley scowled. "You should wait until it's all logged."

"Yes, you're right," Asha said cheerfully, "but we need all the help we can get with this case, so I'm hoping you have something we can use."

"We have fingerprints," Jana said, "but not from the killer, I think. I'm pretty sure he wore gloves, and maybe even a protective suit. The only traces we've found belong to the victim and the old man who found the body. Same with other

68

trace material. We have fabric fibres from clothing, but it all matches those same two men, and a lot of dog hair."

Asha was still focussing on the words "protective suit".

"What makes you think he was suited up?"

"Apart from the complete absence of normal clothing fibres?" Jana waggled her eyebrows grotesquely. "Only this!" She held up an evidence bag that had a tiny strip of blue plastic inside. "I'll test it to be sure, but I think it comes from a set of plastic overshoes, the same as the ones we use at scenes of crime."

Asha wasn't convinced. "Couldn't it have come off one of the sets our lot wore?"

Jana smiled triumphantly. "Nope. Marley found it next to the cooker, and up until then no one had gone all the way into the cottage except Sergeant Birch, who didn't wear overshoes, nor did he go very far inside. We know this because he left his shoeprints in the wet blood."

Asha didn't like the sound of that one little bit. "Surely anyone can buy boxes of disposable plastic overshoes? They must use them in factories and places like that."

Jana nodded. "Yes. We will test and find out where these ones came from, if you want to spend the money. It is the only part of himself our murderer left behind, I think, except for the saliva and the teeth marks."

Beside her, Chris O'Neill shuddered.

CHAPTER 10

The dog whined and put a paw up on Gerren's knee.

"All right, Jack. I'll find us both a bit of breakfast." But when he opened the fridge, there was only one egg and some leftover mashed potato. The cupboard was similarly bare, with only dried goods and a tin of vegetable soup — and the dog food he'd bought yesterday. They'd shared the mince for last night's dinner.

There was no excuse, now he was retired. He'd have to start shopping regularly, especially with another mouth to feed.

There'd been no question in his mind that he would keep Jack. The dog was too old and crotchety to go to strangers, and Gerren was the only soul the dog knew now his master was dead.

He poured dog food into a bowl and put it down for the collie. Jack might be slow, but his appetite was still that of a growing puppy, and the food was gone in a few seconds. The dog whined and looked up at Gerren with a tentative tail wag.

"All right. You can come with me for a walk, lad. I'll buy a bit of bacon and some sausages, and we'll have a treat, shall we?"

The dog wagged his tail and the two of them set off into the village.

He soon realised his mistake. Jack had grown up on the farm and had no idea how to stay out of the way of traffic. A sleek, black car whizzed past them with a blast of its horn and a swerve as Jack trotted out into the street without a glance.

Gerren called the dog to heel, and the old collie came, confused and frightened. "Maybe we should buy you a proper collar and lead first?" Luckily the little general store sold these items, and Gerren picked up a small tin of beans at the same time, as well as a dog chew that claimed to taste like beef. Gerren tried it but could only taste plastic.

Jack whined when Gerren fastened the collar around his thick ruff, being careful to avoid the wounds. "I know, lad. We're both going to have to get used to new things."

He picked up a loaf of bread from the baker's and then stood in the shadows, watching the butcher's shop until May Dunlop disappeared into the back room, untying her apron. That left Walter in charge of the shop.

"Hello, Mr Penrose," the boy said. "What can I get for you?"

Gerren glanced nervously at the bead curtain at the back of the shop, but nothing stirred. "Half a pound of back bacon, rind on, and half a dozen sausages," he said in a hoarse whisper.

"Something wrong with your throat, Mr Penrose?" asked the lad in a clear, penetrating voice. Gerren shook his head. "What sort of sausages would you like? We've got pork and leek or pork and sweet chilli or beef and tomato—"

"Plain pork."

The boy chatted while he weighed and wrapped the meat, but still the bead curtain stayed undisturbed. Then, just as he thought he might get away with it, May Dunlop's voice sang out from the back room.

"Coo-ee, Walter. I've got you a wee sandwich ready. You come and eat it and I'll mind the shop."

Gerren slapped a five-pound note on the counter, grabbed the two packages and ran for it. As he sped up the hill, he heard Walter calling after him, "Would you like a nice bone for the dog, Mr Penrose?" And then he was safe around the corner.

Jack was jumping up and down with excitement on the end of the lead, caught up in the game, and it took a few minutes for Gerren's breathing to come back under control enough to calm the dog down. By the time they reached the house, they were both ready for what was turning out to be an early lunch instead of breakfast.

Gerren dished himself a plate of hot food. He'd made tatie bread from last night's leftovers and a bit of flour, and he was salivating, but he put down a bowl with half a cooked sausage and the bacon rind for Jack before he sat down himself. He tucked a tea towel in around his neck to prevent the fat from staining his shirt, then raised his knife and fork.

The doorbell rang.

He'd ignore it. The first forkful of crispy bacon exploded in his mouth as he chewed, followed by a piece of sausage, dripping juices. The doorbell rang again. Jack growled, but continued to wolf down his own plate of food. The dog had the right idea. Whatever it was, it could wait.

Then a knock came at the window, just behind his back. He spun around on his chair to see a face peering in at him through cupped hands. It was no one he knew; a woman of around fifty with steel-grey hair held back in a severe style that did nothing to soften a hard jaw and flinty eyes.

He turned back around determinedly and took another mouthful, but the joy had gone from the meal.

"Mr Penrose? Could I have a word with you? It won't take a minute."

She had a grating voice, and an accent like someone off the telly. *Coronation Street*, that was the one. Mrs McKee had been addicted to the programme and Gerren had heard it often enough that he could recognise it even through the dirty glass.

He continued to eat, wiping the grease off the plate with a bit of tatie bread, conscious the entire time of her eyes on his back. Well, he wasn't going to give her the satisfaction of getting her own way, no matter who she was.

Finally, he got up and took his empty plate and Jack's empty bowl through to the kitchen. Only then did he go to the front door and open it on the chain. "What do you want?"

Her face pushed up to the gap, and he got a strong whiff of perfume. "My name's Gloria Bryson and I'm from the *Ballyclare News*. I wanted to talk to you about why the police have been interviewing you. Can you spare me a couple of minutes?"

He tried to push the door closed, but she had her foot in the gap. She wore heavy boots, black and shiny, and the door wouldn't budge.

"I have nothing to say. Go away." But of course, she wouldn't, so he did instead. He walked back into his little sitting room and closed the connecting door. As an afterthought, he closed the curtains as well. He opened the book he'd been reading, an academic work on lameness in cattle, realised it was too dark and that his reading glasses were upstairs, and put it away again.

He had a television, but he'd never really learned how to use it and whenever he'd seen it on, when Mrs McKee was still alive, there'd only ever seemed to be the same old rubbish showing. Now, it gathered dust.

A dark cloud settled over him. When he'd been working, he'd longed for some time to himself, for an end to going out in the middle of the night into whatever weather County Antrim could throw at him to grapple with a wet, stinking cow with a prolapsed uterus or a horse with colic.

Now the days stretched ahead of him, each one so very long. Maybe he should take up a hobby? But he couldn't imagine anything he'd enjoy doing. All he could think of was stamp collecting or trainspotting, and neither appealed.

He didn't even have Rob to talk to now.

His fists clenched. Whoever did that to Rob, they were dangerous. Would they really stop at one murder? The savagery had taken his breath away, especially now the shock was wearing off.

"Mr Penrose!" That voice. It could cut glass. "Have you any comment about the police activity up in the hills? I'm told you used to go up there a lot. Do you know anything about what's happened?"

He switched on the television. It came on at the deafening volume his former landlady had set it to. Some quiz show was in progress, all bright primary colours with a host who looked as if he'd taken shares out in Brylcreem and bought his suits from a pawnshop. Terrified-looking contestants tried to guess the answers to ridiculous questions while the host ridiculed their inability to name the winning team in the 1979 FA Cup final and urgent drums sounded the countdown to a klaxon.

He turned it off again. Silence.

"Mr Penrose? People are saying there's been a death and that you were involved. How does that make you feel?"

His chest tightened and breathing became an effort. Beads of sweat popped out on his forehead and ran in a slow trickle into his eyes. He dashed them away.

"Mr Penrose? Wouldn't it be better to make sure the truth is printed rather than just hearsay? I'd like to get your version of what happened, but I have a deadline, so if I can't get it, I'll just have to run with the gossip instead."

He unclenched his fists and forced himself to control his breathing. The sweat slowed and the chest pain receded. Maybe she was right. Maybe it would be better to give his side of things before the gossip started.

She was still at his door, but her foot had moved.

They stared at each other through the narrow gap. She gave him an encouraging smile that almost made him change his mind, then he unhooked the chain, let the door swing open, and walked away from her, back into the sitting room.

"Mind if I sit?" she asked, dropping into his favourite armchair before he'd had time to reply. "I'll just start the recording going." She set a fancy-looking mobile phone on the table, a red light blinking malevolently on its screen.

He'd used a Dictaphone for his visits, recording which animal he'd treated and what drugs and dressings he'd used so he could write up the invoices back at the surgery in the evening, but he regarded the sleek phone with suspicion.

"Tell me all about it," she said in a voice that invited confidence. Jack growled and sat by Gerren's knee, staring fixedly at the interloper.

"What do you know so far?" he asked, pleased at his cleverness. No need to tell her anything if she was just guessing at this stage.

She raised an eyebrow. "I know a very handsome young detective sergeant spent some time with you yesterday and I know something has happened at a place up in the hills. There's police tape blocking off a lane, and apparently that lane leads up to a farm you regularly visit. Who does the farm belong to?"

So, she knew nothing at all. He regretted letting her in, but the damage was done now. He'd tell her just enough to keep her happy then get shot of her. "I heard there was a break-in at the farm," he said slowly. It was true too, up to a point. "The police wanted to know if I'd seen anything amiss last time I was up there."

"So you do know the owner? Lady friend of yours, perhaps?"

Gerren almost stood up, but he managed to keep his cool. "No, just an old farmer. Harris. Got a few sheep. Grumpy old beggar." *Forgive me, Rob.*

"And you were with Mr Harris the night before last, is that right?"

He looked up at her, startled, then realised she was fishing and that he'd given her an answer. "No, as it happens, but I'd like to know where you heard that." As if he needed to ask. There was him, thinking he was avoiding May Dunlop when it was really her avoiding him. And no wonder. Guilty conscience.

"Never reveal our sources," Gloria Bryson said, tapping her nose.

"Well, they're wrong," he said.

"But you were up there yesterday morning, weren't you? Your old jeep was seen coming back down after the police had gone up there. Did you discover the, er, break-in?"

She knew. He'd been a fool.

"I think you should leave," he said.

"That's not very friendly. Are you a suspect, Mr Penrose? There was a police officer asking questions about you this morning. Knocking on doors in the village."

His chest muscles spasmed and a burning pain began in his left arm. Her voice echoed in his ears, and the room was blurring.

It took a while for the pain to subside, and by the time he'd blinked the tears from his eyes, she'd gone. Jack was whining and licking his face. He pushed the dog away but gave his ears a rub by way of consolation.

The front door was open, but there was no sign of Gloria Bryson. She'd left a calling card on the coffee table, with her office phone number, a mobile number, and an email address, as well as a link to the paper's website.

The room was beginning to spin, and he felt as weak as a newborn baby. He needed to close the door to keep the cold breeze out, but it looked so far away.

CHAPTER 11

Aaron really hated post-mortems. Professor Mark Talbot, the state pathologist, kept the Belfast pathology lab clean and fresh-smelling, but there was no way to mask the stench of a freshly dissected corpse. And that stench filled Aaron's nostrils now, before the PM had even begun.

Rob Harris's body was laid out on a stainless-steel table with the dismembered parts placed roughly where they would have been in life. Aaron tried to think of them as props for a movie rather than actual body parts. That was the trick he'd always used, but it wasn't working as well today.

He'd first met Talbot a couple of years before, when he and Asha were investigating a child's skeleton that had been dug up in a garden. The tall, slightly balding man looked as distinguished as he sounded with his plummy English accent, but Aaron happened to know that Mark Talbot had grown up in a sooty two-up two-down in Leeds, and had reinvented himself after he won a scholarship to a public school.

The professor had already told them that he thought Rob Harris had been stunned by a blow to the head with a blunt object before the cutting began. "Tell your SOCOs to look for something heavy and long, like a length of timber or a bit of scaffolding pole. Judging from the impact site and the bruising, it was approximately five centimetres in diameter, so to have caused the fracture to the back of his skull, it would need to be heavy for its width or quite long, to get a good swing in."

"There was nothing like that in the evidence collected by CSI," Asha said. "Maybe we should widen the search?"

"Or the killer took the weapon away with him." He turned his attention back to the body and spoke into the microphone.

"Here we have the right hand. Probably removed first, once the victim was incapacitated, using a very sharp blade wielded with clinical accuracy. Whoever the attacker was, they cut cleanly through the proximal wrist joint, at the distal radius and ulna. Bleeding would have been copious from both radial and ulnar arteries, but the victim may have clasped the stump firmly with his remaining hand, thus stemming the flow. The left hand is heavily bloodstained." He pointed to the other hand.

"Not completely incapacitated, then?" Aaron said.

"The feet were next," Mark went on. "The killer used the same blade, I'm pretty sure, and it became increasingly blunt with each successive amputation, as demonstrated by the slightly ragged edges in the later cuts, right foot first, then left. Last of all was the left hand. By now, the victim would have suffered extreme blood loss and would have been barely conscious, but the killer wasn't quite finished." He pointed to the chest, where several small cuts indicated multiple stabbing attacks. "Same knife, I'm fairly sure. The blade's diameter is . . ."

His assistant, a gangly youth with dreadlocks and a cockney accent, measured the wounds. "Three point five centimetres at the widest point, Prof."

"As to the length of the blade, that must wait until I've opened the chest cavity to see what damage it did inside."

As the post-mortem went on, Aaron became so involved in the detail that he almost managed to forget this was a human being they were discussing. Someone who'd been walking around and talking — and painting landscapes — only a couple of days ago.

"The teeth marks are a bit of a puzzle," Mark said, indicating gaping, tattered wounds around some of the knife marks. "The victim was almost certainly dead by then, yet the killer ripped at the dead flesh with his teeth, tearing away chunks. That must have taken a great deal of savagery and strength and seems in stark contrast to the control exhibited when amputating the limbs."

"It's as if they'd restrained themselves until then, but lost control at the end," Asha said quietly. "So much fury."

Aaron's skin shrank at the thought of someone biting and chewing human flesh. "Is any missing?" he asked. "I mean, did the killer actually eat the victim's flesh or just chew?" Like a dog with a big marrowbone. "And are we sure these are human tooth impressions?"

"Yes, I'm afraid so. Perhaps not good enough to take a mould from, but there's enough to give a partial dental description of the killer, and of course we have their saliva. Hopefully we can get a DNA profile from that." Mark shook his head. "But it depends on the quality of any samples we can get. Still, we'll do what we can. And as for your question about consumption of the flesh, the answer is unclear as yet. I'll let you know as soon as I have more information for you."

He bit his lip, as if trying to decide whether or not to say more.

"Spit it out, Prof," Aaron said. "What aren't you telling us?"

"Well, it's not something I'd be prepared to put in my report — or not yet, at least — but the dentition seems to belong to quite a fine bone structure. You must understand, this is very subjective. It's more an impression than anything, and it could be completely misleading. I'll know more if I manage to get decent moulds, but I think your pseudo-cannibal might be quite fine-featured."

Asha followed Aaron out to his car. "You've been very quiet. What are your thoughts?"

She shrugged. "You both keep saying 'he', but we don't really know if it's a man or a woman, and women have fine features."

"So do lots of men. The level of violence that was used? This is some sick individual, whoever they are."

"We really need to know more about Harris's past. I think you're right, and the clue is in there somewhere. I wonder if we should give Nic a bit of help."

Aaron nodded. "She told me she's hoping to make detective one day, so I think it's important she learns the right way from day one, and you'd be a great role model for her. Her current mentor isn't exactly encouraging."

Asha made a noise of agreement. "Tell me about the greasy-haired fella. Dave?"

Aaron laughed. "PC Dave Stanley — a bit of a grouch. He was promoted to sergeant once, you know? Apparently, it lasted six months, then he begged to go back to constable again. Couldn't take the extra responsibility."

"Interesting. He doesn't strike me as a man comfortable in his own skin."

"You could say that. He's a grumpy old sod, but he's a good officer, just a bit sensitive when it comes to his rights. He's our Police Federation rep and he's mentored a few probationers before Nic."

"I wonder if he'll pick anything up from his canvassing of the locals. It must be quite a small place if one officer is enough to cover it?"

"You have no idea. It calls itself a market town on the sign, but it hasn't had a market worth the name in years, and the locals call it 'the village'. Every Tuesday, a few stalls set up in the square, selling toiletries and clothes and some cheap knock-off handbags. Used to be a fruit and veg stall but that gave up the ghost this year. Back in the day there'd have been a livestock mart there, and people would have come from miles around to see the beasts, but only the old ones remember that now."

"You've been digging a bit into the history of the place?"

He smiled. "Well, I have, but a lot of that came from PC O'Neill. He told me all about it when he was driving me up to the scene yesterday morning. He was born in the place, apparently, but moved away in his teens. Still has family there."

"So that's why you sent PC Stanley in, not O'Neill?"

"Hmm. Although I might use him as my second string, once we have a few basic facts to add to Nic's board. He might get more detail, but I don't want to waste him as a resource."

She laughed. "This role is suiting you, Aaron. You're turning into a really competent SIO." He felt the heat rising. "How's Faith?"

"Good, I think."

"You think?"

"Well. She's away at the moment, studying."

"Yes, I heard. Where did she go? Queen's?"

His deep sigh surprised even him. "No. London. Birkbeck College. She's doing a degree in law and human rights. I haven't seen her since September last year."

He could feel Asha's shock. "But you stay in touch? I mean—"

"Yes, we stay in touch, and her stuff's still in my flat, or some of it, anyway. But honestly, Ash, I don't know what the future holds for the two of us. She seems more interested in her campaigns to protect prostitutes than in me these days."

"I'm sorry," she said. "I hope it all works out."

"So, what about you and Richie Rich, then?" Attack was the best form of defence.

She flushed, her brown skin darkening. "He's well. He's away at the moment too, as it happens. Sailing with his sister. They're heading south to warmer climes. Last I heard, they were halfway across the Bay of Biscay. There's an app I can use to see where they are, but I don't—" She bit her lip. "I'm not sure I want to know."

So, they were both in limbo at the moment. He glanced across at her usually serene face. Asha had been his mentor in his early days as a DC, and they'd worked together on a few cases now. It would have been easy to feel something more for Asha, and perhaps he had once, when he'd been a rookie detective and in awe of her, but their friendship had always been platonic. She was like the big sister he'd never had.

"How's the family?" he asked, moving on to safer territory.

Her face lit up. "Really good. Bapu is currently into wildlife documentaries, so he's looking into ways to save the planet. My mother says he wants to dig a huge hole in the garden so they can have geothermal heating, and he's got solar panel salesmen coming to give him quotes. I think Ma's contemplating moving out for a while until he moves on to his next hobby."

Aaron laughed. Asha's father was a retired bank manager with brains to burn — which he'd passed on to his daughter — and an active imagination. Her mother was ACC Harriet Miller's best friend, and he always felt that Asha had inherited her calm, analytical manner from her.

"What about Peter and the family?"

Aaron sighed. "Haven't seen them in a while, but I think they're okay." He didn't feel like telling her about the tension he'd picked up between his brother and his sister-in-law the last time he'd visited. Even the kids had been affected. They'd been a bit quieter than usual, as if they were afraid of saying the wrong thing. Maybe he'd give them a call this evening, when he got home.

He pulled into his usual space in the station car park and switched the engine off. "Ash," he began.

"It's still your case," she said quickly. "I'm just here in an advisory role. Whatever you say goes, and I promise not to disagree with you in front of your team." She grinned, looking years younger. "What I say in private, however, will be uncensored!"

CHAPTER 12

Nic was becoming frustrated by the time Asha and Aaron had returned from the PM.

"Well," Asha said, "have you found anything more on Rob Harris?"

Nic opened another file. "Sergeant Birch gave me this photo of him at a farming show in June 1995, standing next to Gerren Penrose, so that puts him in the area from at least that date. I have a record of a driving licence in his name that expired in 1994 — no photo — and the passport I showed you went out of date in the year 2000."

Asha made an impatient noise. "We need to find out what our victim was doing before 1995. Have you checked overseas registers? He could have been living abroad, and if so, there must be a record of his arrival in Northern Ireland. Nothing from the rest of the UK or the Republic, I take it? And we really need a photo of your military Rob Harris to compare. Surely it can't be the same man?"

Nic had checked all those already. She shook her head. "Nothing, ma'am. And I have looked. I even contacted Interpol, but they've nothing either."

Aaron butted in. "I wonder if he had any sort of accent. I should have asked Penrose. Nic, will you radio Dave Stanley and ask him to check, please?"

Nic got to her feet. "Yes, sir."

The officer on duty at the front desk was another young PC, all freckles and reddish blonde hair, not much older than Nic herself. He'd joined straight from school, so he'd been here a bit longer than her. He sat by while she radioed Dave, who was, predictably, grumpy at being asked to retrace his steps to the other end of the village. Apparently he'd called on Penrose first, as Aaron had suggested, but found no one home. He grudgingly agreed to go back.

Nic said she'd wait until he radioed in with the outcome. It wasn't that far to walk, anyway. Maybe a quarter of a mile? Half a mile at most. Mind you, her mentor was a bit podgy around the middle, what Ma would call a beer belly. He didn't look as if he did much walking.

"Fancy a coffee?" the young PC asked. What was he called? Nigel?

Nic shook her head. "I don't date fellow officers."

He laughed. "Very wise. Maybe I should have said, 'Do you fancy a paper cup of the brown sludge the machine in the corridor calls coffee?' Because I'm about to have one."

Nic couldn't help but laugh. "Sorry. And yes, please, but not coffee. I'm a tea drinker. Let me buy it though, by way of apology." She fished in her pocket and turned up four pound coins. "Maybe a chocolate bar each if the kitty runs to it?"

"Really letting our hair down, aren't we?" he said, but he took the coins from her. His fingers were icy when they touched her palm. A punishing draught came in through that door when the wind was in the north.

"I haven't yet become depraved enough to risk the sandwiches. Who buys sandwiches from a vending machine anyway?"

He flushed to the roots of his hair. Funny how red-headed people always seemed to have the fieriest blushes. "They're no' bad, those sandwiches," he said. "Well, lettuce is mebbe a bit limp, but I've had worse."

They were still laughing when the radio squawked into life.

"PC Stanley here, over."

"That was quick," Nic said, but that was before she'd pressed the transmit button. "PC Gordon here. Did he remember an accent? Over."

Stanley was out of breath, finding it hard to get the words out. "Call an ambulance. The old fella's collapsed and I can't wake him. Starting CPR."

Nic exchanged a startled look with Nigel, who pushed her aside. He snatched the phone off its cradle and dialled 999, giving the location and as many details about the patient as he could.

"I'd better tell the DS," she said. Nigel nodded and she ran up the stairs to the incident room, crashing through the door without knocking. Two startled faces turned towards her, one dark, one very pale by comparison. "It's Mr Penrose," she gasped. "PC Stanley says he's collapsed. We've called for an ambulance."

"Come with me," Aaron ordered, and she followed him down the stairs and to his car. The shiny new Golf was a far sight from the aged vehicle he'd driven the last time she'd been his passenger, but the deep throaty roar of the engine promised a fast journey. "Radio Stanley," he said. "Get an update."

But Stanley wasn't answering. "And he doesn't carry a mobile," she moaned. "Who doesn't carry a mobile these days?"

She saw blue flashing lights up ahead, about half a mile away at the top of a long rise before the road dropped down towards the village of Ballygroggan. By the time they reached the village, the paramedics were inside the house, all the lights blazing.

"Stay here for now," Aaron said, then he unfolded his tall frame and ran inside.

Typical. She was on the outside looking in again. Nic strained to see what was going on, but dark clouds were massing, causing the light to fade as if dusk was closing around them, although it was barely after noon. She could see nothing inside the house except for the bare bulb in the hallway, swinging a little in the rising wind.

A face at the driver-side window made her gasp. It was a woman with grey hair fastened back in an old-fashioned bun, but her face looked younger than her style. When she saw Nic in the passenger seat, she appeared delighted and opened the door, slipping into Aaron's seat.

"How do you do?" she said, holding out her hand. "I'm Gloria Bryson, *Ballyclare News*. I haven't seen you around before. New, are you?" Hard eyes raked Nic from head to toe, and a flash of recognition dawned in them that made Nic's heart sink. Her photo had appeared in the news a couple of years back, when she'd been abducted, and who would remember better than a journalist?

Nic ignored the hand. "I know who you are. I need you to get out of this car immediately, please."

The woman didn't budge. "I only want a few words," she said, almost pouting. "About the terrible events up in the hills. I know poor Mr Penrose was devastated. Truly devastated."

Nic held her eye. "Ms Bryson, I need you to leave this vehicle immediately, or I will have to report this as an incident." Nic had no idea what that meant, but it sounded like the sort of phrase she'd heard more experienced officers use. For effect, she drew out her notebook and pen. "That was your last warning."

Gloria Bryson gave her a dazzling smile. "Well, aren't you the little tiger, Constable? All right, I'm going, but you should remember that I'm working for the public good here. If there's anything bad happening in this area, the residents deserve to know about it." She opened the door and slid out, then stooped to say, "Do give dear Dave Stanley my love, won't you?"

86

And then she was gone.

Dave had described her as a hard woman with a nose for trouble, and he hadn't been wrong. She wondered if the reporter had expected to find him in the car and been disappointed to find a female officer.

The paramedics appeared in the doorway, carrying a stretcher out to the ambulance. The figure on it looked pale, almost grey, but a bag of fluid hung on a frame above him, and an oxygen mask covered his face, so he must still be alive. Poor old man.

Dave appeared, stripped down to his shirt sleeves and carrying his jacket. Aaron was walking with him, a hand on his shoulder. Nic got out of the car and went to meet them.

"Is he going to be okay?"

"Thanks to PC Stanley's presence of mind," said Aaron, "he has a fighting chance. Dave carried out chest compressions till they arrived. The paramedics said it was a miracle the old fella was still holding on."

Nic looked at her mentor with fresh eyes. "You must be exhausted. That's hard work."

Dave gave her a tired smile. "You do it in first aid training and hope you'll never have to use it, but when the time comes, it's nothing like doing it on a plastic dummy. Yes, I'm knackered. Could do with a pint," he finished with a hopeful look at Aaron.

"And you deserve one, but first, we need to get the basic facts off you. A detailed statement can wait until tomorrow, but can you just run me through the events as they happened for now? Sit in my car, if you like."

Nic sat in the back and the two men in the front. She hung between the seats, elbows propped on the seat backs, and listened.

"I was at the other end of the village when PC Gordon radioed to say you needed to ask the old boy a question, so I set off back up there. He'd been out when I went up earlier, and I planned to go back anyway once I'd finished in the village. This time the front door was open, so I was instantly worried. I was about to call it in as a possible break-in when I saw his feet." He wiped his brow. "Gave me a shock. Thinking about that place up in the hills, you know? But I went in, calling his name, and then he groaned."

"Was he conscious when you found him?" Nic interrupted. Aaron shot her a look and she subsided. "Sorry."

"He was lying on the floor, clutching his chest. His eyes were closed, and he didn't respond when I called his name. I checked airways and circulation, but I couldn't really feel a pulse. Maybe just a wee flicker. His lips were blue too. Fair scared me, it did, but the training kicked in. Chest compressions, singing 'Stayin' Alive' in me head, you know? Even though we're not supposed to do that anymore. No idea how long I'd been at it before the ambulance crew arrived and took over. They checked him over, then used those electric plate things." He snapped his fingers, trying to remember.

"Defibrillator," Nic supplied.

"Yeah, one of them. It must pack some punch because his heart seemed to take off again, and then they did an ECG and loaded him onto the ambulance."

"You did well," Aaron said. "Probably saved his life." But he was frowning. "Did you say the front door was open when you got there? No one else in the building, though?"

"Honest, sarge? I didn't look around. Just concentrated on the casualty, like. But I didn't see anyone there, and I think I'd have noticed if they'd left, 'cos they'd have had to walk through my line of sight to get to the door."

"And Mr Penrose wasn't anywhere near the door?"

"No. He was in the wee sitting room." Stanley shook his head. "But now you mention it, there were two part-empty mugs on the table, so maybe he'd had a visitor before I got there."

"Maybe," Aaron said, "but I had a mug of tea with him yesterday when I was taking his statement. We'll check them for prints, but it's possible he just hadn't got around to washing them up."

"Something must have triggered his heart attack," Nic said. "I wonder if that reporter had been annoying him?"

Aaron shifted in his seat to look at her. "What reporter?"

"That Gloria woman from the *Ballyclare News*. She was here just now, while you were in the house. She wanted to know about the 'terrible events' up in the hills, and said she knew Mr Penrose was very upset about it."

"Bitch!" Stanley spat. "I'll bet it was her, sarge. She'll have been here questioning him, pretending she knew more than she did, and that'll have upset him, all right." His face had darkened alarmingly. Nic hoped he wasn't going to have a heart attack next.

"She sent you her love, by the way, Dave."

"She what?" If anything, his face reddened even more. Nic had heard the expression *beetroot red* when applied to a complexion, but never actually seen it.

"She was yanking your chain, Dave," Aaron said, "but I think we might need someone to have a word with her bosses at the paper. And it's definitely worth looking into. If she's been badgering a witness, and that led to his heart attack, she could be charged with harassment."

"Not to mention leaving him there all alone and in pain," Nic added.

"I'll ask DI Harvey or maybe even the ACC to have a word with the paper. That media blackout would have been a good idea. Maybe this will be enough to tip the balance and get us it." Aaron sighed. "How did you get on with the canvassing, Dave?"

"I think Gloria's been shoving her nose in already and stirring," he said. "Everyone I spoke to had a different theory about what happened. They all seem to know it was up on the hills, and some — like the butcher, a Mrs Dunlop — know the victim's name, but have no idea what happened. The commonest theory seems to be that there's been a break-in up there."

"Were you able to pin down Gerren Penrose's movements at all?"

"That's where that Dunlop woman was useful. Apparently, she had Penrose around for dinner that evening, but she says he got a phone message around nine and had to leave. She thought the message was from his friend, Rob Harris."

CHAPTER 13

Asha held the phone a few inches away from her ear. ACC Miller — definitely not Aunt Harriet now, judging from the frostiness in her voice — wasn't happy.

"Any news on the old man?"

"DC Birch has been in touch with the hospital, ma'am. Apparently Mr Penrose is going to be okay, but he's very tired and woozy at the moment. I think Aaron's heading over there to try to speak to him as soon as he's allowed."

"Terrible thing to happen. I only hope the newspapers don't get wind of it, or it'll be headlines screaming, 'Police brutality pushes old man to collapse,' and we can't have that."

"Actually, I was hoping to speak to you about that," Asha said. "There was a reporter, Gloria Bryson from the *Ballyclare News*, hanging around outside the house. We think she might have forced or tricked her way inside to question Gerren Penrose, because her card was on the coffee table. PC Stanley found the front door open, and Mr Penrose was a long way from it. Bryson tried asking PC Gordon questions, but she very correctly sent her away with a flea in her ear. The thing is, ma'am, this woman is spreading gossip around the village.

Half the folk PC Stanley questioned already knew something was up. Someone's been putting ideas in their heads."

The ACC huffed out a sigh. "I'll have a word."

Asha went back to the incident room to pass on the good news.

Nic was bent over her keyboard, just as Asha had last seen her, but she wasn't typing. Asha cleared her throat.

Nic jumped. Whatever was on the screen had been holding her full focus. She turned her face up to Asha. "Have you seen the news?"

"No. Why?"

"There's been a fatal stabbing at a house in Newry. Multiple wounds. The attack is described as frenzied and with no obvious motive."

Asha shrugged. "Off our patch."

"Yes, I know. Just thinking how awful it is, two violent attacks in such a short space of time."

"Seems to be the way of the world, these days." She peered over Nic's shoulder at the news article. There was a picture of a forensic tent over the front door of a terraced house, with neighbours gathered around in nervous groups. "What's the address?"

Nic named the street.

"That's a mesh of wee housing executive terraces. Couldn't be more different to the scene we're investigating. Not as violent as our case, by the sound of it."

"Apparently, the victim was sleeping in the house with his wife and daughter when someone broke in and stabbed him to death. It's just that phrase, 'frenzied'. Reminded me of our case. I'm sure they're unrelated, but . . ."

"I'll tell you what," Asha temporised, not wanting to shoot the girl down. "Why don't I give the SIO there a call and ask to be copied in to any new data, just in case?"

Nic beamed at her. "Thank you, ma'am."

"Your instincts have been known to hit the mark occasionally, I suppose," Asha said, laughing. Then she wished the words back, because Nic's face crumpled. The last time she'd managed to persuade someone to believe one of her hunches, Aaron had been seriously injured.

The Newry SIO was an older detective, DI Sandy McGurk, whom she'd known when she lived in Rostrevor. He took Asha's request seriously.

"The victim's wife got up to see what was going on, and she witnessed the stabbing. She also heard the killer's voice, and she swears it was a woman."

"A woman?" Did the killer leave any evidence behind? Prints of any sort?"

"Apart from the knife embedded in the victim's chest? There were some boot prints in the back garden where she ran across a flowerbed. Nothing we can use, though. The killer must have been wearing shoe covers, like the ones we wear at a crime scene, and they disguise the tread and the size of the shoe. Also he or she wore gloves, and possibly a coverall of some sort. The wife says they were dressed in something dark and baggy."

"Will you keep me in the loop, please? I expect it's unrelated to the case we're working on, but we can't ignore a second attack so close after the first."

"Will do," he said. "It'll all be on the system soon, though. Feel free to pop in if you're passing, and give my regards to your mother, will you?"

Asha had always suspected the older man had a bit of a thing for her ma.

She stared at the phone after the call finished. Nic watched her with big eyes. "You think they're connected too, don't you?"

"Not really. They might be close together in time, but they're a long way apart geographically. It's about an hour and a half's drive to Newry from here. And what's the motive for either murder? I suppose you could look for a connection between the two victims later, but before that I need you to join PC Stanley. If that reporter has been shoving her nose in, it'll need tact and empathy to find out the truth of what anyone did or didn't really see or hear instead of what the press wants them to say they witnessed."

After she'd gone, Asha logged into the system to see what other evidence there might be from the second murder, but there was very little so far, just a bit of background on the victim and his family. He had been a cabinetmaker, apparently, working for a local furniture-making business. Forty-two years old with a wife and two daughters, only one of whom had been home at the time of the attack.

He had been born in Northern Ireland, but his own parents had moved here from Pakistan with two of his five brothers. All three boys had stayed in the same area their parents settled, carving out careers for themselves in trades. There was a list of names and addresses of the three family groups. The parents lived with the eldest son.

There was nothing here to explain why this man had been chosen as a victim, and nothing obvious so far to tie him to the official owner of the cottage. There was no sign that Harris had been anywhere near Pakistan or that the second murder victim had been near Ballymena.

Nic's notes lay on the desk where she'd left them. Asha leafed through, reading the neat handwriting easily. She'd drawn up a timeline with events above and below a horizontal line. The ones above were labelled *R.H.* and ones below, *H.C.* Who on earth was H.C.?

The earliest note for H.C. was *1960 (extrapolating from army records), born in Southern Rhodesia (now Zimbabwe. Need birth cert.)*, then *Joined BSAP around 1979*, followed by notes for when she thought he'd joined the British Army and the date he left again, in 1996, not long after he'd been promoted to major.

After that, she'd used a different colour, perhaps to indicate her uncertainty about the information from then on. But what was clear was that H.C. disappeared just before their victim, R.H., appeared on the timeline in Ballygroggan. What sort of speculation was Nic indulging in now?

94

It was only when she sifted through the pile of clippings Nic had accumulated that the penny began to drop. Nic was wondering if a Harold Cavendish had taken over Rob Harris's identity after the other man died in Delhi.

Asha bit her lip. She knew from the time she'd spent with Nic in the past that she was a thorough researcher, and she had great instincts. What they needed was someone with the punch to ask questions of international contacts in high places.

There was really only one choice, and Asha quailed a little at the thought of asking yet another favour of the ACC. Still, it was in Aunt Harriet's best interests too if they got to the bottom of this case quickly.

Before she had time to bottle out, Asha called up Aunt Harriet's number from her contacts.

"Asha." Nothing else, just her name with no inflection. Asha swallowed, resisting the urge to clear her throat, which would be interpreted as a sign of weakness.

"Ma'am. We're still having a little trouble tracing our victim's history before 1988, and I wondered if you might be able to help us."

"Of course I'll help if I can, but I can't see what I can do that your very efficient probationary constable hasn't already done."

"We're trying to find out if there's a link between our victim and a second man from his unit in the Gulf War, a man called Harold Cavendish." She took a deep breath, then just said it. "He also had a military background. British Army. And before that, he was in the British South African Police. He disappeared around the time a certain Lieutenant Rob Harris was killed in Delhi, just before the first rumour of our victim, Rob Harris, turning up on a remote farm in the wilds of Antrim."

The ACC was quiet, and Asha wondered if she'd made a mistake calling her. "So you're saying that your victim might have changed his identity and stolen that of a dead colleague?

If he really was Harold Cavendish, you'll need to track down everything you can about the African side of things. If he was British Army back then, he'd need to have British citizenship or prove long-term residency. Maybe that's a good place to start?"

"Yes, ma'am. We're looking into that. Is there any chance you'd be able to help us? There's a limit to what we can access, and it seems this squad was involved in some hush-hush stuff, so anything about them is well wrapped up in red tape."

"I'll see what I can do."

CHAPTER 14

Gerren woke to the muted beeping of hospital equipment. He tried to open his eyes, but the lids seemed too heavy and the lights too bright. Damn, his chest felt bruised. He tried to bring a hand up to touch it but found he didn't have the strength.

"Hello, are you awake, then?" asked a bright voice. "You're in hospital, Mr Penrose, but you're going to be just fine."

He forced open his eyes, blinking until they focused. A young nurse was hovering over him, beaming like a ray of sunshine on an overcast day.

"What happened?" At least that was what he'd intended to say, but it came out as a low moan. He clenched his fist in frustration.

But the nurse seemed to understand. "You had a heart attack, but the doctor says you should be all right with a bit of care."

A heart attack? He remembered a pain in his arm and tightness, and *that woman*! The beeping speeded up a little, and the nurse placed a cool hand on his forearm.

"Easy now. Don't let yourself get excited or you'll undo all the good of the medicine."

He wanted to tell her that he wasn't just some old geezer, that he knew more about the workings of the heart than any young nurse, that he knew what was best for him. But he found he couldn't be bothered arguing, so instead he closed his eyes in protest and waited for her to go away.

Maybe he dozed, but the next voice he heard was male. He opened his eyes a little more easily this time, and was relieved to find that he was thinking a bit more clearly after his nap. If this was the doctor, maybe he'd get some sense from the man now he was feeling a bit stronger, but the tall, slim figure in the dark pullover and trousers didn't look like a doctor. No hospital ID and no stethoscope dangling around his neck.

Recognition dawned, followed by annoyance. Couldn't the police leave him alone and just get on with finding out who killed Rob?

"Mr Penrose. How are you feeling?" DS Birch said. He perched uncomfortably on a hard plastic chair next to the bed. "The doctor says you're going to be fine, but you still need to rest for a while."

"Don't need no rest." He knew his Cornish accent strengthened when he was stressed, but there didn't seem to be anything he could do about it. He frowned at the intelligent face. "What happened, exactly?"

"One of our constables found you collapsed in your cottage. Luckily, he's first aid trained, and he did all the right things. The paramedics say that he probably saved your life."

That was a bit of a facer. Owed his life to a copper, did he? "What was he doing in my place to start with? That's what I'd like to know."

The young sergeant smiled. "You can blame me for that. I sent him to ask you one more question."

"More questions? Haven't you asked me enough already?"

"Just one." But he didn't say what the question would have been. Gerren scowled at him.

"Well?"

"Are you sure you're feeling strong enough? The doctor made me promise not to pester you."

"Just ask the damn question!"

The lad wasn't fazed. "It was just to ask you if your friend, Rob Harris, had any accent that you were aware of? Did he ever say where he was from? And do you have any idea when he moved here?"

"I'm not sure when he came here to live," the old man said querulously. "I met him in the pub, I think. Odd, really, because he wasn't the type to go to the local, but I think that's when I first saw him. Then I went up to the sheep a few times, and we got talking. Maybe mid-eighties? He sounded English to me. Spoke with a posh accent."

And he had, but there'd been that time he'd come in and found Rob singing to himself in a different language. *Siembamba, mamma se baba* . . . When Gerren had asked him what language it was, Rob had laughed and said it was a nursery rhyme he'd heard once from a fellow he'd worked with long ago, but not one you'd get away with today, because the mamma kills the baby. That's why it had stuck in his memory. Such an odd thing to say.

"Have you remembered something?" the DS asked.

"Maybe, but I don't know if it's what I'd call useful." He told him about the song, even managing to reproduce a snatch of the tune in his croaky old voice. The sergeant wrote it all down, except he couldn't write down the tune. Then he did something very odd. He got his mobile phone out and spoke into it without dialling.

"Hey, Siri. What is this song?" Then he sang the same snatch of refrain Gerren had just sung.

Much to Gerren's surprise, the phone answered him back, "*This sounds like 'Siembamba' by*—" and a name he didn't recognise.

"Interesting," the sergeant said, tapping away at his phone screen. "Looks as if it's a South African lullaby, sung in Afrikaans." His eyebrows shot up. "There's a translation here. Wow, and I thought 'Rock-a-Bye Baby' was bad! Could Rob have had a South African accent, do you think?"

"I don't think so. Seemed to me he spoke the Queen's English, public school style, you know? Round vowels and all. Always seemed too posh for his style of living."

"I guess I'm going to have to do some reading up on South Africa. From what I remember, their history's almost as bloody as ours in Northern Ireland. Did you ever ask where he came from?"

"No. Why should I?" He shifted himself a little, trying to make it easier to breathe. "We didn't talk about that sort of thing."

"What did you talk about? Politics? The weather? Religion?"

Gerren snorted a laugh. "Sheep, mostly, and yes, the weather, but only as it related to liver fluke and foot rot. It's damp up there on the hills."

His breath was coming in wheezing gasps now, and an alarm went off on the monitor hooked up to his finger.

A moment later a nurse came in, checked his readings, and told the copper politely but firmly that it was time for him to leave.

After the young sergeant had gone, Gerren laid his head back against the pillows and closed his eyes, trying to bring Rob's face to mind. It disturbed him that he couldn't, any more than he could remember the sound of his voice.

Theirs had been a distant sort of friendship. He hadn't been lying about the conversations they'd had over dominoes and a pint of the black stuff. They'd never really tried to find out much about each other, both equally content to let the past remain undiscovered. Now Gerren wondered if he should have asked more questions. He didn't even know who Rob's next of kin was, or if he'd left the farm to anyone. Did he have children? Had he ever married?

There had been scars on both his hands, puckered edges of ragged wounds, that Rob had laughed off as old rugby injuries, but Gerren had never really been convinced. Once, when he'd surprised Rob up on the hill, cutting peat, he'd seen a nasty scar on his shoulder, front and back. He'd never seen a scar from a bullet wound, but that was certainly what it had made him think of.

Rob had slid his shirt back on without comment, and Gerren had never asked.

Too late for regrets now.

And a South African lullaby? That was a bit of a shock. If he'd wondered at all about it, he'd probably thought it was German or Dutch. As he only spoke English himself, Gerren hadn't worried about it at the time, but now? What did he really know about his friend? That he was a good sheep farmer, with a keen eye for disease, spotting the early signs before it devastated his flock. He was an artist, with a dark vision of the world. And he liked to be alone, discouraging visitors. Gerren thought he'd only been tolerated because he wasn't the sociable type himself either. Rob had been the closest he had to a friend.

The next visitor was even less welcome. A voice out in the corridor alerted him first, a voice he'd heard across the counter of the butcher's shop for decades, and one that made him squirm. If it hadn't been for May Dunlop and her nice leg of lamb, he'd have gone up to visit Rob that night, and then maybe his friend would still be alive.

He just had time to lie back, eyes closed and mouth hanging slightly open. He made his hands relax so the fingers opened like an upturned spider, like they would when he was asleep.

A change of air pressure told him the door had opened, but he kept his breathing slow and shallow and his face relaxed.

"Oh, he's sleeping," said May in a stage whisper. "I'll just sit by him for a while, shall I?"

"Visiting time is just finishing, I'm afraid," said the cool, clear voice of the nurse. "And as Mr Penrose is sleeping, I don't think you should stay. You could always come back tomorrow. Visiting is from two to four in the afternoon and seven to eight in the evenings."

"I won't be any trouble," replied May, sounding as if she was getting ready for a fight. "I've brought him a nice pork pie and a Scotch egg."

Gerren struggled to keep his breathing even. The implication was that hospital food wasn't to be trusted, and that wouldn't go down well with the staff!

"I'm afraid we can't allow visitors to bring in food for patients. Often, they're on a special diet for medical reasons, you see. I can tell him you called by when he wakes, if you like, but I'm afraid I must ask you to leave now."

"Is he? On a special diet, I mean?" May Dunlop sounded affronted.

"As you're not family, I'm afraid I can't share—" The nurse's voice cut off as the door closed behind her. Gerren kept his eyes tight shut, just in case, until the door opened again. "It's all right, Mr Penrose. She's gone now. You can open your eyes."

He did, laughing. "How did you know?"

"Because you were too quiet," the nurse said, twinkling back at him. "I've sat with you while you slept, and your snores would wake the dead." She checked his blood pressure and his pulse. "You need to rest still, so maybe try to go to sleep for real, why don't you?"

"I'll be fine," he said automatically, but he knew he'd been ignoring those chest pains too long, pretending they were indigestion. He hadn't had time to be sick when he was working. Animals needed him, and he couldn't let them down.

There was understanding in her grey eyes. "Still, best do as the doctor says for now, yeah?"

He sighed, noting the slight twinge. "All right." Then as she was leaving, he called her back. "Why's my chest so bruised? Feels like I've been run over by a horse."

"That's from the chest compressions that kept you alive until the paramedics got to you. Resuscitating someone is not for the gentle, you know. It takes serious force to compress the ribs far enough to keep the heart going."

He did know. He'd done it himself, but that was on a dog. The thought of dogs jerked his memory back. "What about the dog? There was a dog in my place, an old farm collie I was looking after for—" He couldn't finish the sentence, as he remembered that Rob wasn't coming back.

The nurse shrugged. "I don't know anything about a dog. I'm sorry."

The machine reflected his anxiety as the frequency of the beeping increased again. "I need to know he's all right," he said. "He's just lost his owner, and now he's lost me. He'll not know what's happened."

She smiled reassuringly. "I'll mention it to that nice detective sergeant, shall I? I'm sure he'll make sure the dog's looked after."

"Would you? And will you let me know what he says?"

She glanced at the monitors, a little frown creasing her brow. "I will. Promise. Now, you need to rest if you want to get out of here anytime soon!"

Her words had a soporific effect on him. As the door closed behind her, he had to fight down a yawn, but he'd not sleep until he'd heard about Jack.

Illness and the warmth of the room finally overcame him, and despite his best efforts, his eyes closed.

CHAPTER 15

Aaron took the call from his car. "Dog? No. There was no sign of it when we were there. I'll see if any of the team know anything about it."

He called PC Stanley first, but the older man said he hadn't seen it in the cottage. In fact, he'd forgotten its existence, or he might not have gone into the place at all. Savage animal, it had been up at the farm, and he'd never have trusted it.

Damn. Aaron called the station and asked for a patrol to do a drive-by of the old farm in case the animal had returned home. PC O'Neill answered, and he said he'd do it himself, since he still had the Range Rover signed out. And he'd contact local animal charities, vets, and the pound in case the dog had been picked up anywhere.

Aaron thanked him. He wouldn't have thought of that.

When he rejoined Asha in the incident room, he found her hunched over a computer terminal, looking not unlike Nic had. Her fingers didn't tap as efficiently, but there was that same intensity of expression.

"Found anything useful?" he asked.

"Not yet, but I have put out a few feelers. I've been looking through Nic's notes, and I think she might be on to something after all, you know."

104

"Her pet theory about a fake ID?"

"Hmm. I've asked the ACC to sound out her contacts in military intelligence about all the squad, but especially Harold Cavendish and Rob Harris. I was also thinking that we've neglected to investigate Gerren Penrose's past in any depth, so that's what I'm doing now. Did you know his brother was jailed for murder nearly twenty years ago?"

"I did not. He failed to mention that."

"Trevik Penrose. Younger brother. Apparently, he took a kitchen knife to the man who was having an affair with his wife. Admitted to it straight away, pleaded guilty, served fifteen years and was then released into the community. I'm trying to find out where he went after that."

Aaron pulled a chair up beside her, looking over her shoulder. There was a photo of a man in his forties with a beard and moustache. It was hard to trace any resemblance to the old man he'd seen taken away in an ambulance that day. "Is that him?"

"Yes. He'd be older now by about twenty years. That was taken when he was arrested. He's eleven years younger than Gerren. Other than him, there's only one sister, Derwa, and she died of breast cancer while Trevik was still locked up. She was closer to Gerren's age."

She opened another file. "Here we go. Trevik went back to the family farm in Cornwall, apparently. There was another police report about him three years ago. Seems he tried to scare his cousin out of possession of the farm, with a spate of theft and sabotage. The cousin never pressed charges, but there's no mention of Trevik anywhere I've looked after that."

"I don't suppose he came over here, looking for his big brother?"

"There's no evidence pointing that way, so we'll have to leave him out of the equation for now. Did you turn up anything new?"

"Only that Gerren Penrose might be lying. According to May Dunlop, the woman who owns the butcher's shop, he did have dinner with her, but he left at nine."

Asha frowned at him. "But that ties in with his statement, doesn't it?"

"Except Mrs Dunlop says he left in response to a text from Rob Harris and he supposedly said he was going straight up there when he left. If that's true, it could put him at the scene sometime during the night, and there's no way of knowing if his Land Rover had been up there all night when he called the murder in or if he'd just gone up that morning as he claimed. He could still have killed Harris that morning."

"CCTV?"

Aaron laughed. "You must be joking. This is rural County Antrim. I've asked Dave to have a look around the village in case there are any on private homes, and the same for the route up to the farm, but I'm not holding my breath."

"Maybe someone saw him."

"Not that they're saying so far, and unfortunately that reporter has really stirred the waters. Most people are that confused now about what happened, they're imagining they saw things they didn't. I could kick her from here to Belfast."

"Is this the same reporter who we think caused Gerren Penrose's heart attack?"

"The very same. Gloria Bryson from the *Ballyclare News*. She's been poking around, asking questions and putting ideas into people's heads. And yes, it's likely she was there when Gerren Penrose had his heart attack. Someone left the front door open, and whoever it was didn't stay to help him or even call for an ambulance. Her card was on the table."

She looked shocked. "Any news about the old man? How's he doing?"

"Worrying about the dog, Rob Harris's dog. It seems to have run off. And I asked him about Harris's accent, by the way."

"What did he say?"

"Said Rob sounded English to him, upper class. But he did remember his friend singing a lullaby that turns out to have been in Afrikaans."

Asha's mobile rang before she could comment, and she snatched it up. "Hello, ma'am. That was quick."

Aaron couldn't hear the other side of the conversation, but Asha took notes as she listened, then rang off with a thank you.

"That was useful. The ACC has given me a contact number for someone Cavendish worked with in the army, a fellow officer. She says this man is willing to help us."

"Go for it," Aaron said. He looked at his watch. "It's getting late. I might just touch base with everyone and then call it a day. Will you let me know if you discover anything? Use my office if you like, for privacy."

She nodded, intent on tapping the number into her phone.

Aaron didn't have an office as such in this station, but he was camping out in the one belonging to the absent Sergeant McBride. It was decorated with photos of the sergeant and her husband on various walking holidays or skiing down mountains. The potted plants she'd placed on virtually every flat surface were looking thirsty and dusty, but he was too scared to water them in case he killed them off.

O'Neill answered eventually, sounding a bit out of puff. "Sorry, sir. I'd left the phone in the car. I've found the dog, and he seems fine, but I can't get near him, I'm afraid. He's halfway to the farm, trotting along the side of the road as if he knows exactly where he's going."

"Is he a danger to traffic?"

"Not at the moment, but it'll be dark before too long, and he's mostly black. I was thinking of phoning the vets or the pound to see if they have one of those dog catcher things, but then I remembered the local vet is in a hospital bed. I don't like calling the pound, because if they take him, he could get put down before Mr Penrose is well enough to look after him."

"Leave it with me," Aaron said. "I have an idea. Can you keep an eye on him for a bit? I'll call you back."

O'Neill agreed, and Aaron rang off, then searched through his contacts for an old colleague, Josh Campbell, whose wife had been a police dog handler before she left the force. It took Josh a while to answer, and he sounded flustered when he did. In the background a wailing sounded, not unlike an air-raid warning from a World War II film.

"Josh, it's Aaron Birch. Bad time to call?"

"Oh, hey, Aaron. No worse than usual. Claire has had a vomiting bug and the youngest is teething. Hang on a mo."

Aaron listened to his fellow officer negotiating with a child, thinking with a small pang of guilt about how long it had been since he'd visited his own nieces and nephews. He'd give Peter and Ellie a ring as soon as he could, and maybe try to pop in on them over the weekend.

A door slammed and the phone went quiet, then Josh's voice came back on. "Sorry about that. What can I do for you?"

"If Claire's sick, maybe nothing," Aaron said. "I have a murder investigation going on up here, and the victim owned an old farm collie. His friend took the dog in, but now the friend has had a heart attack, and the dog's wandering loose along the edge of a fast road."

"You want someone to come and fetch him?" Josh hazarded.

"I was hoping Claire might be able to, but maybe she knows someone else who could? The dog's a bit uncertain of temper with strangers, and he was wounded in the attack that killed his owner."

"I think we might be able to help," Josh said. "Claire's on the mend now, and we have her sister coming to babysit for us shortly, so we could set off in maybe half an hour? We'll bring the van because it has a dog cage in the back."

"You might need one of those long catching pole things too," Aaron added. "The officer I have up there with him says he's not keen to let anyone close."

"No wonder, poor old lad," said Josh, the dog lover. "I'm sure we'll manage."

Aaron let O'Neill know that help was on the way. The stolid constable said he was happy to stay with the dog until they arrived. He made it sound as if he had nothing better to

108

do at this time of night than sit in a police car with his hazard lights on, guarding a dog. A twinge of guilt bothered Aaron. This was all a part of his budget now, and he'd have to explain away any overtime paid to his officers. But what else could he do? He couldn't leave the dog at the roadside when it could cause a crash.

His phone rang. "Dave. Got anything?"

"Not sure, sarge. There's a couple of private homes here with CCTV. One house at the edge of the village has a camera on the front of it, pointing towards the road Penrose would be likely to use if he drove up to the farm. They're going to download the footage for the relevant times and give it to us, but the other house has nobody home, and the neighbours think the family might be away on holiday. That camera looks as if it would take in the front of the butcher's shop and the side of the old vet's building, where Penrose often parks his Land Rover."

"That sounds promising. Have the neighbours any idea when the homeowners will be back?"

"If they went for a week, they should be back today or tomorrow, but if they're on a three-week cruise or something, we might be buggered." He sniffed. "I gave my number to the neighbours and asked them to call me if the owners turn up."

"Good work. It must be getting dark there by now. How about you call it a day? Briefing tomorrow morning at half eight. Maybe the missing neighbours might have come home by then."

He wandered through to see if Asha was still there. She was just putting the phone down, an arrested look on her calm features.

"Anything useful?" he asked.

"Very. This fella knew both Cavendish and Harris. He says Cavendish was a lunatic who didn't know the meaning of fear. He shot up the ranks in the army like a cork out of a bottle — his words, not mine. The sort of stuff they got up to was right up his street, apparently."

109

"Does that get us any closer to linking him to our victim?"

"No, but there's more. The guy I was talking to didn't particularly like Cavendish, but he had a lot of time for his friend, Robert Harris, who was in the same small unit as Cavendish. Apparently the men in that squad were a tight crew, and they kept a lot of secrets. He said that they'd have died for each other. This man confirms that Harris died in 1990 on a mission in the Yemen. Cavendish was on the same mission, and he brought his friend's body back to the family, apparently at great personal risk."

Aaron shrugged. "So, what are you saying? Cavendish took his dead friend's identity and then disappeared until he popped up here as a corpse?"

"I have no idea, but it's looking more and more possible." She shuffled the papers, frowning.

"You have more?"

"Just one thing. Not sure how important it is. Nic noticed there'd been a murder last night in Newry. A stabbing. She's convinced the two might be connected because of the frenzied nature of the attack, but I'm not so sure. I spoke to the SIO, and he said the victim's wife reported hearing a female voice in the house at the time of the killing. They're not discounting, at this stage, that their killer could be a woman, and he's going to keep me in the loop."

"Doesn't sound very promising." Aaron yawned suddenly, one of those jaw-wrenching yawns that take over your whole body. "Look at the time. I'll get people looking at Penrose's brother as well. Then we can see if we can draw a solid connecting line between Cavendish and Harris. Have you eaten yet? We could get pizza?"

Neither of them felt much like eating out, so they bought pizza and took it to Aaron's flat. Asha said nothing to him about the changes since she'd last visited him there. Only now, seeing it through her eyes, did he realise how much Faith had stamped her mark on the place. Her coat and scarf hung on a peg just inside the front door, and her boots were in a corner.

The Denby crockery had been her suggestion, and the smart napkins and placemats.

Since she left, he'd changed nothing, hoping she'd come back to him one day; now he realised he was just in denial. She wasn't coming back. At the beginning, the phone calls and video chats had been regular, and she'd been full of interest in the details of Aaron's life, the cases he was working on, and the people they both knew. But the calls had tailed off over the months, and the last time he'd video-called her, she'd kept her camera off. He was fairly sure there'd been someone else in the room, trying to be quiet, and it had bruised his heart. He couldn't bring himself to ask her outright, and she'd never called him back since.

He bit into his pizza as if it was a condemned man's last meal while Asha nibbled politely at hers and sipped at the white wine they'd picked up from the offie around the corner. Maybe that's why his mouth was full when his phone rang.

He pushed it over to Asha and mumbled that she should answer it.

"DI Harvey here, on DS Birch's phone," she said, punctiliously. Then she listened for a bit, her pizza forgotten. "Hang on, Josh. I'll put you on speaker. Aaron's here too."

Josh's voice rang out across the room. "We got the dog, no problem, but your PC O'Neill says he can smell smoke, and we're just at the end of the lane up to the farm the dog came from. Thought we should let you know we're going up there to investigate."

Asha pushed her almost untouched glass of wine aside. "We're on our way."

CHAPTER 16

Aaron drove with all his mind on the job, aware of the few sips of wine he'd drunk before the phone went. Not enough to put him near the limit, but he knew as well as anyone how even a small amount of alcohol can slow the reflexes. Rain lashed the windscreen, turning the road ahead into a hazy monochrome landscape. They arrived at the end of the lane to find Claire sitting in the blue van she and Josh used as a runabout, and to carry their many retired police dogs as well as the other waifs and strays they picked up on their travels. She got out as they pulled up on the verge and walked over to meet them.

"Josh has gone up with Chris," she said. "It was lucky he had the four-wheel drive, or they'd never get up there, not after all the rain this evening."

A steady stream of dark brown water was running down the lane and across the public road, carrying mud, small stones, and peat with it. Aaron took a deep breath and smelled what the others had smelled. The wind was blowing down from the hills, and it bore with it the unmistakeable scent of smoke.

Asha stuck her head out of the car, blinking in the driving rain. "Josh says the fire's just about out. It didn't reach the cottage, but the barn's just a skeleton now. They're coming back down."

The Range Rover was almost unrecognisable when it finally appeared at the end of the lane, splattered with dirt to its rooftop. Chris O'Neill pulled in behind Josh's van, and they all crammed inside it to hear the report.

"We'll need SOCOs up there in daylight," Josh was saying. "It was hard to be sure in these conditions, but there did seem to be an area that had been much hotter than the rest, and there were bits of rectangular wood, some with gold leaf on them. Maybe picture frames? Do you remember anything like that in the barn yesterday?"

Aaron thought back. He'd walked all around the property and been inside the barn, but there'd been nothing like that stored there. There hadn't even been any unidentified piles of stuff under canvas, or he'd have looked, but there had been plenty of pictures in the cottage. "No. It sounds as if someone might have taken the pictures down from the walls inside the house and set fire to them. As you say, it'll be easier in daylight. I'll send a callsign to secure the scene and then a CSI team over there first thing to take a look." He should have had someone up there, maintaining the integrity of scene. If he hadn't messed up again, the fire might never have been started.

By the time they reached his flat again, both he and Asha were exhausted. He mumbled that the bed was hers and crashed onto the sofa. He didn't even remain awake long enough to know if she'd argued or not.

* * *

Aaron wasn't the only one yawning at the morning briefing. Nic had brought cardboard cups of coffee for everyone apart from herself — she must have trained herself to be able to be in the same room as coffee now, but he didn't think she'd ever drink it again, not with the memories it must trigger. She'd bought a box of doughnuts along as well, from a wee shop around the corner. Aaron eyed them with mixed feelings. On the one hand, they were the best doughnuts he'd ever tasted; on the other, his belt had moved a notch since the place had opened.

He made a mental note to start running again, before he was past the point of no return, and helped himself to a pistachio one with soft, green icing on top. Another twinge of guilt when he remembered that pistachio was Asha's favourite flavour, but it served her right for turning up late. She'd muttered something about needing to make a phone call and disappeared into Sergeant McBride's office. He'd give her another couple of minutes, but then they'd have to make a start.

For a while the only sounds were slurping and murmurs of enjoyment, then he glanced at the clock, swallowed down the last bite, and licked his fingers clean.

"All right. Thank you, Nic, for providing the yummies, but we have a murderer to track down. And it seems he or she might have gone back to the scene of the crime. I've got CSI heading up there this morning, but it looks as if someone has torched the barn at Harris's farm. Maybe burned his paintings too. We only know this because of an escaped dog and Chris O'Neill's nose." He left that hanging cryptically in the air for a moment.

O'Neill nodded. "I phoned the hospital about the dog last night, by the way, and asked them to pass the message on to Mr Penrose, to give him peace of mind."

I should have done that. "Well done. Dave, how did you and Nic get on last night?"

PC Stanley wiped his mouth with the back of his hand and cleared his throat. "We've had a look through the footage from the house at the edge of the village, and there's no sign of Penrose's car passing the night before Harris was killed, but it did go out on the morning he found the body, which fits with his story."

114

It was encouraging that the dour constable was talking about Penrose *finding the body* now, instead of assuming he'd been the killer.

"But he might have gone out on the other road, knowing there was a camera there," Dave continued.

Somehow, Aaron couldn't see the old man even being aware of the existence of CCTV cameras, never mind thinking about how to avoid them, but then people often did surprising things. "Any news about the other residents coming home?"

PC Stanley looked at Nic.

"I phoned the number the neighbours gave us, but it went straight to their answering service, sir. I left this number and asked them to get in touch with us as soon as possible."

"Okay. Let me know if they contact you. I'd like to see that CCTV footage to confirm Penrose's story as soon as we can."

"But sir," PC Stanley interrupted, "we have no other suspects. No one else in the village seems to have known much about Harris, and Penrose is the only one who called him a friend."

"Well, they'd hardly admit knowing him well under the circumstances, would they, since it would automatically put them in our sights?" Nic snapped. She caught Aaron's eye and apologised. "Sorry, but I just can't see that old guy killing anyone, never mind dismembering his body and biting the flesh."

"There's always the chance it was someone who'd found out he was ex-army and decided to use him as a scapegoat for some of the atrocities committed during the Troubles. Or even an old grudge. He was so isolated up there, it seems unlikely anyone would just stumble across him." Aaron glanced again at the clock, wondering where Asha was.

She came in, cheeks red and eyes shining. "Sorry I'm late." She opened her shoulder bag and took out some papers, laying them across the desk. Everyone gathered around. There were heavily redacted documents barred with thick black lines where text had been hidden, but then she produced a photo. It

115

showed a group of men in desert fatigues standing next to an old-style Land Rover with a camouflage net over it. Someone had drawn a circle around one of the men in red, lest there be any confusion, but Aaron was already excited. The resemblance to their victim was clear.

"This is an elite unit about to be deployed just before the Gulf War in 1990." Asha placed another photo next to it.

"This is Rob Harris — the real Rob Harris, taken from his military records." There were similarities, for sure. The same dark hair, similar face shape, but the brows weren't as heavy and dark and there wasn't the same impression of granite in the eyes. Not their victim, and not the man circled in red in the first photo.

Lastly, she laid down a copy of the clipping Aaron had found, of Harris with Penrose at the local agricultural show. With the images side by side, the features of the man circled in the Gulf War photo could be traced through an ageing face. He'd become more stooped in the recent image with the sheep, the shoulders less powerful, but it was the same man, Aaron was certain of it. This was their victim, without a doubt.

"And look at the names of the men with him in the Gulf War photo."

Aaron squinted at the faded print. It said, L to R: Lieutenant Robert "Trigger" Harris, Captain Roy "Forrest" Beecher, Major Harold Cavendish (the man ringed in red), and Major George "Whisky" Bailey. The man on the left was shorter than Cavendish, but the resemblance was obvious even in the old photo.

He took a deep breath. "So, Cavendish did steal Harris's identity." He looked helplessly at Asha. "Now we have confirmation, how can we use it?"

"You said from the beginning that the clue to motive would lie in his past, and with a past like this, and a change of identity, I imagine there'll be plenty of material to work with. We just need to plough through his background to find it. For

116

a start, why the name change? *Something* drove him to hide in a remote cottage in the mountains, so we need to discover what that something was."

"Okay," Aaron said, "we'll concentrate on Cavendish-slash-Harris and divide his life into sections. Nic, I'd like you to take a look at his early life in Rhodesia, please, until he left to join the army."

"Zimbabwe," Nic corrected him.

"Yes, today. But in those days it was Rhodesia, a British colony. In fact, it was Southern Rhodesia when he was born in 1952. And then it became independent in the 1960s — Rhodesia, run by a minority-white government." Aaron, aware that he was beginning to sound like a textbook, trailed off. "It only became Zimbabwe in 1980." Nic flushed, so he smiled to take the sting from his words. "Nic, could you look at his time in the army too?"

She nodded.

"Good. Then I'll look deeper into his time living on the farm, and his relationship with Gerren Penrose. Dave, I'd like you to have a word with our local hack, please, and try to warn her off — gently, mind, but firmly. You know the routine. Interfering with a murder investigation, et cetera."

"Up to now, she's only been guessing that there's been a murder," Nic piped up. "Won't telling her she's right just encourage her?"

PC Stanley gave her a condescending smile. "It's what's called doling out titbits," he said. "Give her a little something she can call a scoop and promise her more at a later date. Enough to make her salivate for the rest of the story. That ought to keep her out of our hair. Right, sarge?"

"Right," Aaron agreed, "but do be sparing with what you give her, Dave. I don't want any details leaking out, or our witnesses will be even less useful than they've been so far. I'm going to the hospital to check up on Penrose and warn him not to talk to the press at the same time. Any questions before I leave?"

117

No one answered. Nic was already attacking her keyboard and Dave was squeezing himself inside that tweed jacket he wore that made him look like a racecourse bookie from the nineties.

Asha followed Aaron out. "Can I use your office again while I speak to the ACC?"

"Yes, for what it's worth. And it's not really my office, so don't judge me on the décor, okay?"

She laughed. "It's all right. Your secret fetish for potted plants is safe with me."

Aaron drove to the hospital, his mind teeming with ideas. The murdered man must have something in his background to explain the barbaric attack, surely? Then he caught himself up. Victim blaming? He wished he could stop second-guessing himself all the time. It wasn't really victim blaming, was it? Whatever he'd done in the past, it couldn't be enough to justify such a savage murder. Whoever killed Rob Harris — he corrected himself: Cavendish — must have carried hate in their heart for a long time to drive them to not only stab but dismember and then tear into the man's flesh with their teeth.

His phone rang just as he was parking up at the hospital. It was Asha.

"I've just had a call from the SIO in the Newry murder case that happened the night after Rob Harris's murder. He's had a preliminary report from the PM and forensics, and it looks as if it might have been the same knife that was used in our murder."

"Do they have the knife?"

"It was left at the scene, the SIO thinks accidentally. Apparently, the victim's wife and daughter both woke, and the killer fled. It's a fairly ornate affair, possibly an antique of some sort. We're trying to trace its origins, but so far all we have is that it might have come from the Indian subcontinent. Sandy says it would have been worth a lot more money if someone hadn't replaced the jewel in the hilt with glass."

Aaron drummed on the steering wheel with his fingers. "If it's the same knife, this puts a new perspective on the whole thing."

"Yes," Asha said in a sober voice. "It's early days, but we could potentially have a serial killer on our hands."

Aaron walked into the hospital deep in thought, trying to make sense of the two crimes. On the face of it, they had nothing in common. Jibreel Khan had been in his forties, the father of two daughters aged five and fifteen. His neighbours said the family were quiet, kept themselves to themselves. They still had to trace the elder daughter, who wasn't at home at the time of the murder, but Aaron couldn't see a fifteen-year-old girl as a double killer. Not for this sort of killing, anyway.

Gerren Penrose looked far healthier, sitting up in bed with a little colour in his cheeks. He was tucking into a plate of toast and jam when Aaron knocked on his door and entered.

"Morning, lad. Thank you for finding Jack. I was proper jumping to think the old boy had been through all that and then got isself lost." His Cornish accent seemed thicker this morning, but Aaron got the drift.

"It's all right, sir. We didn't want him to get hurt. He's with a colleague of mine now. They've dogs of their own, but they're keeping him apart in a kennel, and they said he settled in well enough. Ate a good dinner last night, so he can't be too bad." He nodded towards the plate on Penrose's tray. Only crumbs were left.

The old man laughed. "You're not wrong there, boy. I feel like a new man this morning and can't wait to get home. Dratted doctors want to keep me in for observation, whatever that means, but I reckon I'll be out of here later today."

"I hope so," Aaron said politely. "But in the meantime, mind if I ask you a few more questions?"

"Ask away. It's not as if I have anything better to be doing, is it?"

CHAPTER 17

Asha had amassed a pile of notes by the time Aaron reappeared. She rubbed her eyes, suppressing a yawn. It was only half ten in the morning, and she already felt drained.

"Did you get anything useful from Gerren Penrose?" she asked as he pulled a second chair across to the desk.

"Not as much as I'd have liked — he was pretty vague about dates — but I still feel he's telling us the truth. He hasn't stayed in touch with his brother, the convicted murderer, but he gave me a few starting places to search for him. He seemed genuinely shocked when it dawned on him that we might be looking at him for his friend's murder."

"What did he have to say about the text from Harris?"

"He says he invented that text as an excuse to get out of May Dunlop's house! He was embarrassed. Said he should have admitted to it sooner, but he'd had too much to drink that night, and he wasn't thinking straight. I think he sees our Mrs Dunlop as a bit of a femme fatale."

"But he was originally planning to go up to the farm that night, wasn't he? I'm sure he said that in his statement somewhere."

"He says he was, but that May Dunlop ambushed him and as she's such a good cook, he couldn't bring himself to turn down a meal with her. She'd bought in his favourite local beer and everything, and before he knew it, he was three sheets to the wind and feeling trapped. He said he'd assumed her son would be eating with them, but he went out and left them alone."

Asha laughed. "Poor man!"

"Yes. He wore a bit of a hunted expression when he was telling me about it. He gave me his mobile so I could check for texts, and there isn't one from Harris from that night, not that that proves anything." He shoved an evidence bag across the desk with an old-fashioned brick mobile in it. "I brought it along for Bishop to check, in case any texts have been deleted, but I can't imagine they have. What have you got?"

Asha leaned back in her chair and steepled her fingers in a bad imitation of their former boss, Yvonne Patterson. "I thought you'd never ask. I asked the ACC for a favour. She's prodding the army, trying to make them give up all their secrets."

"Wow, you're really bringing in the big guns!"

"Yeah. I'll probably pay for it later, but she says she'll take it to the very top if she has to. I think she's enjoying herself, actually." The affair last winter, when she'd become embroiled in the hunt for two rogue ex-policemen, had really given Aunt Harriet a new lease of life. "Anyway, her help has freed me up to take a look at this second murder."

"The Newry stabbing?"

"Yes. The only connection that I can find is the possibility of a similar knife, but the SIO is sending me details as they come up. They're still looking for the missing elder daughter, and the local press are already stirring up trouble, hinting that she might be the killer. I just hope they manage to find her before she reads about her father's death in the newspapers."

Her phone rang and she glanced at the screen before picking up. She raised her eyebrows. "Speak of the devil. DI Harvey here."

"Morning, Asha. Sandy McGurk here. We think we might have a sighting of the eldest daughter, Hadhira Khan.

121

She was seen getting onto a bus for Belfast two nights ago, so we've been on to the bus company to see if their driver remembers her."

"I'm putting you on speaker, Sandy. I have DS Aaron Birch here with me." She tapped the speaker button. "Did the bus have cameras?" Many of them did, these days, in case of trouble.

"Vandalised," Sandy said. "The bus went all the way to the Europa Bus Station, off Great Victoria Street, so we've asked them to review their footage from the bus's time of arrival, and we've picked her up. I'm sending over some images now. The thing is, we lost her when she left the station. It was dark, the streets were busy, and we've not been able to find her in the crowd, but she turned right heading towards Shaftesbury Square, and she was carrying a rucksack."

Asha's laptop pinged as an email arrived. She opened the first attachments: a series of stills showing a young woman in jeans and a loose sweater, wearing a hijab and carrying a black rucksack. Nothing much could be seen of her face, but she was lightly built and walked with a long, fluid stride.

"I've got the pictures." She opened another photo. This was a family photo showing the four of them, on a beach-front somewhere. The women all wore scarves, but in this one, Hadhira's face could be clearly seen. She looked very young.

"Her mother has identified her from the clothing and rucksack in the footage," Sandy said. "The thing is, she doesn't seem to have checked into any hotels in the area, and her mother says she'd have had very little money with her. Are there any hostels or anything around there that she might have stayed at?"

"Yes, tonnes. At this time of year they're full of visiting students, tourists on a shoestring budget . . . and perhaps people running away from home. Do we know why she left home late at night with hardly any money?"

Sandy laughed without humour. "The mother is pretty cagey about that. She says she's too upset to talk about it. I'm guessing there was a bust-up of some sort. I've got a family liaison with them, so I'm hoping we might pick something up, and I've put in a request to child services to ask the younger daughter a few questions, but she's only five, so I don't rate my chances."

"Do you want me to get someone to call around a few hostels and show them Hadhira's picture?" Asha asked.

"That would be really helpful, if you can spare the manpower with your high-profile case going on. Is that okay with you, DS Birch?"

"We'll manage," Aaron said. "Any more on the knife yet? I take it there are no prints?"

"No prints. The killer wore gloves, a suit, and overshoes from the looks of it, because we haven't found a trace to identify them yet."

"Apart from the female voice the wife heard," Asha prompted.

"Apart from that, but if it's the same killer, a woman carrying out a murder as violent as the one you guys are dealing with doesn't sound likely, does it? That sort of loss of control is usually associated with male killers."

Aaron opened his mouth to answer but Asha got in first. "Sandy has a degree in psychology, and he's been working as liaison with the National Crime Agency's psychologists."

Aaron nodded. "I'll admit I thought the same thing," he said. "But the pathologist did say that the dentition of the bite marks was quite fine, and might have belonged to someone with fine features. He wouldn't put it in his report because it was too subjective an opinion."

"Interesting. Well, I suppose it's not unheard of, but we need to keep an open mind for now."

"Thanks for bringing us up to speed, Sandy," Asha said. "We'll do the same for you as soon as we have anything more concrete. For now, we're still digging into our victim's past in case we can find a motive hidden there. And we're still looking for a link between our victims, of course."

"Okay. Speak soon."

After she'd ended the call, Aaron looked at her with a quizzical expression. "When you say, 'send someone to check the hostels', who did you have in mind?"

Asha laughed. "We can both go, if you like? But maybe I should get Nic to draw up a list first."

Nic was humming to herself as she worked, with at least a dozen tabs open on the browser. She looked up with a start when Asha walked in.

"How's it going?"

"I'm working my way through the members of Harris's squad, starting with Cavendish, but it's surprisingly hard," the young woman said. "My mum did a bit of genealogy research a year or two ago, and I remember how she used to track down distant relatives using birth certificates and marriage certificates and all that. This is very similar, but Cavendish doesn't seem to have married or had any kids that I can discover. He grew up on a cattle ranch in rural Zimbabwe — or Rhodesia as it was then — just outside Fort Victoria."

Asha had met people like Cavendish, who'd grown up in Africa and had it easy until rule was taken from the white overlords and returned to the Black Zimbabweans people. Some of them had lived on tobacco farms or Arabian horse studs that had belonged to their family for decades, with black servants rearing their children and running their farms while they partied with other white folks. When the political climate shifted and apartheid became a dirty word, they'd fled to Europe with little but the clothes they stood up in, filled with resentment at having had their perfect lives wrenched from them. They'd get together in little cliques, bemoaning the loss of lands they considered their own but no mention of the way those lands had originally been acquired from the black population.

She'd been to school with some of their children, very independent kids who didn't always adapt well to living in a city when they'd been used to having hundreds of acres of farmland to roam on horseback.

"Go on," Asha said.

"Well, he joined the mounted division of the police there in 1979 when he was still eighteen — they had national service, but he stayed on beyond the usual three years. Apparently, they were deployed alongside the regular army, because the horses could move quickly and quietly over rough terrain. And although they were called police, they sound much more like an army to me, battling black resistance fighters — Rhodesia was under white-minority rule. It was a civil war, I guess, and pretty nasty with it." She was reading this from one of the web pages she had open. "He made it to inspector, by the way." She gave Asha a sideways look.

"Hmm. I don't think I would have, not in those days. And not with my skin colour."

"You could still progress up the rankings if you weren't white, one of the few places it was possible," said Nic. "But somehow I don't see you galloping across the veldt with a rifle slung over your shoulder and a bush hat on your head."

"Oh, I don't know," Asha said vaguely. She'd ridden horses competitively in her youth, including some eventing. Riding was like cycling: once learned, you never forgot the skill, and the thought of galloping a good horse beneath the blazing sun didn't sound too bad at all. She dragged herself back to the job in hand, trying to zone out the sound of rain hammering the windows outside.

"I need you to do another job for me, if you don't mind. A list of hostels and other cheap places to stay in Belfast within walking distance of the Europa Bus Centre. Probably out Shaftesbury Square direction. We have a possible sighting of the missing daughter from the Newry stabbing case, and the SIO has asked us to show her photo around."

"So the two cases *are* connected?"

"Maybe. Similar weapon, at least, and the killer left it behind in Newry, so that should give us a bit of help. I'm going to give the Prof a call from the car to see if he has a description of the weapon used on Cavendish for comparison."

"I'll get onto the hostels," Nic said. "But I can name a couple off the top of my head. Hazel — you remember my sister? — she volunteers for a hostel for the homeless and she's mentioned a few other places." She scribbled a couple of names and street addresses on a Post-it note and handed it to Asha.

"That's great. We can start with these, and you can text me with any more you find."

She joined Aaron just inside the back door that led out to the car park. The small glass panel was blurred with the rain that drove in waves against the door. They both fastened their raincoats and pulled up their collars ready for the sprint to Aaron's car. Maybe a stint in Zimbabwe with blazing sun and dry heat wouldn't be so bad — was it still hot there in winter?

Professor Mark Talbot sounded pleased to hear from her. "Asha, my dear. You must have read my mind. I was about to give you a call, but you beat me to it."

"Oh? What about?" She crossed her fingers.

"There's an interesting link between two of the cases I'm dealing with at the moment. The weapon left in the body of our Newry victim is a pretty close match in shape and size to the knife used on your victim, so I ran a few tests on the edge, and it turns out there's blood from two victims on it. Blood group of the earlier sample matches your victim. I'm waiting for DNA to confirm, but it seems likely the same knife was used in both murders."

* * *

It felt strange to be back in Belfast again. As Aaron threaded the streets, expertly slotting the Golf into a tiny parking space against the kerb, a pang of nostalgia struck her. She'd spent years working from the Lisburn Road station, but the good memories were laced through with poison, and she hadn't much felt like coming back here since she'd left for Bangor.

The first hostel, and the closest to the bus station of the ones Nic had given her, was an international one, very smart and not at all what Asha had expected for some reason. Aaron stayed in the car in case of traffic wardens while she went inside to speak to the duty manager, a tall man with a neat beard and a warm manner.

She identified herself, showed her badge, and asked if he kept records of people who'd stayed at the hostel.

"We do," he said, eyes wide with curiosity. "We ask for photo ID and payment on arrival, but I really shouldn't be sharing people's personal details. GDPR and all that, you know?"

"Yes, I understand. I'm hoping you might have had a young woman called Hadhira Khan staying here recently." She showed him the photos on her phone.

"Hard to recognise her from those," he said with a nervous titter. "We get a lot of ladies wearing hijabs, and honestly, I'm not sure I could tell one from t'other, as they say." When he saw the full-face image, there didn't seem to be any more recognition. He shrugged.

"What about the name? Can you check your register? If they have to show photo ID, she'd have had to use her real name, unless she used a fake ID."

He flushed. "This isn't the sort of place where fake IDs are used. We're a very respectable hostel, not some party venue, you know. We keep strict hours with no loud music from—"

Asha cut him short. "The register?"

He flounced across the small distance to the back office and produced an old-fashioned register in book form. The place was so modern Asha had expected digital records, but apparently not.

He ran his finger down the page. "Let's see. Khan. It's so hard to read their signatures. Ah, here we are. But not Hadhira Khan. This guest signed herself Fatma Khan."

Maybe the girl had stolen a family member's ID. She'd need to ask Sandy. "What dates was she staying?"

"Well, she signed in on the evening of the fifth, two days ago, and she hasn't signed out, so she should still be here. She paid for three nights, it seems, so tonight would be her last night unless she decides to stay longer."

127

"Can you take me to her room?"

"She's sleeping in a dorm room, but it's mostly empty. She was sharing with one other woman, but she left on the sixth, so Fatma should be on her own." He was talking too much, his eyes darting from his register to her face and away again, dying to ask why she wanted to know, but fearing a snub.

Asha smiled encouragingly.

"Well, I suppose there's no harm if I knock on the door and ask if she'll speak to you. But you'll have to wait outside in the corridor. Our guests' privacy is very important to us."

The hostel was a maze of modern carpeted corridors that could just as easily have belonged to a commercial office building. The manager stopped outside a dark purple door and knocked.

"Hello? It's the manager. Anyone home?"

No one answered, but there was the sound of something heavy falling over, followed by a scraping that made Asha think of a stiff window latch. But up here on the third floor, all the windows would be restricted opening, wouldn't they? To prevent would-be suicides or people high on drugs from trying to fly.

"Open it."

The manager spluttered, then took a look at her face and unlocked the door with his master key. Asha barged past him, just in time to see a very slim young woman trying to squeeze through a small gap where the window opened just enough to let air in.

"Stop!" she cried, but the girl was in a flat panic and hearing nothing. Asha dashed across the room and grabbed her ankles, pulling. A foot slammed her in the mouth, and she tasted blood, bitter and metallic. "A little help?"

The manager was worse than useless. He fluttered around, making unhappy little noises, but didn't seem able to bring himself to touch the escapee. Asha shifted her grip, pinning down the other ankle as well, and hauled.

With a slither and a pop, the girl was dragged back into the room. She collapsed on top of Asha and went limp.

Asha pulled herself free and bent over the still form. A small, pale face, fine-featured, lay fully exposed. She carefully pulled the scarf back to cover the girl's hair and smoothed her fringe. When the girl's eyes opened, they were dark brown and swimming with tears.

"I won't go back," she sobbed. "I won't."

"It's all right," Asha said, as soothingly as she could, keeping her distance. "I'm a police officer, and I'm not here to hurt you. Are you Hadhira?"

The eyes flashed past her towards the door, as if seeking an escape route, then back to Asha's face. "No. Who is this Hadhira?"

Asha turned back to the manager, who was now wringing his hands. She was momentarily distracted: she'd never seen anyone actually do that before. Then she recovered herself. "Could you please tell my colleague who's parked outside the hostel that we've found her? He'll know what to do." They needed this child taken somewhere safe immediately, and Aaron would have a social services team out here to her as quick as he could.

The manager reversed out, still muttering complaints and questions that Asha ignored.

"Leave the door open, please." She waited until she heard his tread retreat down the corridor before turning back to the girl. "I'm going to sit here with you for a wee while, all right? My colleague will get a team here from social services, and we'll have you safe in no time."

There was a pair of sinks against the wall. Asha dampened a bit of paper hand towel and handed it to Hadhira, who dabbed at her cheeks and eyes. They sat side by side on chairs that wouldn't have looked amiss in a school staffroom.

"What are you so afraid of, Hadhira?"

A deep, sobbing breath. Then, in a tiny voice Asha could barely hear, "My father." She closed her eyes. "I ran away from him. I thought he'd sent you to bring me back and make me marry that pig, but the police wouldn't do that, would they?" A thought seemed to startle her. "How do I know you are police?"

Asha pulled her warrant card out of her trouser pocket. "I'm sorry. I should have showed you this straight away, but my hands were a bit full. I won't ask any more questions for now. There'll be time for those later, once we have you safe."

The girl bit her bottom lip, looking even younger than her fifteen years. She wore not a trace of make-up, but she was beautiful with those fine, clear eyes and a heart-shaped face beneath naturally arched brows. She'd never need make-up. "I'm sorry. Did I hurt you?"

Asha touched her lip with a fingertip. It was fat and bruised, but that was all. "I've had worse."

CHAPTER 18

It felt like ages to Asha, but eventually footsteps sounded on the stairs, and a moment later, a harassed-looking older woman appeared at the door. She wore a lanyard with a photo ID dangling from it. "Sally McCreight, Children's Services," she said, sounding out of breath. She smiled down at the girl, and Asha was relieved to see kindness in the slightly myopic eyes. "You must be Hadhira, you poor wee thing. Is that your bag? It looks as if you've packed already, have you?" Then she turned to Asha. "I can take things from here, Inspector. I have another colleague on her way here."

"I'm not leaving," Hadhira said, and set her lips in a thin, stubborn line. "I want to stay here until my friend returns. She told me I never need to be afraid again. She promised."

Asha froze in the doorway, knowing she should leave. Whatever the girl said couldn't be used in evidence: Hadhira was a minor and needed a parent or guardian with her before she could be questioned, but she couldn't resist waiting to hear what else might spill out.

She noticed that although only one bed had been recently slept in, the upper bunk of the bed opposite also had a rumpled look as if someone had made it in a hurry. Was this

131

Hadhira's mysterious friend? She opened her mouth to ask, but the social worker gave her a hard stare, and she changed her mind. Later.

In the entrance area, the manager was fussing around, shuffling papers, clearly determined not to miss anything. He looked up as she appeared. Asha walked past him and stuck her head out of the door, glancing up at the front of the building. There it was: a CCTV camera pointed down to record the entrance and the pavement for a few feet either side. She went back in to confront the manager again.

"Does that CCTV camera work?" she asked. "Do you have any CCTV inside the building?" She couldn't see any.

He pouted, but there was a glint of interest in his eyes. "It works, but I believe you'll need a warrant before I have to show it to you."

"I can certainly get a warrant," she said agreeably, "but it would be much easier if you just let me have a look at the recordings, or better still gave me a copy."

"We take our guests' privacy very seriously," he said, but his heart wasn't in it. He wasn't about to let an opportunity like this pass him by. She gave him another nudge.

"It's possible that a person of interest in an ongoing serious investigation may have been picked up on the cameras. It would be an immense help to know if it's worth applying for a warrant."

He bit his lip, dragging out his reply, but she knew she'd won. "All right. But you'll need a warrant if you want copies from me. Is that clear?"

"Of course."

It was disappointing. Asha went back over the last couple of days in fast forward, slowing every time a female figure appeared.

"That's the young person's roommate," the manager said unexpectedly. "I remember she always wore that long coat with the hood pulled up, and those sunglasses."

Asha examined the figure. Tall, slim build, mannish stride. That was all she could determine. The quality of the footage wasn't great either, but she got the feeling this woman might be purposely hiding her shape and appearance behind the baggy clothes. "Did you ever see her face?"

The manager shook his head. "I didn't really see her at all. Both times I was on duty, she just whisked past the desk and up the stairs before I could even say hello."

Damn.

* * *

Aaron was waiting where she'd left him. "Tell me," he said.

She related what she'd heard Hadhira say, and they speculated all the way back to the station about what it meant.

"Some woman told her that her father wouldn't trouble her anymore?"

"Words to that effect, yes."

He whistled. "Interesting."

"I'll get Sandy McGurk to ask her more about that when he interviews her," she said. "But I expect Hadhira's case is going to be passed on to the Forced Marriage Unit, once Sandy's got her story for his murder case. They'll need to get her sister under protection and question the mother. What a mess."

"When did she check into the hostel?"

"The evening of the fourth. Rob Harris was killed on the fifth, early in the morning, and Hadhira's father was killed in the early hours of the sixth."

She left him to get the ball rolling while she went through the reports from Newry again. It was sometime later before Aaron reappeared.

"Sandy's sent us a transcript and video footage of Hadhira's preliminary interview," he said. "Want to see it?"

The video was in colour, and of reasonable quality. Hadhira sat with her knees drawn up to her chest, feet on the chair and backpack held as a protective barrier in front of her.

"Apparently the mother is in custody, based on whatever Hadhira said informally before she was brought in, so there's

133

a social worker been appointed as her temporary guardian."
That would be the motherly figure sitting on the same side of
the table as the child but sitting sideways on so she wouldn't
look too intimidating. "They've already broken the news to
Hadhira about what happened to her father."

Sandy wasn't in the interview room; perhaps he'd thought
a female officer would be a less threatening figure, given
Hadhira's relationship with her father. The sergeant took
Hadhira through the questions as gently as she could, trying to
win her confidence, and gradually the story unfolded.

Yes, her mother had known about the beatings. No, she
hadn't helped Hadhira. When appealed to, she'd been sympathetic but told her that her father's word was law and that
she should do as she was bid. Asha felt sick, listening to the
matter-of-fact little voice.

"So I ran away," the girl said. She hadn't cried throughout the interview, but now her eyes filled with tears. "I didn't
want to go. I love my little sister, Nadira, but I couldn't stay.
My cousin is old, much older than my father, and he is not a
good man. His wife died last year in Pakistan where they live.
She took her own life, my mother says." She frowned. "Well,
she did say that at the time, but my father was angry that she
had said that, so then she told me she had been wrong and
that my aunt died of cancer, but I know that is not the case. I
think she did take her own life because she was so unhappy."

Pakistan. That would make it difficult to check Hadhira's
story. Asha took a note of the names of the uncle and the aunt
and the town they lived in, just in case.

The interviewer asked Hadhira about her journey to
Belfast. Hadhira had taken some cash from the jar on the
mantlepiece where her mother kept her housekeeping money
and bought a ticket to Belfast, leaving straight from the holiday club she was supposed to be attending all month. She'd
told her mother that she would be going to her friend's house
to work on GCSE coursework with her, so they wouldn't start
looking for her until late in the evening.

"Was the money the only thing you took?"

Hadhira looked away. "I am not a thief. I would have paid my mother back, and returned her passport."

"Is that what you used when you checked into the hostel? Her passport?"

"Yes. We are very alike, my mother and me, and the receptionist didn't look closely. I didn't want to use my own name."

"You mentioned a woman who promised you your father wouldn't hurt you again. Tell me about her."

This was the important part, but Hadhira didn't know that. She was happy to describe the woman who'd held her in her arms and listened to her as no one had ever listened before. From what Hadhira said, it sounded as if her own family didn't go in much for hugging, or sharing emotion for that matter. It must have been a new experience for this girl to have someone's full attention and feel their sympathy.

Because that's what the woman had given her: first sympathy, then understanding, and finally hope. And money. She'd given Hadhira enough cash to allow her to stay in Belfast until she found herself a job.

But when the interviewer tried to draw a detailed description out of the girl, she failed. It seemed she'd spent much of the time with her head buried in the woman's shoulder, sobbing out her story, and the woman had held her there.

"Then what was she wearing? Smart clothes? Denim?"

Hadhira shook her head. "I'm sorry. Something soft and fleecy as a top, because I said I was worried I'd ruined it with my tears. She smelled of the outdoors, you know? A sort of wild smell. And of smoke too."

"That's really helpful, Hadhira. Thank you."

A dark look met her words. "She did nothing wrong, that woman. She was kind to me, that is all. You need not look for her. Besides, she is gone by now."

"Still," the interviewer said carefully. "It'd be nice to find her so we can thank her for looking after you, wouldn't it?"

"You think she killed my father." She shook her head. "No. I don't want you to find her. If she killed him, she did it for me, and I will do nothing to help you find her." Her face twisted in disgust. "I shouldn't have told you anything at all about her. If you had told me you suspected her, I would not have. You do not fight fair."

After that, she clammed up. The social worker indicated that she'd had enough for one day and the interview ended.

Asha turned to Aaron. "We need to find any CCTV cameras in the area around the hostel. The woman that shared a room with Hadhira smelled of smoke: maybe it was from burning oil paintings."

"We've got a preliminary report from CSI and the Fire Service," he said. "The barn fire was almost certainly arson, and it *was* picture frames that Chris and Josh saw last night — someone took the paintings from inside the cottage and burned them. They're looking for any evidence that might identify our arsonist, but there's nothing yet. The rain overnight won't have helped."

"I've a feeling there won't be anything. According to the eyewitness in Newry, she was probably wearing a forensic suit or something similar, as well as gloves and overshoes."

"She really knows how to stay invisible, doesn't she?"

"All too well," Asha said. She blew out a frustrated breath. "It feels too uncontrolled and vicious to be the work of a contract killer, but if I say to the ACC that we might have someone from law enforcement involved, she'll say I'm jumping at shadows after spending two years hunting down those two creeps from Lisburn Road."

Aaron's phone vibrated. He looked at it and then balanced his paper cup precariously on the corner of her desk. "Sorry, I should probably take this. Peter and Ellie have been going through some difficulties recently."

Asha had always thought of Peter and Ellie as the perfect couple, with their nice house in Lisburn and their two bright, intelligent children. What could possibly have gone wrong for them?

136

CHAPTER 19

It was a beautiful day in Phoenix Park and Ellie would have been enjoying her day out in Dublin if it hadn't been for the row she'd had with Peter before she left the house.

"Mummy! I wanna go home." Lizzie's persistent whine was beginning to fray her nerves. "My feet hurt."

Not as much as Ellie's own head throbbed, and her arm too. She wondered if she'd taken more damage than just a bruise.

Before she could snap that Lizzie should have thought of that when she refused to let her bring the pushchair, Simon piped up. "If Daddy was here, he would carry her." That was Simon all over. At seven he was the eldest and considered himself, in Peter's absence, the man of the house.

"Well, Daddy isn't here, and we don't have the push-chair, so we'll just have to manage."

"There's a playground over there," Simon said with a speculative glint in his eye. "And a coffee van."

"All right," Ellie agreed. "We'll stop for a drink."

"And ice cream?" Lizzie asked, perking up.

"We'll see." Which both children recognised as the total capitulation it was.

This day out had been Peter's idea. They were supposed to be here as a family, visiting the zoo and spending quality time together to heal their rifts, but then he'd pulled out at the last moment, saying he'd been called in to work as an emergency.

What sort of emergency occurred in an accountancy firm? Urgent sacking of hundreds of employees? It wouldn't be the first time her husband, so kind to the children and so well-liked in their church and by their friends, had signed a piece of paper that would change lives for other families, apparently without regret.

He said it was what he'd been trained to do: to spot redundancies in the system, people who hadn't been earning their keep in years and who were just a waste of space in their companies. Sacrificing the few to save the jobs of everyone else in a company which might otherwise have gone bust.

"And is that what you're doing to us?" she'd asked. "Getting rid of the redundancies?"

He'd flushed and tightened his lips, with that mulish expression that had always yanked her chain. Guilt? When she asked him outright if he'd been having an affair, he hadn't been able to answer her. He'd just clammed up, face as white as it had been red the moment before.

She'd wanted to hurt him as he'd hurt her. "You are, aren't you? Having an affair. Who is she? That new secretary of yours, the one who's so efficient that you still have to work late?"

He'd tried to turn away, but she'd wrenched him back, fury lending her strength. "Answer me, Peter!" she screamed, specks of spittle landing on his charcoal suit and turning into dark spots on the expensive cloth.

"Why? You won't believe anything I say."

It was exactly the same thing she'd used to shout at her mother when she was a teenager. The shock of it! Did he really see her like that — an untrusting nag? She'd lost her hold of his sleeve and he'd scurried out and slammed the front door like she was poison.

Running after him, determined to get the truth, she'd tripped over the edge of the rug and landed hard on the parquet floor of the dining room. Her head had hit the edge of a sideboard as she went down and her forearm had struck the doorframe, sending electric shocks of pain down into her hand.

She'd heard him drive away into the night, and wept — silently, in case she woke the children. This morning, he'd still not returned so she'd packed a picnic and put out summer clothes for Lizzie and Simon. To hell with Peter. They'd go without him.

It had seemed a good idea at the time, an act of defiance. Now, with two tired and grumpy youngsters dragging at her coat, she wanted to scream aloud.

Luckily the little coffee shop in an old horse trailer was open and although it didn't serve ice creams, it did sell a variety of packets of sweets and bars of chocolate, all at cinema prices.

Ellie counted out the unfamiliar euro coins to the hard-faced teenager behind the counter, then glanced over at the playground to check on the children. Simon was making his way up a small climbing wall, face creased with concentration, and Lizzie was on a swing, her feet barely able to touch the ground. Ellie had ordered herself a cappuccino and a traybake, with fizzy drinks and sweets for the children — she knew she'd regret it later, when the sugar rush hit, but for now it might hold back the floodwater.

By the time she'd stored the cans and sweets in her shoulder bag, and managed to balance the traybake on top of the coffee so she could open the gate into the playground, wincing as her bruised arm pressed against the cold metal, Lizzie had found someone to push her on the swing.

Her new friend was a tall, slim woman of indeterminate age with a sun-creased face that could belong to anyone from thirty to sixty. She was well dressed in a trouser suit and camel-coloured overcoat for the chilly breeze, and Lizzie was chatting away to her, trusting as only a child raised in a loving home could be.

When Ellie appeared, the stranger smiled apologetically. "I hope you don't mind. I always come here for my coffee break from the office." She nodded towards a bench a little way along the path from the playpark, where an open paper bag and a takeaway coffee suggested the woman had been in the middle of eating when Lizzie had distracted her. "I don't make a habit of speaking with little girls behind their mothers' backs." Her eyes crinkled at the outer edges as if smiling was what they'd been designed to do.

"Oh no, I understand," Ellie said. "Lizzie can be very persuasive when she wants to be."

Simon ran over to join them. "What did you get, Mum? Did they have ice cream?"

She produced her trophies. "No ice creams, but they had Coke bottles and fizzy chews." His eyes widened at these usually forbidden treats. "And I got you a can of Fanta each too."

They snatched the goodies before she had chance to change her mind and ran off together giggling, to clamber up one of the climbing frames and disappear inside a den together.

The stranger laughed. "That's two happy children. Do you want to share my bench while you eat your own snack?"

So they sat together in the summer sunshine, and for the first time in forever, Ellie found herself unwinding with another adult who wasn't Peter, or one of their friends from church, or another parent. It was just what she needed.

"Do you have children of your own?" she asked.

"No!" The word came out like an explosion. "Sorry. There's nothing wrong with having children, but it's not for me. I don't feel I'm a fit person to be in charge of another's life from cradle to adulthood, that's all." She took a sip of her coffee. "Besides, I don't have time for a relationship. My work keeps me busy."

"What do you do?"

"I work for the Garda, over there." She pointed vaguely towards the zoo.

"What a small world. My brother-in-law is in the police too. He's a detective with the PSNI."

"Oh, I'm not anything like that," the woman said quickly. "I'm a civilian, working in cybercrime. Bringing down hackers, that sort of thing."

"I suppose it's a different sort of detecting, but I expect you use some of the same methods."

"Maybe." A long finger picked at the edge of the plastic lid, shredding it.

Just then, Simon and Lizzie ran over, bickering. "Mummy, Simon said Daddy's gone away and isn't coming back. It's not true, is it?" Lizzie's little elfin face was blotched with tears and her eyes swam with more, as yet unshed.

Ellie's hesitation was mostly due to the presence of a stranger, but Simon pounced on it. "I *told* you," he said. "Mummy won't say it's not true, 'cos it *is* true."

"No," Ellie said weakly. "Daddy's just had to go into work today at short notice, that's all. He'll be home tonight. Wherever did you get that idea from, Simon?"

"Heard you arguing. Last night. Daddy slammed the door when he left."

"Daddy was just stressed. He wasn't happy that he had to miss this trip with us, that's all. He'll be back." She sincerely hoped she was right. The stranger was looking at her phone as if she wasn't listening, which was kind of her, but Ellie was sure she'd heard every word. Her children's clear voices could probably have been heard at the other side of the park. In fact, a couple of other mothers inside the swing park were looking her way now with interest and sympathy.

"We've got to go," Ellie said. "It was nice talking to you, but I've a long drive ahead. Like a fool, I parked the car in the Lords Walk car park and that's a way off from here."

"Carry me, Mummy!" Lizzie was overtired.

Ellie closed her eyes. This whole day had been a disaster from start to finish. Her head was pounding, and her vision beginning to blur. She hadn't had a migraine since she'd left

141

school, and this didn't really feel like one yet, but it would be a miracle if she got home without losing her temper with one or both of the children, and that was something she and Peter had always promised they would never do.

"Nice lady," Lizzie said, at shoulder height. Ellie blinked. While she'd been having her little moment of breakdown, the stranger had lifted Lizzie and now held her on her hip. A crease of concern marred her forehead.

"Are you okay?" Her eyes darted to Ellie's forearm, where her sleeve had ridden up to expose a dark bruise.

She tugged the cloth back down, embarrassed. "I'm fine. Thank you for asking. I can manage now." She reached out for Lizzie, but the child clung to her new friend, with that inborn perception that tells a daughter exactly which of Mummy's buttons, when pressed, were most likely to be effective. Ellie sighed. "You need to go back to work."

"I'm in no rush," the woman said. "The place is hardly going to fall down if I'm a bit late back from my coffee break, and they need me too much to give me a hard time over it. I'll walk back to your car with you."

And she did, chatting to Lizzie and Simon all the way as if they were old friends. Ellie appreciated the break from having to provide answers to all of Simon's "for why?" questions, and she allowed herself to drift off into memories of her harsh words last night until something Simon was saying caught her attention.

"No, Daddy's a good man. He probably didn't mean to hit Mummy. He was just cross."

"Simon! What on earth are you saying? Daddy has never hit me. Don't tell fibs!"

Lizzie reached out and gently touched the place on Ellie's arm where the bruise was. She flinched, not meaning to. "Did Daddy do that?"

"No, he didn't. I fell over the rug," she said truthfully. But there was doubt in all three of the pairs of eyes that watched her, and even to her own ears, the words sounded hollow and unbelievable.

142

CHAPTER 20

"I just fell." How many times had she heard some variation on that theme over the years? Used it herself, in fact, to explain away the bruises she'd carried to school as a child.

What was it about the psychological make-up of women that made them hide the brutality of men? Fear? Nothing so simple, perhaps. Why had she never spoken out about her father? Had it been fear of further punishment, or something else?

Caro had once asked her mother why Pappie still hurt her, even when she tried so hard to be good, but her mother had told her not to be so silly, that the maid might hear her and that she surely didn't want people to think bad things about her pappie, did she? So little Caroline had learned that speaking up gained her nothing.

And none of her school gym teachers or swimming coaches had ever asked questions about the bruises. She'd been written off as a clumsy child, always knocking herself on things or falling over. She did fall over, but it had been from sleep deprivation, not lack of balance.

So now, whenever she heard a woman covering up for a man, it roused her to a cold hatred that she couldn't ignore.

Maybe no one had helped her, when she needed it most, but she'd survived and escaped, and she was safe now with a new name and a new life. No one would hurt her ever again.

When she'd killed Jibreel Khan, she'd finally tasted a little of the release she'd expected to feel from killing her own father. Not enough, but a taste that reassured her she was on the right track at last.

She laughed, surprising herself by the harshness of the sound. What was she thinking? Did she aspire to be a superhero in a cape? A vigilante?

No. Just Lady Justice, blindfolded, weighing people in her scales, and deciding which side they came down on. And there was no doubt in her mind which way the scale would tip for the man who had hit that poor woman today.

The car ahead indicated and moved off the dual carriageway onto a slip road. Three cars behind, Caro shadowed it all the way to the neat house on a modern development in Lisburn. She cruised past slowly, not stopping, as the woman and the two children carried their bags inside the house.

There was a car park just around the corner, so she parked up there and opened up her laptop. Her phone gave her a hotspot as she used her access codes to dig up information on the family, now that she had a car registration and an address.

Peter and Helen Birch. Within minutes, she had their entire backgrounds at her fingertips, and Helen's (Ellie's) social media too. The woman had made no attempt to keep anything private online, but the man was a different story. He had no social media, and the only accounts she could find for him online, apart from work-related ones, were subscriptions to porn sites. Soft porn.

She imagined plunging a knife into the fat belly that bulged beneath his shirt in his work photo, watching the white skin splash with crimson and smelling the stench of punctured guts. No quick death for this man. He'd die slowly and in agony if she had anything to do with it, and a long way from help.

Oddly enough, the women he watched on his porn sites were as different to his own wife's type as it was possible to be. Online, he preferred curvy brunettes with enormous breasts and generous hips, whereas Ellie was slim and blonde with a boyish figure.

Ellie reminded Caro a little of her mother, Grace. As she laid her plans, she remembered Pieter, her father — stepfather — and the way he'd always watched her from his office window as he worked, even when he was on the telephone. She'd learned not to look his way, in case the expression on her face annoyed him. The slightest glance might be considered provocation — he'd call it insolence.

Her mother must have known, but had never lifted a finger to help her. Caro had run to her that first time, incoherent with tears, showing the welts where he'd laid into her with his belt. Her mother had held her, comforted her, told her it would all be okay, but it hadn't been. The next time, she hadn't needed to run to her mother, because her mother had walked in on them when Pieter was hitting her. Caro had screamed for help, but Grace had ducked her head and backed out of the room, closing the door gently behind her.

She'd seen Grace applying make-up to cover her own bruises. As she grew older, she became better at spotting the signs, but neither she nor her mother ever mentioned it. It was as though the beatings never happened. Once she was old enough, she left home for a university halfway around the world, as far away from the man who took the name of father as she could.

"Goodbye, Mother. I wish you of the life you've chosen for yourself," she'd said as she left. Even the choked sob her mother couldn't hold back hadn't been enough to make her turn around and go back to her.

Of course, she hadn't known the full story back then. That hadn't unfolded until Mother was dying in hospital, her body riddled with cancer, before she took her own life to save herself from the pain of a slow death.

In the short time since Caro had left home, her mother's fragile beauty had drawn in on itself, revealing that spectacular bone structure in skeletal mockery with yellowish, parchment-dry skin hanging in loose folds at her neck and the once-glorious flaming hair hanging dull and lank around her face. Only her eyes had retained their brilliance, sparkling beneath the hospital lights with the fervour of a burden that had to be laid down.

"I'm dying," she said, unnecessarily. "I've known for a while, but it took an . . . accident to make the doctors aware."

Caro had already spoken to a nurse before she came in. Grace had been admitted with a broken thigh bone after she'd "tripped" in the house and fallen. The X-rays had revealed bone cancer, and further investigation had proved that the osteosarcoma had spread to other bones and to her lungs.

"Is it because of all the injuries he's inflicted on you over the years?" Caro asked in a cool voice. "Seems a coincidence."

Grace put her finger to her lips, still afraid to talk about it even after all this time. "Never mind that." She rolled her eyes, checking for anyone who might overhear, but the room was empty apart from the two of them. "You did right to leave, Caroline."

Caro laughed. "What other recourse did I have?" Why had she even come back here? Back within *his* reach?

Her mother licked dry lips. Her voice was weak, as tiny and frail as her body, but she had a determined glint in her eye. "Thank you for coming, darling." She flinched when Caro made a dismissive gesture at the term of endearment. "There are things you need to know, and I haven't got long. Please, just listen, then maybe you'll understand a little better."

Nothing could ever make Caro understand, but she'd flown all this way, and her return flight wasn't until the next day, so she might as well hear her mother out. "I'm listening."

"Thank you." A sigh so feeble it didn't stir the fine hair that had drifted across her mouth. "Pieter isn't your father."

Those bald words, delivered with no preamble, shocked Caro to her core. Then the dark clouds that had inhabited her mind for so long shifted a little, not enough to allow the sun through, but a change of shade perhaps, from deep purple to bruise.

Before she could ask, her mother went on. "I'm not sure, even now, if he knows for certain, but he must have some idea, or surely he'd never have treated you so roughly."

Is that what Grace was calling it? A bit of rough treatment?

"Who is my father?" she asked, her voice sounding stiff and unfamiliar.

"Your father and I, your real father, grew up together. His name doesn't matter, darling, because he's dead now, but I felt you needed to know."

"Know what? That my abuser might not be my dearly beloved father after all? That I've kept quiet all these years to protect a man who isn't even related to me?" The words poured out in a torrent, but there were no tears. Hers was a cold anger. "Why did you marry him?"

"You wouldn't understand. In those days, a young woman in the circles we moved in couldn't get pregnant unless she was married. When he . . . left, he had no idea. My parents — your grandparents — didn't approve of him as a husband for me, so they sent me away. I thought he'd follow me, track me down, but he never did." She swallowed. "I guess he didn't care so much, after all." Grace had never been very strong-willed. Caro wouldn't have rolled over so easily, allowing herself to be torn away from the man she loved. "When I got here, I found work as a model for an agency." She smiled. "It was like a dream come true. I was talent-spotted at a party and offered a contract. Before I knew it, my face was on billboards all over the city. And then I discovered I was pregnant."

She closed her eyes, exhausted. Caro lifted the non-spill baby cup of diluted juice from the bedside table and held the spout to her mother's lips. "Drink. You'll feel a bit better."

Grace sipped wearily, but it did seem to revive her a little. "Pieter was mad about me," she said, a slight smile of reminiscence hovering about her lips. "It was like the answer to a prayer. Everyone wanted us to marry: our friends, our families, a society magazine even ran a sweepstake for the date we'd get

147

engaged. We were like royalty in those days, and it was a heady mix for a frightened young girl from the country. Besides, as soon as I was certain I was pregnant, I *had* to marry."

Caro had shaken her head in disbelief. "This was the eighties! You can't be serious."

Grace smiled faintly. "We're talking South Africa, not Soho. It was very conservative here, and even more so in Rhodesia. My father would have killed me."

"So you married Pieter. And you never told anyone I wasn't his daughter?"

A slight headshake.

"Not even my 'real' father?"

A haunted look and a tightening of the lips.

"You did tell him, didn't you? What did he say? That he didn't want you?" She was being cruel, but she wanted to hurt this pale, sunken woman, and if she couldn't do it physically, she'd do it with words.

"He never replied," Grace said quietly. "I still don't know if the letter ever reached him."

Voices in the corridor broke in on Caro's thoughts, followed by a heavy tread on the tiled floor. She knew that determined stride and automatically looked about her for somewhere to hide, but Grace grasped her hand and held it with surprising strength. "Stay. Please."

Too late, anyway. The door swung open and Pieter van Rooyen strode in, his white silk shirt straining over a belly rounded by too many industry dinners. He stopped halfway through the door, one hand on the frame, staring at Caro. She tilted her chin, meeting his stare, determined not to be the first to look away. Then that cynical smile curved his lips and she felt herself disintegrating, bits of her floating away: her confidence, her strength, her very *self*.

Now so many miles away and so many years later, her eyes fixed on the photo of Peter Birch. Even the names were the same. Pieter and Peter. It had to be fate. This was surely the act of kindness that would free her forever from the chains Pieter van Rooyen had draped over her year after year.

CHAPTER 21

"What's up?" Aaron asked cheerfully. "Sorry to miss your calls earlier."

"I think I might have lost Ellie." Peter sounded depressed, his voice heavy and low.

Lost? Lost as in dead, as in missing, as in what? He took a deep breath. Peter would have said if it was anything as bad as that, he told himself. "I'm in Belfast. Want to meet for a coffee?"

"Okay."

It was left to Aaron to suggest the place and the time. His brother seemed to have lost all his decisiveness and drive.

Peter was there before him, an Americano set in front of him, but he wasn't drinking, and he hadn't bought anything for Aaron, which was unlike him. He was usually generous to a fault and always thoughtful. Aaron bought himself an espresso and went to join his brother, who still didn't look up.

"Peter, you're scaring me. What's happened?"

"I blew it, that's what happened. We were supposed to be going to Dublin Zoo today, as a family, but I had to cancel at the last minute. Work," he added, as if that explained everything.

"That's not unusual, is it? You often have to go in at funny hours." In fact, Aaron had teased him that he worked

149

nearly as many overtime shifts as a peeler. It always seemed odd that an accountant would be required to work outside business hours, but apparently when you reached Peter's dizzying heights in the firm, it was assumed you'd be available whenever you were needed.

"No. That's part of the problem. Ellie thinks I'm having an affair."

Aaron almost laughed out loud. His big brother was about as loyal and faithful as it was possible for a man to be. He adored Ellie and his children. "Why would she think that?"

For the first time, Peter raised his eyes to Aaron's. His were bloodshot, and his face deathly pale. "I don't know. She just came out with it last night. She accused me to my face of having an affair with my new secretary."

"And are you?" The words were out before he could stop them. It was the sort of banter they'd always exchanged, but his timing was off. "I didn't mean that. Of course you're not. Surely you told her that?"

Peter looked poleaxed. "That's the thing. When she said it, I just couldn't find the words. I never expected . . . It never occurred to me that she'd think . . ."

Aaron reached across the table and patted his brother's hand. They'd never been good at expressing their emotions, either of them. "It'll be all right. Do you want me to drive over and have a word with her? On your behalf?"

The haunted eyes started back at him. "It's too late. She's gone. With the children. I went back there this morning, as soon as I could tear myself away from work, and the house was empty; her car had gone. She didn't even leave me a note."

It all flooded out in disjointed phrases that reflected Peter's confused state of mind.

"Are you sure she hasn't just gone shopping or taken them to the cinema? It's the middle of the summer holidays, after all."

"She'd packed a bag with some of their clothes and taken food from the fridge."

"Oh, Peter." It was all he could think of to say. "Maybe I should go and have a look around with a policeman's eyes. Would that help?"

His gratitude was a pathetic. "Would you? I can't bear to go back. The place seemed so empty and cold. I had to get out of there."

Aaron left him sipping another coffee and drove the twenty minutes to the house in Lisburn. It was a pretty house, one of many on a development where the builders had tried not to let the houses look like little boxes. Each had unique features and they were finished in a variety of coatings that included grey local stone and cream rendering.

Peter and Ellie's house was surrounded by a black wrought-iron fence and sat on a corner, not really overlooked by any other houses. The garden was mature and filled with colour: dark reds and deep greens and some tiny white flowers on a bush. The glossy crimson front door opened to the key Ellie had insisted he kept, so he could "treat their home as his own".

As soon as he walked inside, he recognised what Peter had described. There was a coldness, an emptiness to the place that he'd never experienced there before. He closed the door behind him and looked around.

Everything was in its place. Nothing appeared to have been disturbed. He could see down the hall into the kitchen, and the black granite breakfast bar on the island Ellie had been so proud of when they chose the kitchen design. No breakfast dishes or coffee mugs lying about. As he walked along the hallway, his eye was caught by the first sign of trouble. In the dining room on his left, a deep-pile rug sat askew on the floor, one corner turned under like a dog-eared book page. That wasn't like Ellie.

He took a closer look. The parquet floor had a scrape on it, just a thin line as if someone had slipped and their shoe heel had caught the wooden blocks.

Then he saw the hair, caught on a splinter of wood on the edge of a sideboard just inside the door. No, not a splinter;

it was stuck to the wood with something dark and glutinous. Blood. *Oh no.*

He went through the rest of the house, feeling like a burglar. When he caught himself holding his breath, he pulled a wry face, even knowing there was no one there to see it. The main bedroom was tidy, the bed made, but the two children's rooms were not. Both beds were rumpled, the quilts thrown back as if they had got up in a hurry, and there were clothes scattered around, hanging out of drawers.

Perhaps they were always like this? Although Aaron couldn't imagine either Peter or Ellie encouraging their children to be untidy. It certainly gave the impression of a hasty departure. His heart sank.

He went back down to the kitchen. The part he hadn't been able to see from the hallway wasn't quite as tidy as the rest. One worksurface had crumbs scattered across it, and there was a chopping board and a knife with butter along its edge. Had she stayed long enough to make sandwiches?

Then he heard a car draw up outside. The front door opened and running feet came down the hall towards him.

"Uncle Aaron!" Lizzie flung herself into his arms, burying her face into the hollow of his neck. She was damp with tears and snot, but he held her close, not caring. "We've had a terrible time!"

Simon marched along the corridor, his little round face serious. "Daddy hit Mummy," he said. "But she says he didn't." Then, apropos of nothing, "We got burgers on the way home. With chips, and 'mato sauce."

"Oh, for heavens' sake!" Ellie said. She stood in the doorway, loaded with bags and coats and looking exhausted. "Peter didn't hit me." She tried for a smile, but it was watery at best. "What are you doing here, Aaron?"

Instead of answering her, he put Lizzie down and took some of Ellie's burdens into his own hands, catching the cool bag just as it slipped from her grasp. He turned and led the way to the kitchen, where Simon was already foraging in the freezer.

He emerged bearing a box of chocolate waffle cones, which he opened clumsily, then handed one to Lizzie. Her tears instantly dried up and she began unwrapping it straight away.

Simon held one out to Aaron, who shook his head. "Why don't you two help Mummy by taking your bags upstairs? You can take the ice creams with you and eat them upstairs, yeah? I'll help Mummy put everything else away."

They scurried away with their treats and Ellie gave a hard laugh. "I'll be cleaning ice cream off every surface tomorrow."

"Sorry." Then they stared at each other, and he didn't know where to start.

"Why are you here, Aaron?" she repeated in a tired voice.

"Peter thinks you've left him," he said, deciding that he might as well just come straight to the point. "He's a mess."

"He's not the only one," she snapped, eyes flashing. "I'm too knackered for this sort of talk tonight. I just want to get the children bathed and to bed, then I'll be right behind them."

"How about I bath them and get them ready for bed, then I can read them stories until they're asleep. You look dead on your feet, Ellie."

Her face crumpled. "Would you? I do love them, but right now I'm not sure if I can bear to look at either of them. Simon's managed to convince a perfect stranger that I'm in an abusive marriage, and now Peter thinks I've left him. Can this day get any worse?"

"No, but it can get better. Why don't you have a shower in the en-suite while I bath them both, then we can open a bottle of wine and you can chill for a bit while I make us some dinner. How does that sound?"

The children were delighted to have Uncle Aaron bathing them and chattered continuously the whole time. By the time he had them in clean pyjamas, faces pink and scrubbed, they were both yawning, and it took only minutes before Lizzie was fast asleep, her long lashes laid across her rounded cheeks. Simon wasn't far behind. Aaron closed the book and lifted his nephew in his arms, carrying him through to his own bed.

As he tucked him in, the little boy grabbed his hand and held it, eyes still tight shut. "Don't go, Daddy," he mumbled.

"I won't," Aaron said. The pudgy fingers loosed their grasp and Simon sighed, turning over. "Love you," he said.

Ellie looked just as pink and scrubbed as her children, and very young in her Disney pyjamas and tartan dressing gown. She'd poured two big balloon glasses of red wine and was curled up sideways in an armchair, her head on her arm, eyes closed.

Aaron opened the fridge to see what was available to cook. A packet of mince was close to its use-by date, and there was a jar of tomato sauce and some pasta in the cupboard. "Spag bol okay by you? Or did you eat burgers too?"

"No. It was hard enough to keep those two fed without thinking about myself, and I hate fast food. Spag bol sounds lovely, and there's garlic bread in the freezer." She opened her eyes. "You don't need to do this, Aaron. I can cook."

"You need to rest. How's the head wound?" he asked neutrally.

Her eyes widened. "How do you—" Then she shook her head. "Oh, blasted detectives."

"There's some of your hair glued to the edge of the side-board by blood. Not enough for you to have bled to death, but I guessed you bumped your head when you fell. Is that when you got the bruise too?"

She tugged her sleeve down self-consciously. "Yes."

"And that's what's caused all this talk of Daddy hitting Mummy?" He waited for her to meet his eyes. "I know he's my brother, but you can tell me, Ellie, if—"

"Oh, Aaron, not you too." She groaned, but she sounded more cheerful than she had before. "We had a row and he shot off — couldn't wait to get away from me — out the front door and into the car. And I ran after him because I wanted to *know*, and then, *splat*—" she mimed with her hand —"I tripped over the rug in the dining room. Bumped my head, dinged my arm. By the time I'd picked myself up from the floor, he'd gone. He was supposed to come with us to Dublin today, a trip to the zoo. We've been planning it for ages, a family day out, a picnic in Phoenix Park, the works. It was going to be such a lovely day."

"Then he went and spoiled it all by getting called into work."

She scowled. "If that's what it really was. Aaron, I've been worrying about him for a while now. He's getting home so late some nights and he's too tired to talk or eat the dinner I've been keeping warm for him. How can a job as an accountant be such a big deal? He's supposed to be working nine to five!"

"He said you think he's having an affair," Aaron said quietly.

She let out a shuddering breath. "I know I said that, but I didn't really think it. I said a lot of things I'm not proud of, but he's so frustrating!"

"Always was," said Peter's little brother unrepentantly. "I'm amazed I didn't push him off a cliff before he ever had the chance to meet you."

This time, her laugh was genuine. "Did he send you over here to discover the lie of the land?"

"Not exactly," he admitted. "I offered to come. I really ought to phone him and tell him you're okay, because he's worried sick about you. He thinks you've taken the kids and left him. Maybe you two should talk, I mean really talk, now the kids are asleep?"

She bit her bottom lip. "Okay. Phone him and tell him to come home."

CHAPTER 22

"The doctor says you can leave now," said the young nurse. "Have you anyone to give you a lift?"

Gerren shook his head. "No, but I can get a taxi."

She looked worried. "Don't you have a family member who could come and pick you up, or a friend?"

"No," he said shortly. "No one." He'd never felt so alone before. It was getting dark outside, the passing cars switching on their headlights. Still, he'd manage. He always had. "I'll be all right. Don't fuss!"

She looked as if he'd slapped her, but left him alone to get dressed. He was glad to be rid of the stupid hospital gown with its wide-open back that showed his arse if he tried to walk anywhere, but his own clothes smelled musty, and he picked up a whiff of BO.

When he was dressed — it had taken more out of him than he expected — he clutched the blue plastic bag of medicines close to his chest and opened the door.

On the chair outside in the corridor, opposite his room, sat a middle-aged man running to flab, with greasy dark hair and a scowling face. Where did he know the fellow from?

The stranger stood up when he saw Gerren and came forward with his hand outstretched. "Hello again, Mr Penrose. I heard you were being discharged and wondered if you'd like a lift home?"

Then the penny dropped. This was one of those police, wasn't it? He hadn't recognised the man out of uniform. "Now what do you want? I've answered all yer bliddy questions."

The man's face remained cheerful. "I'm not here as a police constable today, Mr Penrose, just as someone who wants to see you get home safe."

A suspicion dawned. That young sergeant had said something about one of his officers keeping Gerren alive until the ambulance reached him. Or had it been a nurse that said it? Either way, he'd a suspicion he knew which officer it had been now. "Are you the one who gave me CPR?"

The man shrugged. "Anyone would have done it. I just happened to be there. Anyway, I was in town for something, and I knew you didn't have a car here, so I thought I'd see if you wanted a lift."

It was blatantly untrue. The man had gone out of his way to be here, that much was clear. This was the man, if he remembered rightly, who'd thrown up at Rob's place the morning they found his body. He hadn't thought much of the bloke then, but maybe everyone deserved a second chance.

"That's kind of you. Much appreciated." But he shook off the man's hand when he tried to help him down the stairs. "I can manage. I might have one foot in the grave, lad, but the other one's still working just fine."

As he fastened his seatbelt in the battered old Ford the officer drove, he decided to make a bit of an effort. "Not sure I ever caught your name."

"Stanley. Dave Stanley." He went silent for a bit while he negotiated a roundabout. "I always wanted to be a vet when I was growing up, but never had the brains."

"Sounds as if you'd have made a good vet, if what I hear about you is true. Did you really keep the chest compressions going for nearly an hour?"

Dave Stanley nodded, eyes still on the road ahead. It was misty with that light, drizzling rain they got so often in Ireland.

Not unlike Cornwall, Gerren thought, except Cornwall was generally warmer.

Once they were clear of the busy town roads and onto the main road that led north towards Ballygroggan, Stanley made a phone call. Gerren listened in amazement as the man spoke to his phone, which sat in a holder on his dashboard, and told it to call someone called Josh.

A male voice answered. "Dave, are you on your way?"

"Yeah. ETA roughly thirty minutes from here."

"Gotcha. All sorted."

"What was that about?" Gerren asked.

"Just letting a pal know when I'll be home," he said, but even in the flickering headlights from oncoming vehicles, Gerren could see the blush. Maybe he was gay, but surely no one blushed about that these days, did they?

There were lights on Gerren's cottage. He tensed. What the hell?

"It's all right," his new friend said. "I asked someone to open up and get the kettle on for you coming home."

As he got out of the car Gerren took a deep breath, inhaling the unmistakeable aroma of peat smoke. He looked up to see a thin stream of grey coming from his chimney.

The front door opened before he could touch the handle, letting out a rectangle of warm orange light that drove away the mist. A dark shape rocketed out of the house and flung itself at him, growling with delight.

"Jack! Lad, what are you doing here?"

Dave Stanley ushered him inside and he went as if in a dream. The place was warm, and a smell of fresh bread came from the kitchen, along with something else, meaty with herbs.

He wandered through to the kitchen to find a woman bending over his stove. She took out a casserole in one of the oven dishes he'd inherited with the cottage but never used. The smell made his mouth water, and Jack was salivating too, his tail wagging in big circular motions as he looked up adoringly at the cook.

"Hello, Mr Penrose," she said. "I'm Claire and this is Josh. We went up and fetched Jack for you when he tried to go home the other night."

The dog was clearly on excellent terms with her, and with the big, quiet man seated at the kitchen table.

He found himself seeing everything through a haze, as if a veil had been drawn down over his eyes.

"Poor fella's overwhelmed," Claire said. "Get him a chair, Dave."

A kitchen chair appeared, and Dave Stanley helped him down onto it, then he was pushed up to the table and a plate of food placed before him.

After dinner, Claire and Josh left but Dave Stanley stayed on. They sat together in Gerren's sitting room, sipping mugs of Horlicks in peaceful silence.

"I had a word with that reporter," the policeman said after a while. "She won't be bothering you again, Mr Penrose."

Gerren blinked, remembering, and shuffled around in his chair to look behind him at the window where her face had appeared. "She was right there," he said. "Shouting through the window. She made me let her in——" He tried to take a deep breath, but his lungs weren't working.

Dave Stanley ripped open the bag from the hospital and opened a small brown pill bottle. "Open up," he commanded, and Gerren obeyed without thinking. Dave popped a small pill under his tongue, and he closed his mouth. "Don't swallow it, just let it dissolve. Nitroglycerin."

The pain subsided after a few minutes, and he could think clearly again. "I was wrong about you being good enough to be a vet," he said. "You should have been a doctor. How did you know what to do?"

"My granny had angina," Dave said. "She had a spray, but it's the same thing. I knew they'd probably send you home with some of the stuff."

"Thank you, again." It was usually quite hard for Gerren to thank someone, but then he'd not had a lot of practice. Maybe it would get easier with use.

"I didn't kill him, you know. Rob."

"We've guessed that much. Did you know there's been a second murder?"

The shock of those words nearly sent Gerren off into another spasm of pain, but he controlled his breathing, and his pulse rate came back down. "No, I hadn't. Nearby?"

"No, Newry. Looks like it was the same knife, though."

"Who? Who died?"

"A cabinetmaker called Jibreel Khan — killed in a home invasion. It's been on the news already, so I'm not telling you anything you shouldn't know, except that it's probably the same killer. I'm trusting you to keep that to yourself, Mr Penrose."

"Newry? Why Newry?"

"Why Rob Harris?" asked Stanley. Then he hesitated as if he wanted to say more.

"Spit it out, lad. What aren't you telling me?"

"Your friend, Rob Harris. Did you ever suspect that might not have been his real name?"

Gerren opened his mouth to deny it, but then all the doubts he'd nurtured over the last few decades, all the little mysteries and questions about Rob that he'd never found the answers to, began to trail through his mind. There'd been the gun, for a start. He'd never explained that. And the Afrikaans song. And the way he was so suspicious of strangers, refusing to come into the village for anything, as if he was afraid he'd be seen and recognised.

"No. It never occurred to me," he said slowly, "but I suppose I knew, deep down, that he wasn't quite all he appeared to be. And then there was the gun."

Dave's eyebrows shot up. "What gun?"

"Well, he had a shotgun, obviously, to hunt rabbits and the like and to chase the crows away from the new lambs, but he had a handgun too, hidden in a drawer in the sideboard. Came across it once when I was looking for matches."

"Do you know what make or model?"

Gerren snorted. "Not me. The only sort of gun I know about is the humane killer. The one I saw at Rob's place was a pistol of some sort, black and shiny, like it had been oiled. That's all I know."

"Do you think you'd recognise it if you saw it again, say in a photograph?"

"Maybe. It was years ago, mind, and I only caught a glimpse of it in a drawer. Didn't you find it when you searched the place?"

"I'll check, but I don't think so."

"What was his real name, if it wasn't Rob Harris?"

"We're not sure yet. Does the name Harold Cavendish mean anything to you?"

"Never heard the name before. Harold Cavendish." Gerren tried it for size, pulling an image of Rob's weather-beaten face to mind. Yes, it fitted him. There was a poshness about the name that suited Rob's aloof manner and his rounded vowels. "From South Africa, you say?" Dave hadn't said, but Gerren could put two and two together as well as the next man. "What was he running from?"

"We don't know yet," Dave said. "But the sarge thinks the clue to his killer lies somewhere in his past."

Gerren looked at him suspiciously. "How come you're telling me this all of a sudden? Last time we spoke, I reckon you thought I'd killed him. Am I right?"

Dave Stanley looked away from him. "Maybe, but you have to admit, it was a bit suspicious-like, you being covered in blood."

Gerren sighed. "I suppose it was. You were just doing your job." He decided not to mention the vomiting. "So, what was it about Rob's previous life that caused someone to murder him, then?"

Dave shook his head. "We're trying to find out. I don't suppose there's anything that stood out to you, is there? Anything that made you uncomfortable or curious at the time but that you shrugged off because he was your friend?"

Gerren started to shake his head, then he remembered one thing, quite early on, not long after he first met Rob. Gerren had brought the newspapers up, and Rob was skimming through them, commenting on world affairs and complaining about politics. Then he'd gone very quiet, staring at a small column on one of the inside pages. When he realised he was being watched, he'd folded the paper with a snap and thrown it across the room as if he didn't much care for it.

Later, Gerren had sneaked a look at it, but the only article on the part of the page Rob had been looking at was an obituary for some military fellow who'd been found murdered. Funny name. Something to do with alcohol?

It had been around that time that Rob had become even more reclusive. He'd stopped coming down into the village at all, and had deterred visitors, except for Gerren, who he needed for his sheep in any case.

"You've thought of something?" Dave asked.

"It's nothing, really. Can't be relevant."

CHAPTER 23

Nic was first into the building the next morning. She took her coat off and fired up the computer, wondering if she should risk the machine tea or steal some more of the absent Sergeant McBride's good stuff. Then she remembered that she'd used most of it up and needed to refill the tin. Damn. Machine it was, then.

The door opened and PC Stanley came in backwards, carrying a cardboard tray with two paper cups on it and holding a paper bag in his other hand. This was so unusual that she knew she was staring at him as he put everything down on an empty desk. The aroma of bacon and fresh bread drifted across to her, and her stomach grumbled.

"Saw you go past while I was in the shop, so I got you a bacon butty. Hope you're not veggie?"

"Who are you and what have you done with PC Stanley?" she asked, laughing. "You're a lifesaver, Dave." She snatched a butty before he changed his mind.

He looked embarrassed. "Well, you know. I thought you needed feeding up a bit. Wasn't sure if you took sugar, so I brought some sachets just in case."

"No sugar," she said, taking a sip of the hot, strong tea. "Thank you. What brings you in here so early?"

163

"I was over at Gerren's place last night," he said, surprising her again. "He told me something that might be relevant to the case, and I thought you might be the ideal person to look into it."

She should have known. Breakfast was a bribe to get her to do his legwork for him. Mind you, it was good tea. And the food would buy him quite a lot of favours. "What do you need me to do?"

He told her what Gerren had told him the night before, about a newspaper article that had seemed to shock Harris so much that he'd changed his behaviour.

"Any idea which paper and roughly what year, or better still, what month?" she asked as she typed into the search bar, *murder of soldier, alcohol*. There were dozens of useless links, various celebrities who'd drunk themselves to death, but none of them, at first glance, appeared relevant.

"Gerren says it was the *Irish Times* and probably a Sunday. It was winter, because he remembered they were wearing their outdoor clothes inside the cottage, it was that cold. It must have been after 1995, because there's that photo of him at an agricultural show in that year, isn't there? And Gerren said he really turned into a recluse after he read that piece in the paper."

"Okay, I can work with that." Her fingers flew, refining the search terms in the online newspaper archives.

Dead soldiers, sadly, were common news. There were articles about an actor who'd died of an overdose, a former beauty queen, the wife of an industrialist, who'd taken her own life, and a sports star killed by a hit-and-run, but nothing that leaped out of the page at her. One news item made her slow down, because it spoke of a victim with the name of de Beer stabbed in Johannesburg, but he was a politician, a plump, self-satisfied looking character with a greased combover, not a soldier. The link to alcohol had initially caught her eye, but she hit the back button and moved on.

Most of the articles were too recent. Maybe she'd need to go old-school and actually visit a newspaper office to stare at pages and pages of blue microfiche, but then she had a thought, and turned instead to the printed notes she'd shown the ACC. One of the articles was from the *Irish Times*, dated 2005. She let out a breath.

> ### FORMER SOLDIER BRUTALLY
> ### MURDERED IN COUNTY CAVAN
> *Major George "Whisky" Bailey, a former member of the British Army, was found murdered at his home in Ballyjamesduff, County Cavan.*
>
> *Residents of the quiet country town were shocked this morning to find themselves at the centre of a sensationally gruesome murder enquiry. The victim, a former soldier, was brutally attacked by a knife-wielding maniac and died of his wounds before help arrived.*
>
> *"It's awful," said market stall holder Biddy McGuirk. "He was such a nice fella, and a regular churchgoer. Why would anyone want to kill someone like him? Young hooligans, I expect."*
>
> *Police are so far baffled, as the killer left no traces behind, even taking the murder weapon away with him. Garda promise a statement will be released later today.*

There was a photo of the dead man in his full regimentals, aged in his late twenties.

"Could this be it?" she asked.

"Yeah! Gerren said something about alcohol, so I thought maybe he was from a brewing family, you know? Like Arthur Guinness. What's the date?"

"February 2005. Will I print out a second copy so you can ask Mr Penrose if he recognises it?"

He thanked her gruffly, then the rest of the team began to drift in, and he moved away.

"Okay, everyone," Aaron said. "Let's have a recap, shall we? Where are we now with the investigation into Harris's past life? Nic, do you want to get us started?"

She glanced uncertainly at Dave, who looked as if he might burst with suppressed excitement. "I think PC Stanley might have found something that we can use, sir. Maybe he should go first?"

Aaron looked surprised but nodded for Dave to speak.

"Well, sarge," Stanley began, "I had a word with that Gloria Bryson, like you said, and she won't be bothering Mr Penrose anymore. I gave her the third degree, and she finally admitted she'd been there when he had his heart attack. She says she ran off because she was frightened and didn't know what to do, but I can't imagine that old cow frightened of anything, can you?"

Aaron grunted.

"I made noises about him maybe wanting to press charges, thinking that would keep her walking small for a while, but then I hinted that there might be exclusives for her if she stayed on her best behaviour." He looked worried. "I hope that's okay, sarge?"

Aaron sighed. "I'm not sure what we're prepared to give her, but we can deal with that later. Is that all, Dave?"

Nic glared at him and he cleared his throat. "No, sir. I drove the old fella home from the hospital last night, and those dog handler friends of yours brought the dog back. Claire made a hot meal for him."

"Get on with it," Nic hissed. "The newspaper!"

Asha straightened up from where she'd been sitting hunched on the corner of a desk, her attention sharpening, and Aaron frowned.

"Well, I asked him if there was anything Harris had done over the years that was a bit odd, like. You know? Maybe nothing much, but anything that didn't quite ring true, or seemed a bit unlike him."

"And was there?"

Dave told them all about the newspaper article, and how he'd asked Nic to look into it. "She thinks she might have found it, sir. I was going to go over to the old man's house today and show him a printout, see if he recognises it."

Nic had already sent the image to the printer, so she picked the copies up and passed them round. Aaron shook his head. "What does this have to do with Harris-slash-Cavendish, I wonder."

"Apart from the fact that the man was in the same small squad as our victim?" Nic said. "Of course, I'll wait until PC Stanley has checked with Mr Penrose, but I've a feeling it might be significant."

"Another hunch?" Asha asked with a twisted smile.

Nic looked down, a little ashamed. She'd promised herself she'd never listen to hunches again, after Aaron had been injured.

"Get that printout down to Gerren Penrose, Dave," Aaron said. "Then let Nic know straight away if he thinks it's the right article. Nic, you can spend today following that lead if it pans out. Anything else from your research yesterday?"

Nic summarised what she'd found out about the young Harold Cavendish. "Seems to have been a bit of a lady's man, sir. I found some gossip pages about the social circle in Rhodesia, and the magazines were flooded back then with photos of him and fellow officers in the Rhodesian Mounted Police, each one with a pretty woman on his arm. All white, of course." She flicked through the tabs she'd bookmarked. "Different woman nearly every time . . ."

She broke off, staring at one of the photos from 1985. The chestnut-haired beauty he was escorting looked familiar. "Hang on a mo, Dave." She hit the History button on the web browser and tracked down the article about the dead beauty queen. Dave was looking over her shoulder, maybe picking up on her enthusiasm. She put the photo of the dead woman up on the screen and compared it to the one of Cavendish with a very young woman on his arm.

"Is it just me, or is that the same woman?"

Everyone crowded round. "I'm not sure," Aaron said. "Send it to the projector."

There was a few moments' confusion while Chris O'Neill tried to get the projector to link to Nic's laptop, then the screen appeared on the whiteboard.

The two photos were very different. In her obituary photo, the young woman wore a full-length ball gown with a high-necked fur coat. This one was in colour, and her hair was a glorious coppery red, whereas in the black-and-white newspaper photo with Cavendish she wore a knee-length tea gown and her hair appeared so dark as to be almost black.

But the features were very similar.

"Is there no caption for the society photo?" Asha asked.

Nic checked, zooming in on the small print beneath the photo. "It just says, 'Inspector Harold Cavendish of the Rhodesian Mounted Police with his beautiful cousin, Grace.'"

"His cousin?" Aaron said. "Interesting, but I don't see that it gets us any further."

"Maybe not," Nic muttered, not quite under her breath. "But I have a feeling she's important somehow. Can I spend some time following her up as well as the rest of Cavendish's squad? Anything that gives us more about Cavendish's background might help, right?"

"Okay," Aaron said, clearly already thinking of something else. "We'll leave you to it, then."

Nic was already typing. She could spend a bit of time researching Cavendish's beautiful cousin before someone gave her something more urgent to do.

It didn't take long to track down a more comprehensive obituary, written by a lifelong friend of the former model, written shortly after her death in 2007.

Grace van Rooyen (née Craig) was born on a ranch near Fort Victoria in 1968. Her father, Paul Craig, was a partner in a successful tobacco-growing business with his best friend, Matthew Cavendish. Matthew Cavendish was married to Grace's aunt, Honor.

I was fortunate enough to spend much of my childhood on the ranch with young Grace and her older cousin, Harold

168

Cavendish. There, we rode horses, swam in the reservoir, climbed trees, hunted and lived a life that is sadly no longer viable in that part of Africa. Today, the old ranch lies derelict and abandoned, the once-verdant plantations grazed to bare earth by goats.

Those were the golden years. Grace was much admired, but she had eyes only for Harold, despite the difference in their ages.

In the late summer of 1985, everything changed for "The Three Musketeers", as we called ourselves. Harold came home on leave that summer, recovering from a minor wound received in action, and immediately after, he joined the British Army, so he shipped overseas and out of our lives. I took up a very junior position in politics, which became my life's work, and Grace moved over the border to Pretoria in South Africa, where she began a successful career as a fashion model. She stayed in touch with me by letter over the next few months, but I could tell she was depressed. Her spark had gone.

She met Pieter van Rooyen at a society function, and he swept her off her feet. Within a month, they were married and before long, Grace gave birth to a daughter, Caroline. Subject to severe postnatal depression, Grace never regained her looks or health and went into a slow decline until she finally took her own life last month after a short struggle with bone cancer.

Those of us who knew and loved Grace in her youth could barely recognise the emaciated, haunted woman she became. Her husband stayed at her side to the end, always protective of her. He shielded her from the public eye and brought in the best medical care, but to no avail.

Grace touched so many hearts and minds in her youth, but like a perfect rosebud, perhaps she bloomed too soon. She will be sadly missed, but I feel her warm, beating heart had already gone before her into the grave.

It took her a moment to notice the byline at the bottom of the obituary, and when she did, her breath stilled. Willem de Beer.

She went back over her search history and found the article again that she'd passed over in her search for the dead soldier. Three years ago, Willem de Beer had been stabbed in his home in Johannesburg with his own knife, an ornate Indian dagger with a jewelled hilt. She searched for more details, but it seemed the killer still hadn't been found. There'd been a streak of violent home invasions in the district and the newspapers implied the murder might have been an escalation rather than a targeted crime, but Nic's instincts were screaming at her. Too many coincidences by half!

So what connected four soldiers, the beautiful South African socialite who'd taken her own life, and this politician, murdered in yet another knife attack in his home in Johannesburg? Cavendish. He was the common factor. He'd known all the dead people, and he'd disappeared.

Then the name "Caroline" leaped off the page. The daughter who'd been born soon after her parents' wedding. And Grace had been in love with her older cousin, Harold Cavendish, if this person was to be believed. Cavendish, who was sent abroad with the army at around the same time. It was all beginning to come together.

The door opened, bringing in a whoosh of cool air, and Chris O'Neill appeared at her shoulder. "Do you have something, Nic?"

"Maybe, but I don't know if it's relevant."

She explained her findings, and he read the obituary carefully, going back over sections of it. "You might be right. We should tell the DS."

Aaron came back into the room, and Chris squeezed her shoulder in a way that managed to be conspiratorial but not intrusive. Nic liked the older constable. She'd wished, when she first came here, that he'd been her mentor instead of Dave, but Dave had begun to grow on her.

"Sarge? Can we have a word?" O'Neill said.

Aaron looked weary. "Sure. In private, or—?"

"It's Nic's story, sarge. It's her who turned up the information."

170

His tired eyes brightened. "Oh?"

Chris nodded encouragingly, and Nic began to explain what she'd been up to, hesitating at first, then with more conviction as the idea took a firmer shape in her mind.

"So you see, sir, it looks as if our murders are only the latest in a trail of killings. No wonder Cavendish tried to bury himself in the wilds of County Antrim."

"Yes, it does seem that way doesn't it? But why? What is it that makes all these men a target?"

CHAPTER 24

Asha's phone rang, the display showing a familiar Belfast number. "Hello, Lonnie. Missing me?"

"Well, it's certainly a lot quieter here without all the cloak-and-dagger shenanigans you and young Birch got up to." The rich laugh of Sergeant Lonnie Jacob, from their old station in Belfast, made Asha smile despite her worries. "We had an alert from the ACC to check CCTV in the area for your case. There's some footage from a car park near the hostel that you'll want to see. It caught your woman on camera, but much good it'll do you. She knew the camera was there, and she kept her face hidden." No surprises there, then.

"Could you send over a copy?"

"Of course, but I've seen it, and I don't think you'll get anything useful at all. If she was that camera-aware, she might even have disguised her build and way of walking. I'm sending it over now."

Lonnie was right. The woman wore dark clothes with a pattern that broke up her outline and made it hard to see, in black-and-white, what her build was. And there were no deleted texts on Gerren's phone, according to Bishop, so that let him completely off the hook.

The next time her phone rang, it was the ACC at her frostiest. "My office. One hour."

Asha checked her watch. There was just time to catch up with the team before she left. Only Nic was in the incident room, but she quickly filled Asha in with the new developments. Asha took a copy of the printouts of the obituaries and the army photos with her.

The road to Belfast was busier than she'd expected, and she arrived late. The ACC was striding up and down in the car park outside the main door to HQ. If she'd been a horse, she'd have been pawing the ground.

"Walk with me."

Confused, but not prepared to question Aunt Harriet, Asha walked with her along the busy main road until they turned off onto a greenway track. The noise from the road was still invasive, but they could hear each other now. The ACC didn't mince her words.

"Your team needs to tread carefully around Harold Cavendish."

"Why?"

"It seems he and his team were involved in some rather nasty cloak-and-dagger work in the late eighties. Apparently Britain's enemies believed him to have died in 1992 and it can't be leaked that he lived in isolation as Rob Harris for many years after that." She sounded furious. "It's proved difficult to wring an explanation from the authorities concerned, but out of the public eye there are always deals being done and compromises being made. If it became public knowledge that the government had allowed him to go to ground instead of eliminating him as it seems they'd agreed to do, certain very influential people would not be happy, and that could adversely affect international trade dealings at a very sensitive time."

"So, let me see if I understand. Cavendish did something so bad that it became necessary for him to disappear. To die, in fact?"

"But he also made deals of his own. He wasn't a nice man, Asha, and he knew things about several people who were rising stars at the time. Now they're shining high in the firmament, and they can't afford to allow clouds from the past to dim their light. People with serious clout, it seems."

"Should you be telling me all this?" she asked gently.

"No, I shouldn't. But equally, I can't stand by and allow you and your team to continue in ignorance, digging up a past that's best left hidden. It could be dangerous for you, Asha, and I couldn't face your mother if anything happened to you on my watch."

"What did Cavendish do that was so bad he's still a potential embarrassment all these years later?"

Harriet paused. "I really can't say."

"Can't, or won't?"

"Asha, really, you're better not knowing. I know you, and I know you'll go on looking whatever I say, but can you at least promise me to be circumspect?"

Asha sighed. "All right."

Harriet Miller huffed out a breath. "Harold Cavendish wasn't *just* a member of the Rhodesian Mounted Police, and he wasn't *just* a major in the SAS. He was an undercover operative with numerous high-profile missions to his name."

Asha took a moment to assimilate that information. Then she asked the inevitable question. "Who did he kill?"

"I don't have that information. I only know that once he 'died', he could no longer be brought to trial in the international courts, and it would make certain people very angry if it ever got out that he was still alive." Her voice had dropped almost to a whisper, which made Asha more afraid than the words she was hearing. Nothing frightened Aunt Harriet.

"It seems someone decided that he deserved a peaceful old age, and that person helped Cavendish to a new life, maybe one of his old friends."

"I think I might know who that someone was," Asha said. She showed the ACC the obituary for Willem de Beer.

"He might have been powerful enough to help Cavendish disappear; his family are extremely wealthy — old money."

Aunt Harriet nodded, the lines at the corners of her eyes showing her tension. "Possibly, and look what happened to him. Stabbed to death in his own home."

Asha silently produced the other printouts, telling the story of a team of men hunted down and killed one by one. The ACC's lips thinned a little more. "Asha you can't get involved in this. I can't protect you."

A little rush of anger heated her face. "I can look after myself, *and* my team." Then shame washed over her. "I'm sorry, Aunt Harriet. Thank you for the warning, but we really can't let this drop. You must see that." She produced the obituary for Cavendish's cousin. "What about Grace Craig, later van Rooyen? Is she a red herring, do you think?"

"Maybe. The name van Rooyen is familiar — another powerful South African family. I really don't know."

"Could you ask some of your sources? If it's a powerful family, maybe they're involved?"

"I can ask."

"Circumspectly?"

"Very."

"But why now, ma'am? What has changed that made him not just a target, but the victim of such a vicious attack? He was dismembered while he was still alive, and his killer sank her teeth into his flesh." She dropped her voice as a dog walker passed them, looking startled. "And then there's this other murder in Newry. Same knife, so almost certainly the same killer, probably a woman."

"Yes. That, I don't understand. But look at the timing of the de Beer murder. What if he was killed after he'd shared what he knew about Cavendish? That would certainly set the hunters back on his trail."

Asha nodded, thinking aloud. "I'll see if I can get information from the Johannesburg police about the murder weapon, and any forensics they might have on record. We need to find out which particular powerful enemy had it in for Cavendish."

"Maybe it's just coincidence," Aunt Harriet said, but her bleak expression gave the lie to her words.

"I don't believe in coincidences."

CHAPTER 25

Aaron sat in the empty incident room, trying to marshal his thoughts. It felt as if he was dragging his feet through a shallow lake of treacle: the more they knew, the less sense it all made. Asha came back in a whirl of fresh air with the faintest hint of lavender from her shampoo. Aaron smiled, despite his stress about this case, then noticed the tightness around her eyes as she looked around to check if they were alone.

"What's happened?"

"I've just come from a meeting with the ACC. It seems we're swimming in hazardous waters here."

He almost laughed. "Really? Two gruesome local murders, and now a chain of international killings linked to our first victim? What's to fear there?"

She gave him a grudging smile. "Exactly, but it's worse than that. It seems Harris-slash-Cavendish might have been some sort of spook in the past. He's made powerful enemies, and they might not be too happy if we track them down. That's why he faked his own death."

She filled him in on the background, and he felt his own facial muscles contracting. No wonder Asha had looked so tense.

She shrugged. "So, now all we need to do is work out who, of the many people who had it in for Harold Cavendish, actually did the deed."

"Or even hired someone else to do the deed." Despite the viciousness of the attack, it still felt professional to Aaron, and there'd been little or no forensic evidence left, which reinforced his suspicion.

Asha nodded. "The victims who were murdered before him might give us a clue." She brought the sheaf of printouts Nic had given her and spread them across the desk.

In date order, there was presumably Rob Harris, then George Bailey, whose death appeared to have sent Cavendish into hiding. After that there'd been a gap of a few decades: the deaths of Willem de Beer, Grace van Rooyen, and Captain Roy Beecher had been more recent. He pointed to the last article, Grace's obituary.

"We can't include the beauty queen, can we? She took her own life."

"We'll leave her in for now. Her death could still be linked in some way, and maybe the suicide was just a cover-up. She's definitely linked to Cavendish."

A knock on the door interrupted them. Dave Stanley edged into the room, his face glowing with fresh air and suppressed excitement. Chris O'Neill and young Nic followed him in, paper cups from the drinks machine in their hands.

"Sarge," Dave said, "Gerren Penrose recognised the article about Bailey from the *Times*. He says it's the same picture too."

"That confirms it," Asha said. "It was the death of his old army friend that sent him deeper into hiding. He must have known they'd be out to get him."

Aaron nodded. It was useful, but they needed to know who was behind the killings, and with no witnesses left alive, that would be a struggle. "How have you got on with your research, Nic?"

Nic gave him a cheeky grin. "Grace's daughter, Caroline van Rooyen, began a degree in computer science in London not long before her mother's death, only going back once around the time of the funeral, it seems. After her degree, she disappeared and I can find no trace of her. That was in 2008."

"Maybe she changed her name too," Asha said. "I assume you've looked under different variations of her name, Nic?"

Nic nodded. "Yes, and under Cavendish too, just in case. I'm still not straight on the timing, but she could theoretically be his daughter, couldn't she?"

"That's a bit of a stretch," Aaron said. "Another hunch, Nic?"

Her lips tightened, but she went on. "I was thinking that if Grace was in love with Harold, maybe the child could have been his. In those days, she could have been sent away in disgrace and a husband found for her to hide her family's shame."

Aaron pulled the pile of news articles over and leafed through them. Grace's obituary claimed that Grace adored Harold Cavendish, but there was a bit of an age gap between them. Eight years wouldn't matter later in life, but when Cavendish was on leave in 1985, he'd have been in his mid-twenties and Grace would only have been seventeen. "I wonder what her parents would have thought of the age difference."

"Maybe that's why she was sent away," Nic said. "And he was her first cousin too, so I'm sure the parents wouldn't have encouraged the pair of them."

"If Cavendish *was* Caroline's father," Asha said slowly, "did she know, or did Grace keep it to herself?"

"My cousin has always said that people in that part of the world were really conservative, even in the eighties, so I'd guess she'd have kept it to herself," Nic said. "Might have come as a bit of a shock to Caroline if she did find out, maybe when her mum died."

"Deathbed confession? Possible, I suppose." Aaron stood up. "Good work, folks. Keep digging, but tread carefully around Cavendish's past. I don't want any alarm bells sounding, and we know for sure our unknown suspect has killed at least twice without compunction; we don't want her hunting any of us down next!"

There was an uneasy silence, then Dave cleared his throat. "I showed Gerren Penrose that photocopy and he's really got the bit between his teeth now, sarge. I left him rummaging around in drawers, looking for anything of Harris's he might still have. I think he wants answers as much as we do."

"I can't see what damage he can do on his own," Aaron said. "There was no sign of a computer in his house, so I assume he's old-school and doesn't use one. Even his phone is a brick. Hopefully he won't look like a threat to our killer, if she even knows he exists. Keep on digging into Caroline van Rooyen. Try to find out where she went after her degree, and who she might have had contact with. If Nic's right, and she has been known to guess well occasionally, she could be a person of interest."

"The woman's a ghost after she left uni," Chris O'Neill grumbled, but he started tapping away at his keyboard.

Nic, who'd been working away quietly throughout the discussion, stopped typing and drew in a sharp breath.

"Got something?" Asha beat Aaron to it by a heartbeat.

"Not sure, ma'am. Have a look at this and see what you think."

Once again, she had two photos side by side on the screen. This time it was the one of Cavendish from his military days and a graduation photo of a young woman with long blonde hair and a serious expression.

"This is Caroline van Rooyen's graduation photo from the yearbook. What do you think?" Nic asked anxiously. "Can you see it?"

Aaron examined the photos. There was a look about the eyes, and something in the wary expression that was similar, but that's where the resemblance ended. Cavendish had black hair and a hard mouth with thin lips, whereas this woman had flaxen hair and a wide mouth, the lips full even when pulled into a straight line as they were in this photo.

"Maybe," Aaron said.

Asha was still bending over Nic's shoulder, looking at the photos. She tapped a long finger on the printed page. "Where did you go after university, Caroline?"

Nic replied, although Aaron thought it had been a rhetorical question. "I have her booked onto a flight to Johannesburg, but I'm not sure she ever boarded it. I haven't found any trace of her after that, not anywhere, so I'm assuming she changed her name." The words *like her father* hung unspoken.

"If she did, we'll have a hell of a job tracing her," Dave said.

Aaron's phone rang, showing Ellie's number. "I'd better take this," he said, already on his way to the office for some privacy.

"Aaron? I'm a bit worried." Ellie's tight voice reflected her emotions.

"I thought you and Peter had made it up?"

"We have. It's not that. It's something Simon said this morning. You know how obsessive he can be? Well, currently it's makes and colours of cars. He keeps a wee tick list in a notebook he got from some comic or other. There's a grid with make on one side and colours along the top, and he has to tick every time he sees a particular colour of each make until he's filled the grid."

"A bit like bingo?"

"Yes, just like that. Anyway, Lizzie slept much of the journey back from Dublin yesterday, so he was playing his game most of the time, and this morning he said the same car had followed us all the way from Phoenix Park to home."

A chill came over Aaron. "Did he say what make and colour it was?"

"A blue Ford Fiesta."

One of the most popular cars in the UK. Simon might have seen several blue Fiestas on the long drive, and he was only seven, for God's sake.

She interpreted his silence correctly. "He says he knows it's the same car because he recognised the driver. Aaron, you know Simon's as sharp as a tack, despite his age. I believe him, especially because . . ."

"Because?" he prompted.

"Because he says it's a woman we talked to in the park. She helped me take the kids back to the car when Lizzie was really exhausted. The children liked her, and so did I, but she did seem a bit overly curious. She was asking about the bruise on my arm, and Simon told her Peter had hit me. I'm not sure she believed me when I told her the true story."

Aaron stared out of the window without seeing anything. "When did he last see the car?"

"I don't know. I think I must have let my worry show, so he got upset and clammed up. I got the impression she followed us almost to the door, but maybe I'm reading too much into this."

"What if Uncle Aaron comes to visit, and uses his amazing interrogation skills to find out a bit more?"

"Oh, Aaron! Would you really? I haven't said anything to Peter about it because things are still a bit strained, but it is worrying me. I don't know why."

182

CHAPTER 26

Aaron told the team he was going out, but not where. Asha followed him into the corridor, waiting until a uniformed PC had passed them and gone into an office before tugging on his sleeve.

"What's so important that you're leaving at this stage of the case?"

He explained. "It's probably nothing, but I'd rather go over there. Ellie's dead sensible, so if she's worrying, I think I ought to try to get to the bottom of it."

"How reliable is young Simon?"

"I'd have said he's like his dad: born with no imagination whatsoever, but then he's still only seven years old, so he might have misunderstood what he saw."

Asha's phone rang, and she glanced at the screen then took a quick breath. "It's Sandy. I'd better take this. Let me know how you get on."

As Aaron drove, he tried to ignore the nagging fear at the back of his mind that Ellie's call had stirred up. Simon might only be seven, but he was already a sensible wee lad, as solid and serious as they came. And he had a quick eye and the sort of steady, logical mind that didn't leap to conclusions.

Aaron envied his brother his lovely wife, with her ready smile and her easy manners. You wouldn't catch Ellie rubbing shoulders with prostitutes and criminals.

He blew out a frustrated breath. That was so unfair. How could he even think such a thing? Faith had risen above a horrific childhood and become a role model for girls who had grown up in the gutter. She was a pioneer for women's rights and a crusader against people trafficking, and she was working hard to gain legal qualifications so she could take her battle into the courts.

Why should he resent that? The woman was a titan. But, said a tiny voice that he usually managed to silence, if she really cared for you, wouldn't she have put your relationship before everything, even her campaigns?

He sped past a service station and moved into the left lane, ready for his turn-off. Time to stop thinking about Faith and concentrate on the Lisburn traffic.

Fifteen minutes later, he pulled up outside Peter and Ellie's house. Simon and Lizzie were both watching for him from the front window, waving like frenetic little windmills.

By the time he reached the door, Ellie had it open. Her face was set with worry, and there were fine lines around her eyes he hadn't noticed before.

"Aaron. Thank you for coming. Simon just said he saw the car again this morning."

The worry sharpened. "Where are my two rascals?"

"Here, Uncle Aaron!" Lizzie was first, leaping into his arms as she always did with total trust, expecting him to catch her. It would last until the first time she caught him unawares and he dropped her.

Simon followed her, but he too was filled with pent-up excitement. "Lizzie, leave him alone. Mummy says Uncle Aaron needs to interview me," he said, as pompous as his dad was at the same age. Aaron struggled to keep the laughter down.

He straightened up, donning the serious detective face he might wear for interviewing a hardened criminal. "Perhaps I should caution you first?"

Simon's eyes widened. "What's that mean?"

"It means that I have to warn you that everything you say might be used as evidence."

"Yes," Lizzie said, wriggling until he put her down. "Caution him!"

"Very well." He cleared his throat theatrically. "You do not have to say anything, but it may harm your defence if you do not mention when questioned something which you later rely on in court. Anything you do say may be given in evidence." He glared down into two pairs of startled eyes.

"That was actually quite scary," Ellie said, laughing.

Ellie made Simon a chocolate milk and Aaron a coffee and loaded a plate with homemade cookies. "You can use the dining room, if you like. It gets the sun at this time of day."

And formal enough for the charade, Aaron thought. Clever Ellie.

Simon sat on one of the dining chairs, his feet nowhere near touching the ground, and Aaron sat opposite him with his notepad, a pen, and a pocket recorder he'd discovered in a drawer recently. He hoped it looked suitably official.

He clicked record on the device. "Please speak your full name for the recording."

Serious-faced, Simon spoke clearly. "Samuel Aaron Birch."

"And this is Detective Sergeant Aaron Birch interviewing," he said. "Mr Birch, please could you describe to me the recent events in order?"

Simon's face creased up.

"I mean in the order they happened," he explained.

His face cleared. "Oh! Yes. Daddy was meant to be coming to the zoo with us but he had to go to work and Mummy was cross with him."

"Okay. Tell me about the lady in the park in Dublin. When did you first see her?"

Simon took him through the events from a child's eye perspective, which was both refreshingly simple and at the same time filled with contradictions.

"So the lady was sitting on a bench, drinking coffee when you first noticed her?"

"No! She said she was, but she wasn't. She was watching Mummy. She followed us to the park, then she got her coffee and sat down while Mummy was taking Lizzie's coat off. Then she went over and pushed Lizzie on the swing while Mummy got us drinks and sweeties."

The niggle sharpened again. "Why did you think she was following you? Maybe she was just going the same way?"

"She wasn't," he said. "She was going the other way. She passed us when Mummy was carrying Lizzie and she stared at her, then she turned around and walked after us, but on the grass not the path."

"Was she staring at Mummy or at Lizzie, do you think?"

Simon blinked slowly. "Lizzie? I think."

Aaron's breath caught for a moment. The faintest whiff of a threat to either of his brother's children made him sick to his core. He took a deep breath. "Okay. So then she followed you to the swing park. What happened while she was pushing Lizzie on the swing?"

"Nothing. Mummy came over and said thank you to her, then Lizzie and me took our food to the high-up den and Mummy sat on the bench with the lady and talked."

"Could you hear what they talked about?"

Simon shook his head. "No. Then Lizzie got cross and ran to Mummy, telling tales on me." He flushed at the memory, his full lips flattening into a thin line. "Just 'cos I told her that Daddy wasn't coming back."

Aaron swallowed back his reply. "What did Mummy say?"

"She said it was true!"

Aaron said nothing, feeling slightly ashamed of using an interview trick on a seven-year-old, but it worked. Simon's face became very pink as he stared down into his lap, twisting his fingers together in a complex pattern.

"We-ell," he said eventually. "She didn't actually say it was true, but she didn't say it wasn't and that's the same thing, isn't it, Uncle Aaron?"

Aaron tilted his head to one side encouragingly and raised an eyebrow.

"We-ell. Then she said it *wasn't* true, but she had that look, you know, that said I'd be in trouble later, then Lizzie started to cry and said she wanted to be carried, and Mummy looked like she was going to cry, and the nice lady lifted Lizzie up and carried her and helped us back to the car." He folded his arms as if glad to get a difficult task finished, but Aaron still had questions.

"Go back a bit, Simon. You said the lady carried Lizzie. Did she go all the way back to the car with you?"

Simon nodded. "She was nice. I think she was worried about Mummy because she asked me about when Daddy hit her."

Maybe the woman was some sort of social worker or campaigner for women's rights and was genuinely just worried about Ellie, but the feeling of approaching danger wouldn't go away.

"What do you mean about Daddy hitting Mummy, Simon?" asked Aaron carefully. "You've said that a couple of times."

Simon blushed at that. "I didn't actually see it, Uncle Aaron," he admitted, "but I heard Mummy and Daddy shouting and then the door slam and then a bang, just like Pingu on YouTube when his daddy hit his mummy with a fish. So that's what I thought happened, only not with a fish." He grinned, then became serious again. "But Mummy said she'd tripped over the rug, and that's how she'd got her bruise, only I don't think the lady believed her. She went away after that, and we came home. Lizzie fell asleep."

"When did you see the lady again, Simon?"

"Outside our house," he said. Aaron tried not to react physically, but the words jolted him.

"When?"

"When we were coming in yesterday and you were here. She stopped and watched for a bit then drove off."

"So you didn't see her on the road at all, just back here?"

187

"I did," he said enigmatically. "But I wasn't sure until I saw her outside the house. Up till then, I just *thought* it was her."

"Do you have your notebook?" Aaron asked. "The one you write down makes of cars in?"

Simon produced it from a pocket. It was A5 size and battered, with the name of a popular children's comic blazoned across its front cover.

"Show me where you first recorded seeing the lady's car, before you knew it was her."

Simon found the page, limp and stained. He pointed to an entry with lots of tiny ticks crammed into the box for Ford and Blue.

"Is there a tick for every time you see a car of that make and colour?"

Simon nodded. "But I think they were all the same car, 'cos it was the same number."

Aaron kept his voice steady and calm. "You weren't clever enough to take down her number were you?"

"No." Uncompromising. "I didn't need to, 'cos it was easy to remember. It's UGG then one-one-oh-one. It was funny because it spelled ugly one!"

Aaron wrote it down on his notepad. UGG1101. The lad had a great eye for numbers and letters too, it seemed. "I've a feeling you'd be wasted as an accountant," he said.

He couldn't wait to initiate a search for the owner of that car. He had a feeling it was going to be very important, but first he needed to put Ellie's mind at rest if he could.

He left Simon in the dining room with his notebook, drawing a picture of the nice lady, and went to find Ellie. She had dark circles under her eyes when she looked up as he came into the kitchen. She'd rolled up her sleeves to wash up some plates, revealing the bruise on her forearm, which looked angry and very sore. He took up a tea towel and started to dry the dishes after she rinsed them. For a few minutes they worked together in silence, then he had to ask. "How's the arm?"

188

"Not as bad as the head. I had trouble sleeping last night for the thumping. I think someone was using a pneumatic drill on the back of my skull."

"You should probably get that checked," Aaron said, but he knew she wouldn't. Lisburn A&E was only part-time, and in any case, she had no one nearby to take the children while she sat in a queue for hours, waiting to be seen.

"Just what I said." Peter had entered the house on silent feet. "But she won't go." He looked unusually quiet and even more serious than normal. "What's this Simon's saying about someone following you, Ellie?"

He looked as drawn and tired as Ellie, with deep worry lines either side of his mouth. Tension frizzed in the air between them.

"It's nothing," Ellie said, but she was hopeless at hiding her emotions and she licked her lips nervously. "Simon has been playing detective, that's all."

"He's not the only one, by the sound of it." Peter turned a baleful glare on Aaron, who began to appreciate the core of steel that enabled his brother to make decisions based on purely financial considerations.

"I think Peter needs to know what's been going on, Ellie," Aaron said. "If you don't tell him, he'll only imagine something worse."

She sagged, and sat down hard on one of their tall barstools. "Oh, for God's sake, Aaron. You tell him."

So Aaron explained to his brother about the woman in Dublin and how Simon thought he'd seen her following them. "But you know what boys his age are like," he finished. "They love the thought of adventure."

"Not Simon," Peter said. "Have you tried tracing that number?"

"I was just about to. I can call the station and get someone to run it through the computer for me." Although he didn't remember ever seeing a UGG reg before; not here, anyway.

"Do it," Peter said, his eyes fixed on Ellie.

Chris O'Neill answered the phone, and he traced the number while Aaron waited. The answer came as no surprise. "There's no record of any vehicle with those plates, and I checked a couple of close variants just in case the lad misread it, but nothing. What was the colour, make and model?"

Aaron told him and Chris groaned. "This year's top-selling model, and a popular colour to boot. It couldn't have been a lime-green Alfa Romeo, of course."

"Do me a favour and have a look anyway," Aaron said. "Maybe check the stolen vehicle files, North and South, and especially whether it might belong to a member of the Garda."

"No luck?" Peter said when he hung up.

"Not yet, but the woman said she was a Gard, so maybe we can trace her through them."

"She said she worked close by," Ellie added.

The Garda HQ was right next to Phoenix Park. Aaron had been there on a cross-border initiative a few years ago. "I'll ask one of my colleagues to put out some feelers," he said, wondering if the ACC could be persuaded. If not, Asha would certainly help him out. "In the meantime, I'd better get back to work, because we're dealing with a huge case right now, but please don't worry about this, either of you. If it would make you feel better, I can ask the local station to send officers for a drive-by every so often, to keep an eye on things."

Both of them immediately said they were fine, and definitely didn't want to cause a fuss, but Aaron decided it would do no harm. One of the sergeants in Lisburn station owed him a favour, and it was time to call it in. Besides, he'd learned not to ignore his instincts.

CHAPTER 27

Gerren couldn't stop thinking about that handgun. If the police didn't have it, and it wasn't in the cottage, where could it be? Maybe the murderer had taken it with him?

Unless Rob had hidden it somewhere, but if he had, then where was it? Gerren had never seen it again since that drunken night. And it hadn't been long afterwards that Rob had read the article the policeman showed him. That's when he'd become even more of a recluse. Until then, he'd occasionally come down to the village — not to the shops, but to Gerren's work, waiting patiently in the waiting room until he'd finished treating the local dogs and cats.

Then he'd have nodded at his friend, and Gerren would have locked the door, pulled down the blinds, and they'd have shared the bottle of whisky Gerren kept in his desk drawer. But all that had stopped after the newspaper article.

He shook his head. The gun would just have to remain a mystery, and exhaustion was catching up with him. He trudged up the stairs to his bedroom under the eaves and sat on the edge of his bed, only intending to rest for a few minutes. Somewhere in the house, a fly buzzed against a windowpane, battering itself against the invisible barrier. The warmth of the afternoon sun streaming through the low window lulled him, and he when he felt himself drifting off, he didn't fight it.

The dream, unsurprisingly, featured Rob. For some reason, he'd been inside Gerren's cottage, drinking Gerren's tea and eating his biscuits, then he'd gone upstairs and fallen asleep in Gerren's bed.

In the dream, Gerren had tried to wake him, telling him he couldn't be there. That his landlady, Mrs McKee, would have a fit if she caught him there with his muddy boots on the good bedspread.

But Rob had just lain there, eyes open, staring at the ceiling as if he was dead.

Gerren awoke with a gasp. He was lying just as Rob had been in the dream, arms folded across his chest like a corpse. He blinked up at the ceiling, willing himself to calm down. Between him and the ceiling, dust motes danced in rays of light cast across the room by warm sunshine, hypnotic in their stately movements. His heart rate gradually returned to normal.

He focused on the ceiling, which, like many old houses in the village, was lined with thin planks painted with gloss — in this case, a soft sage green. The parallel lines of the planks held his attention, so neat and tidy.

But no. Not quite. All the gaps were filled with paint except for three, and these were thin dark lines as if the paint seal had been broken at some time. As if someone might have prised loose a couple of planks in order to access the space between the ceiling and the floor of the attic. And when he looked closer, there were several fresh nail heads there too. Or unpainted, at least. They were hard to spot at first because the dust and rust had given them a patina.

The dream was still fresh in his mind, and so real that he was sure Rob really had lain here and stared up at the ceiling, just as he was doing now. And if he had, would he have noticed the way the planks were different in that one area?

Or *had* they been different then?

Rob had been in his room once, a good few years ago. Had it been before or after the newspaper article? Gerren couldn't be sure, but he thought it must have been before. He'd followed Gerren up here when Mrs McKee was away down at the shops, still talking to him about something. What was it? Something about lambing and some newfangled way to find out how many lambs were in a ewe's belly before times, so you could plan for singles and triplets. That was it. He'd been trying to persuade Gerren to buy one of those scanner things, but he'd said he was too old to learn new ways.

He smiled to himself. He'd been young enough, then, if only he'd known it.

He couldn't take his eyes from those boards. It looked for all the world as if someone had prised a few of them loose and then replaced them, and with copper nails too. Someone who knew that copper doesn't stay that colour for long but turns a sort of green that would hardly be noticed against the green-painted boards.

He sighed. A clamber onto the bed would have been wee buns, as the locals would say, all those years ago. Now, he'd need to be careful in case he fell, but he reckoned he could still manage it with a bit of imagination.

He climbed onto the narrow bed, springs creaking as his full weight came down onto it through his feet, and tottered for a moment, arms out for balance. He'd been lighter in those days too, and he'd never been as tall as Rob.

At full stretch, he could just reach the ceiling with his fingertips, but not enough to lever out a board. He'd need a tool of some sort, even a kitchen knife or a screwdriver, and a bit more height would help.

Getting back down, he almost fell. He windmilled his arms and managed to save himself but landed heavily on the floor, shaking down dust in clouds.

When he reached the kitchen, he realised his hand was shaking, and his legs felt like rubber. A wee rest first, then he'd have another go. A cup of tea would help steady him.

It was an hour later before he felt strong enough for a second attempt. This time he was armed with a chisel from the garden shed and a spindle-backed chair from the kitchen. He puffed and panted his way up the stairs, dragging the chair behind him step by bumping step.

He pushed his bed aside, trying not to see the balls of dust, odd socks, and bits of long-forgotten paper beneath it, then sat on it again until the room stopped spinning. Once he had his breath back, he dragged the chair beneath the suspect boards and climbed carefully onto it. Now he'd given it some thought, he decided it was just the sort of place someone might choose for a hidey-hole.

The boards didn't give up easily. One cracked and splintered as he forced the chisel into the gap, levering the board out from the nails that held it. But when the dust had cleared and he was able to peer into the space, he was sure he could see the edge of something metallic.

With renewed vigour, he attacked the second board, ignoring the first warning signs of breathlessness and pain. If he didn't do it now, he might never manage, and there was no hiding the damage he'd already done to the ceiling.

A squeal of tortured metal and the second board came loose.

The box was an old metal biscuit tin with a Christmas design on it. It was secured with duct tape to keep the lid on and, hopefully, the damp out. It weighed heavily in his hands as he carried it downstairs. He was glad to put it on the kitchen table, taking a moment to draw the blinds and lock the door before shaking out another of the little pills and placing it under his tongue.

Another cup of tea — the box had waited long enough that a few more minutes could do no harm — and he began to feel better.

His fingers struggled with the tape, which seemed to have fused itself into a thick, sticky mess over the years, but finally he loosened an end and began to pull it away.

The edges of the lid showed rust spotting but no serious signs of decay, so Gerren felt a lift of hope for the contents, whatever they may be. He raised the lid and peered inside, expecting to be disappointed, but there it was, dark and gleaming even after all these years: the handgun.

He lifted it out, holding it gingerly by the tip of the barrel and using a handkerchief in case of fingerprints. The police were already suspicious enough of him without him adding to that by leaving his own prints on the gun.

At first, it seemed it was just a few letters beneath the gun, held together by a faded ribbon, but that was only the top layer. He examined the neat, flowing hand. The top one was addressed to someone called Harry Cavendish at a PO box address in Rhodesia. He set the letters aside and moved on deeper into the box.

There was an A4 envelope that had a bit of weight to it. He slid the contents onto the table, and they came out in a slippery rush: photographs. Most were black-and-white, but there were colour images too. Maybe a couple of dozen in all, covering a long time period.

He laid them out in sets, oldest first. These ones showed an idyllic lifestyle in what was almost certainly Africa, with baobab trees and dusty open plains in the background. The foreground showed three people in various poses: two boys and a much younger girl. They seemed to be the best of friends, both boys showing off, monkeying around in trees and riding spirited-looking horses.

The young girl, however, was always turned towards the same boy and she was too naive to disguise her love. The boy he recognised immediately: Rob. Already he had the promise of the older man's strong build, eyes staring arrogantly into the camera lens.

He turned one of the photos over. Someone had written *The Three Musketeers* on the back, but no names. Presumably, with the arrogance of youth, they'd assumed that anyone looking at the pictures would already know who they were.

There was a larger black-and-white photo of a group of horsemen, rifles slung across their backs and bush hats on their heads. The ones at the front were all white. Grown to a man and sporting a moustache, the one in the lead was unmistakeably Rob. Behind him and the other white men were dark-skinned men mounted on dark horses with their manes cropped short. They all looked hard and competent, and determined. Written in pencil on the back was *The Squad*, which was no help at all.

The colour photos were very different. These appeared to have been taken with a powerful zoom lens and showed a beautiful, rambling house with a turquoise swimming pool and black servants carrying trays. The first picture showed the hint of a figure inside the house, just visible through the open French doors.

Gerren found the magnifying glass he sometimes used to read crossword puzzle clues and applied it to one of the photos. Yes, there she was: a slim figure in a gauzy wrap that did little to conceal her gravid state. The distance was too far to be certain, but he was pretty sure it was the same girl from the other photos, but a few years older.

Now he knew what to look for, he could spot her in more photos. This *was* the girl in the black-and-white pictures, but grown into a beautiful woman. Her bump disappeared and a glorious golden child crept into the photos. Had Rob taken these?

The next in the sequence made Gerren slam the whole stack down onto the table. He stared into the distance, unseeing, sickened. The golden child featured often, but so did her mother, along with a broad-shouldered, blonde man with a leather belt in his hand who towered over the little girl. The sequence of pictures showed a pattern of violence that continued over years, as the girl grew into a teenager and the lovely mother aged prematurely, both of them often wearing long sleeves to hide bruises.

Bile rose in his throat. Gerren had no children of his own. He'd never married, but he'd always had time for children.

196

They were the future, and they needed to be cherished and nurtured. Guided along the right path with patience and firmness, yes, but not abused like this girl.

He clenched his fists, making plans to pay this man back in kind until he remembered it was all long ago. Some of the colour photos had date stamps in the bottom corner. They covered the time period from the mid-1980s to the early 2000s. The woman would be old by now and the child a woman grown.

CHAPTER 28

Once Aaron had gone back to work, Ellie stood facing Peter across the kitchen. She was as tongue-tied as she had been when they first met at a school disco for the boys' and girls' grammars.

"I'm sorry," he said. And she thought he meant it. "I'm sorry for not coming with you yesterday, I'm sorry I've been working so much, I'm sorry for hurting you."

She opened her mouth to protest, but he spoke over her.

"No. Let me say it. You asked me a question and I never did answer it. I'll answer now."

This was it. He was going to tell her she was right and that he'd been having an affair. She didn't think she could bear to hear it from his lips, so she turned away and put her hands over her ears.

He came up behind her and gently pulled her hands down, holding them with clammy fingers. "I'm not having an affair, Ellie. The reason I couldn't answer was that I couldn't believe you could even think such a thing of me, and that made me angry. Too angry to speak, too angry to stay and talk. I'm so sorry."

It was like picking a scab. She knew she should let it go, take his word for it, for the sake of the children, but she

198

couldn't. "Why are you spending so many late nights and weekends at work?" She still had her back to him, which she was beginning to realise was a tactical mistake, because she couldn't see his face to read the truth, or otherwise, in his expression. And he held her facing that way with the grip he had on her hands.

His chest rose and fell against her back in a deep sigh. "My company is in danger of a takeover from PFC. We're fighting for our lives, but I was determined you shouldn't have to carry the worry that's been haunting me for months now. We've been having board meetings at weekends, and there've been conference calls to and from the States at weird hours too."

Ellie felt the tension easing from her shoulders. It could be true. She could tell herself it was true.

He turned her around, perhaps because he'd got through the trickiest part. His face was open and honest, with that little-boy-lost look that she'd first fallen for. Simon used the same strategy when he was trying to hide something he didn't want her to know about.

He was going to kiss her, and she didn't want him to, so she pulled back, breaking the circle of his arms around her. "Why couldn't you tell me?"

"We've all been sworn to secrecy." Glib, fluent, said with conviction. If she checked the satnav in his car, would it show only his trips in and out of the office or would it show him driving to restaurants or, worse still, hotels out of town? Did she even want to know?

"And will this be continuing?" she asked in a level voice.

He smiled tentatively. "No. We think we've managed to raise enough from a new backer to keep us afloat for now, but there might need to be some changes. We might need to tighten our belts a bit until things settle down. The financial markets have been volatile recently, and share prices are all over the place. It seems Mark has been speculating, and this has caused us further problems." He frowned down into her face.

199

"Ellie, what I'm telling you now can go no further. You do understand? I shouldn't be breathing a word of this, but I couldn't let you go on believing . . ."

He really did seem worried about telling her this. But was it because he was worried in case she phoned Mark to check his story or because he was genuinely feeling guilty about revealing the depth of his company's problems?

"Mark used funds for investments that should never have been touched. If it got out into the open, we'd be finished. I'd be finished. I'd never again be able to get a job in finance, and I—" He gasped. "I don't know how to do anything else."

She'd heard about this on the news: companies that had gambled with their pension funds and lost. Even banks.

She clutched his hands, trying to send some of her strength into him through the contact. "We'd manage," she said. "We'll always get by. I'm not wedded to this house, or the private schools, or the designer clothes, and I'm a trained teacher, Peter. I can get a job."

He stared down at her with love. How could she ever have doubted him? Then he pulled her to him, his belly pushing against her front, keeping them apart so she had to bend forward to let him kiss her.

"I love you so much, Ellie," he said, almost unintelligible through his tears. "You've always been the strong one, and I've hated lying to you. Hated it. But I won't lie again, not ever."

He reminded her so much of Simon in that moment. "Pinkie promise?" she asked, and held up her little finger.

He laughed, with an edge of hysteria, and met the gesture with his own pinkie finger. "Pinkie promise and cross my heart."

"Now, tell me about these shares Mark so unwisely invested in," she said, and they sat down together on the sofa, hands entwined, while he unburdened himself.

* * *

The next morning, she awoke feeling refreshed for the first time in ages. A luxurious stretch and yawn brought her all the way to full wakefulness.

There was whispering and suppressed giggles from downstairs. She listened, head on one side, identifying two immature voices in stage whispers and one deeper adult voice trying to keep them quiet. When the footsteps reached the landing, she pretended to be asleep.

The door brushed open across the deep-pile carpet and a change in air pressure made her stir, stretching again like, she hoped, a Disney princess being awoken by her prince.

"See? She's awake! I told you she was." That was Lizzie.

"You woke her with your noise," said Sensible Simon. "Of course she's awake now!"

Ellie opened her eyes, blinking. "Why, what's this?" She hadn't done seven years of school drama club for nothing.

"We brought you breakfast in bed," Lizzie said. "But we had to get Daddy to carry the tray in case it spilled."

Peter put his head around the door, a glint in his eye. "Ah. You're awake, I see. Good."

She answered his look with a twinkle of her own. Make-up sex was always the best. She knew herself to be dishevelled and disreputable, but the children would never notice or draw any conclusions, so their secret was safe.

Simon and Lizzie jumped up onto the bed, rearranging her pillows for her and "helping" her sit up so Daddy could put the tray on her lap. There was toast, a little burnt, but someone had kindly scraped off the worst black bits and covered it with so much butter it was hard to see the bread beneath.

There was fresh orange juice, most of it still inside the glass, and a half-cup of coffee, thick and dark the way Peter liked it and with very little milk. Ellie preferred a creamy latte or cappuccino, but she was hardly about to complain.

"Wow! This is a real treat! What have I done to deserve this?"

Simon piped up. "Daddy thought you'd been working too hard, and were tired. He said we should spoil you today."

Lizzie touched the yellowing bruise on her arm. "And you need nursing to get better, so we're going to nurse you, and Daddy says he's going to cook and clean today so you can rest."

Ellie's eyes filled with tears, turning the three beloved faces to swimming blobs. "I feel like a queen," she said. "Thank you, all of you."

When the children had gone back downstairs for their own breakfast, Peter plumped down on the other side of the bed. "I meant it, by the way. I've phoned the office to say I won't be in today, and I'll do all the jobs."

"Even taking the kids to holiday club?" she asked, mischief bubbling in her voice. He hated taking the kids to their school holiday clubs with their queues of Chelsea tractors and parents with more money than sense.

"Even there. *And* I'll be polite to the cougars at the bullpen."

"They're not cougars, Peter. Most of them are happily married. You're imagining things." Then she realised how close they were to dangerous territory and dried up. He'd realised too, she thought. He'd stiffened and looked anxious again.

She licked her lips. A day off from running their children about would be amazing. "If you're sure? Maybe we could go out for a coffee somewhere once they're dropped off?"

He brightened. "I'd like that. What about the new garden centre that's opened out Ballinderry way? Martin mentioned it the other day. Apparently they do their own home baking, and it's really good."

Her heart lifted. That was just what her bruised spirits needed.

"You take your time. Eat your breakfast, have a leisurely shower, there's no rush. I'll sort the children and deliver them, then I'll come and collect you."

She smiled, feeling like a schoolgirl going on her first date again. That had been Peter too. They'd neither of them looked at anyone else since they were sixteen.

The toast and coffee had gone cold, but she dutifully ate the soggy bread and then poured the remains of the coffee down the toilet in the en-suite. A shower would invigorate her, and she was going to have a huge latte in the garden centre with chocolate powder on top and some home-baked yummies as well. The waistline could go hang itself.

Noises typical of a morning in the Birch household vaguely filtered through to her over the running water as she soaped her body with lavender shower gel. Lizzie's indignant squawk was followed by Simon's loud accusation about something he felt his sister had done wrong. Probably taken the last of his favourite cereal. That was the usual complaint.

Peter's deep voice overrode them both, but even with her ears filled with bubbles, the note of exasperation was clear. It would do him good to experience all this for a change. And do the children good to understand that Mummy wasn't the only parent to become impatient when pushed too far.

She was just towelling herself dry when the front door closed and peace descended on the house. It would take him about thirty minutes to do the return journey in the morning traffic, meaning she had until maybe 9.15. She often felt guilty that she didn't walk the journey more often, thinking she was teaching the children bad habits — laziness as well as destroying the planet — but whenever she gave in to the guilt, she soon repented.

Lizzie would drag her feet, complaining all the way that her legs hurt, her shoes rubbed, and her bag was too heavy. When Ellie lifted her, Simon would take up the complaint until she was ready to throw them both over the next hedge.

So she usually drove. At least her car was an eco-friendly model, unlike Peter's great big diesel four-by-four. He was one to speak of Chelsea tractors!

She was ready to go, her hair pinned up in a style he'd once called sophisticated, by the time he was due back. The traffic must have been worse than usual this morning, maybe because of the slight drizzling rain, because he still wasn't home by twenty past nine.

She wandered into the kitchen and began to tidy away some of the breakfast dishes for something to do, then, after a few minutes, she took her coat off, rolled up her sleeves, and began to clean the place.

When she glanced at the clock yet again, the hands had moved to 9.45 and there was still no sign of him. Maybe he'd stopped off to buy her a gift, something to cement the peace they'd begun to forge last night? It would be like him to buy her flowers if he was feeling guilty, never remembering that she hated to see the blooms cut from the plant and would rather see them out of her window, still growing in her garden.

She switched on morning television, resolutely ignoring all the jobs that were screaming for her attention. If this was to be a day off, then she should behave as if it really was one. But *where* was Peter?

CHAPTER 29

Sandy was as helpful as always. He gave Asha the final results of the post-mortem on the murdered man, but Professor Talbot had been at a meeting, so a different pathologist had handled it. Asha didn't find the report as illuminating as she would have liked.

"Was there anything else useful, off the record? Any hunches or suspicions?"

Sandy snorted into the receiver. "You've got to be kidding. This is Prof Hall we're talking about. His father was a medical dictionary and his mother smelled of formalin. He doesn't do hunches."

She bit her lip, thinking. "But we're still sure it's the same killer? Our Prof Talbot says the knife matches the wounds on our victim perfectly, and there's more than one blood type in the traces of blood on the knife. We're assuming some of it belongs to Rob Harris, although the DNA results aren't back yet from the lab to confirm the theory."

"Prof Hall says it's unlikely the results will be clear cut anyway, with so much cross-contamination. But yes, we do still think it's the same killer. Whether it's a woman or a man, I can't be certain. Judging by your crime scene photos and the

PM report, the killer must have been very strong physically, and had nerves of steel to take on a man with a history like your victim seems to have had. Wasn't he some sort of army hero or something?"

Asha winced. Had she really shared that much detail with Sandy? Or maybe one of the team had uploaded those facts onto the system. "We don't know anything much about him for certain," she said, backing and filling. "We're still trying to find out more, but we've stalled a bit."

"Want me to help? I've a real computer whizz on the strength here. Maggie's barely out of school, but she can find pretty much anything or anyone, and those who don't want to be found are her speciality."

"Thanks, Sandy, but no. As it stands, I think your case might be the best way to trace our killer. We might need to request permission to interview Hadhira and her mother too. The preliminary interview under the auspices of social services threw up some unpleasant ideas."

"I heard. Abusive father, mother turning a blind eye. It's not the first time we've come across something like this, is it?"

"No, but I'm really worried about Hadhira. The woman she spoke to, the one we believe may be the killer, seems to have had quite an impact on the girl. She seemed delighted that her father had been murdered."

"What are you saying? Do you think she'd try to protect this woman?"

"I'm really not sure." Asha sighed. "Why would the woman go off and murder a perfect stranger? She surely can't have known Hadhira's father before. It sounds as if Hadhira's story about an abusive parent was enough to trigger a second killing."

"I ran that question past the forensic psychologist from the NCA," Sandy said, sounding a little smug. "Apparently it's not uncommon for someone who has been abused as a child to either become an abuser themselves in later life, or to become protective of other abuse victims. Usually, this manifests itself as commitment to charity work, or campaigning for changes in legislation to protect the vulnerable, but occasionally it might veer off into psychotic episodes, where the person loses touch with reality, or even develops sociopathic/psychopathic behaviour. They're both levels of antisocial personality disorder but neither features elements of empathy, as are suggested in this case. The killer is empathising with the girl, Hadhira, and has removed a threat to her in the form of the girl's father, so it is by no means certain that the killer is exhibiting such a personality disorder; nevertheless, it should be considered a possibility that the killer was also abused at some stage in their life."

"Are you reading that straight off the page?" Asha asked, amused.

Sandy laughed. "How else would I manage all that psychobabble? Yes, I'm reading it from her email."

"So we're looking at a killer who's been abused and is now, what? Taking revenge on his or her abusers? Perhaps Rob Harris was an abuser, and now the killer has a taste for revenge. But if she killed Hadhira's father as a favour to the girl, that suggests she might take a notion to kill anyone she perceives to be an abuser, doesn't it?"

His voice became sober. "That was one of the other things the forensic psychologist warned about. Oh, her language was vague — aren't they always? — but that was pretty much what she was saying. There might be further killings."

Asha put the phone down and stared at the dying potted plants around the absent Sergeant McBride's office without seeing them. More murders. She shuddered. And how were they to prevent them, if they still had no idea who the killer was?

Except maybe they did have a clue. They were having trouble tracing Caroline van Rooyen after she finished her degree course. There was definitely something about that woman that didn't quite ring true, but Asha couldn't put her finger on what it was.

She wandered through to the incident room. Only Nic was there, still tapping away at her keyboard with a deep frown. She didn't look up until Asha closed the door behind her with a clunk.

"How are you getting on with Caroline van Rooyen?"

Nic huffed out a tired breath. "The woman's a bit of a puzzle. I keep thinking I've found a trace of her, then she's gone again. I'm little further than last time anyone asked."

"Do we have any pictures of her?"

"Only that one I showed you, the graduation photo."

"What year was that?"

"2008."

"Send it to Bishop. See if he can run it through that facial recognition software thing. And maybe ask him if it can be aged to give us an idea what she'd look like now."

Nic's mouth curled up into a smile. "Onto it, boss."

Nic sent the digital image, but then she began fiddling around with it herself. Asha leaned over her shoulder. "I didn't think we could do that on the work computers."

Nic flushed with pleasure. "You'd be surprised at what we have on the system, if you know where to look."

As Nic played with the image, the features remained basically the same but the hair changed, thinning and greying a little. She drew down the mouth, thinned the lips, and added creases around the eyes. Then she tilted her head and regarded the image critically.

"Do you know, I don't think that hair is naturally blonde. Look at the eyebrows, and her colouring. I think she has darker hair, but she bleached it for the graduation photos."

Asha peered more closely. "I think you might be right, unless she had the brows darkened too, and her eyelashes."

"Red? Who would pay to have red eyebrows and lashes?"

Asha laughed. "Me?"

Ignoring her, Nic fiddled around a bit more with the image, selecting the hair with a series of clicks, and then choosing a colour from a palette along the side of the page. "How about this?"

An older woman smiled out at them from the screen, with slightly greying auburn hair. Nic was right. The hair colour did match her skin better than the blonde. "Print a couple of copies, will you? And send one to my email. I'll ask around and see if it nudges anyone's memories."

The door opened, sending a draught across the desk that reshuffled Nic's notes, fluttering some to the floor.

"Dave! Seriously? Were you born in a barn?" Nic took the edge from her words by laughing as she bent to retrieve the lost notes.

"I've been talking to Gerren Penrose," he said, babbling with excitement. "Guess what he's found?"

He plonked a square, old-fashioned tin onto the desk between Nic and Asha.

Nic frowned at the fading images. "Christmas shortbread?"

PC Stanley made an impatient noise and lifted the lid of the box. A gun lay there, looking old-fashioned but dangerous. Someone had oiled it before fastening down the lid. As Asha moved the box, it caught the light as if it had a life of its own. Beneath it, a pile of letters sat on top of a brown envelope. She felt a small frisson of hope as she reached inside and drew out the letters, which had been tied together with a ribbon until recently. The ribbon was faded and crumpled as if it had been undone and refastened numerous times.

"Never mind those," Dave said. "Look in the envelope."

Asha slid the contents out onto the table, then donned a pair of nitrile gloves before handling the photographs.

"I haven't touched them," Dave said, "but Gerren has. His fingerprints will be all over them. Other than that, I'd guess just Rob Harris-slash-Cavendish, or whoever he is."

Asha didn't think the prints would give them anything useful, but old habits die hard. She laid out the photos in rows along the desk, with Nic hurriedly shuffling papers out of the way to make room for them. She had to steel herself to look at the images with detachment — to read them as a detective, not as an empathetic human being.

The story they told fitted with Sandy's forensic psychologist's hypothesis almost too neatly. If this family was who she thought they were, and she was pretty sure the glowing young woman in the earlier photos was the one from the obituary, then there was no wonder her daughter had run away from home as soon as she was able to.

Nic had a hand over her mouth, and her eyes swam with tears. "How could anyone take these photographs and do nothing about this abuse?"

"You'd be surprised what people can do," Asha said, more drily than she'd intended, but her own nerves were scraped raw from the effort of controlling her emotions.

"Gerren thinks the photographer must have been Harris," Dave said soberly.

"Oh God!" Nic shook her head. "How could he bear to watch this happening and not intervene? This was his own daughter!"

"We don't know that for sure," Asha reminded her. "And maybe he did intervene." She was thinking of something the ACC had said about all the enemies he'd made over the years. What if he *had* intervened, and made himself a deadly enemy at the same time?

"Nic, how much do we know about Pieter van Rooyen? Have you looked into him at all yet?"

Her blank face was answer enough. "I only looked at Grace, and even then, only in relation to Cavendish."

"Well, now I'd like you to turn your research towards Caroline's father, or stepfather, or whatever he is. I want his background, details about his life with Grace, where he is now, if he's still alive. If he's dead, how did he die? Was it natural causes or was there anything suspicious about his death?"

"Got it." Nic turned back to her computer and began typing. "There should be plenty of material out there, as he's so rich and famous, but it might be hard to cut through the sheer bulk and find the answers we need."

Asha had already tuned out. She had opened the top letter in the pile, assuming it to be the oldest, judging by the faded ink on the envelope.

It read:

Dear Harry,

I hope you're well and having as much fun as you expected when you took your commission. It's wonderful to think of you in the British Army. I expect you look glorious in your regimental uniform.

In case your letters have gone astray, I thought I should let you know my address. I'm staying in an old hotel near the station that even has its own ghost, but I may not be here for long. If you direct any letters to the Victoria Hotel, Paul Kruger Street, I'll make sure to leave a redirection in place when I move. It's really quite exciting, Harry, because my very first interview has led to a photo shoot for a magazine. Apparently, redheads are all the rage here, and I've been "talent-spotted" by a modelling agency. I've already taken part in a competition, and guess what? I won! They want me to compete for the title of Miss Northern Transvaal, and that's the reason I might be moving. They'll be putting me up in a much nicer hotel, and I won't even be paying for it!

I really hope you're receiving my letters, wherever you're posted, because I so want to tell you all my news. Please do write, dearest Harry.

Yours,
Grace

The next one that caught her eye was heart-wrenching. That young woman, alone in a strange town with few friends. How lonely she must have been.

Dear Harry,

I'm sure you read in the newspapers about the fire. They think it was arson! The police are looking for the houseboy,

211

Philip, who turns out to be not the upright character we all believed him to be. It seems he has links with anti-apartheid terrorist groups.

If I'd known, that night when Daddy was shouting at me and Mummy crying, that it would be the last time I'd ever see them again, I'd have behaved differently. I can't bear to think that the last thing I said to Mummy was that I hated her for her prejudice.

I'm sure you're glad your parents weren't still alive to be victims too. Better to die in a car crash than tied up in your home while it burns around you. My heart aches with grief and guilt.

They were wrong about you being too old for me, darling. Please, please write to me. I need you so much.

Yours,
Grace

Asha skimmed a few more, tracking the rise to success of the beautiful young woman and her growing self-confidence, until she came to one that was well-thumbed, judging by the limp edges of the paper. The tone of this one was lower key, almost depressed.

Dear Harry,

I'm almost certain by now that my letters are not reaching you. Are you even still alive? Would anyone know to tell me, now Mummy and Daddy are gone?

Anyway, I've been putting off telling you my really big news, because I've been hoping you might

— the next section had been scribbled out, the words unreadable —

but I realise time is running out, so I've made a decision. The owner of the hotel I'm staying in, Pieter van Rooyen, has asked me to marry him. He's very much in love with me and buys me such expensive gifts. I really don't know how to say no to him.

You will probably laugh at this point, and say that I never did learn that skill. And that brings me to the hardest part of this letter, my dear Harry. This is so hard to write. I really do have to marry Pieter, because, you see, I am expecting a baby.

Perhaps we should have been more careful, dearest, but who could have dreamed that that one night of love would have such far-reaching consequences? When Mummy and Daddy sent me out here, I didn't have any idea, or I'd have been braver and stayed put, but I'm not brave, you know that. I never have been, and Daddy was so angry when he caught us kissing, I think he might have killed you if he'd walked in ten minutes earlier. I left as much to keep you safe as in obedience to Daddy.

I have become famous in this town now, and there is nowhere to hide my secrets. Very soon, I won't be able to disguise my condition, and refusing to allow bathing costume photographs won't be enough to keep tongues from wagging. So you see, dearest, this is the only option open to me.

Pieter believes the baby is his, and that is how it must remain. He loves me, but there is a violence to his lovemaking that I do not like, and I am a little afraid of what he might do if he suspected the baby belonged to another man.

There. That is the hard part over.

I can only hope this letter reaches you. The date he has set for the wedding is 25 March, barely a couple of weeks away, so even if you wanted to, I'm not certain you could reach Pretoria before that time. I think I will just have to go ahead with it, and live a life of my own making.

We dreamed of so many wonderful adventures when we were younger, didn't we? If only dreams could come true. But this is real life, Harry dear, and dreams hold no power here.

Please find it in your heart to forgive me.

Ever yours,

Grace

So Caroline really was Cavendish's daughter! Asha checked the date of the letter: 11 March 1986. Had the letter ever reached him? Had he tried to find her, or had everything just happened too late? He'd tracked Grace down not long afterwards, as evidenced by the candid photos of her carrying their baby, but perhaps he'd decided not to contact her in case he caused her more heartache.

The steady *tap-tap* of Nic's keyboard stopped. Asha looked up to see the probationer frowning at her screen. "Found something?"

"Maybe." She licked her lips. "Pieter van Rooyen came from a wealthy family and inherited a chain of hotels and a shipping business from his father when he was still only in his early twenties. That was about the time he met Grace Craig."

"An attractive catch for a girl in the city, alone and pregnant," Asha said levelly.

"Mm. He continued to build the businesses, adding more and more to his portfolio by buying out struggling companies, often by calling in loans he'd offered to supposedly bail them out of trouble. By the mid-nineties, he was probably the wealthiest man in South Africa, but then things started going wrong for him."

"In what way?"

"Looks like he had a run of seriously bad luck. He lost ships with valuable cargoes that were never recovered. Businesses didn't thrive. Factories he owned burned down. Sabotage was suspected, but apparently never proved. His empire began to totter, and by the early nineties he was no longer topping the lists of the world's wealthiest. His reputation suffered too. Rumours had been flying around for a few years about dodgy dealings, and the authorities were beginning to look into his financial affairs, especially the main company, South Africa Holdings." She took a deep breath. "And then there was his wife."

Asha's attention sharpened. "What about her?"

"We know she took a fatal overdose in 2007, when Caroline was eighteen, but apparently she'd been treated in hospital numerous times before that for head injuries, fractured ribs. Classic abuse picture. Fits in with those photos, doesn't it? Maybe that's why she took her own life. Or maybe she was even helped along the way?"

Asha inhaled. "That's quite a leap of imagination, Constable. I think we should avoid speculation without evidence, don't you?"

Nic, chastened, bent to her keyboard again. "Yes, ma'am. Sorry. But that van Rooyen character doesn't seem particularly pleasant, at least not if his business dealings are any guide to his character."

The young woman couldn't have seen the photos clearly, Asha thought. The man was a monster. "Is he still alive?"

"Yes, I think so. He's not so much headline news these days, but the last report I have of him was that he was living in England, somewhere in London. That was a couple of years ago. He's still wealthy, according to Companies House, but not the shining star he used to be. He's been under investigation by the financial ombudsman service more than once since he moved to the UK, but they've never managed to pin anything on him."

Why London? Was he trying to track down his daughter? "Anything linking him recently to Caroline?"

Nic shook her head. "Nothing. I'll keep digging."

"Do it tomorrow," Asha said. "It's getting late."

CHAPTER 30

Peter Birch seemed completely unaware of Caro's presence as she followed him through the traffic on the powerful BMW bike. The helmet hid her distinctive hair, and the leathers disguised her figure. She'd be just another anonymous biker, making her way through rush-hour traffic.

She was surprised when he stopped his big four-wheel drive at the school gates — wasn't it the school holidays? But from the number of children being dropped off, something must be happening. Perhaps a holiday club of some sort. As his children climbed out, a teacher with a clipboard spotted them and called them over. Peter called them back and gave them each a kiss before watching them run off to join their friends. A flicker of doubt distracted her, but then she remembered the way her own father had behaved when there were eyes on him, and she hardened her heart once more. It was all about appearances with men like him.

When he pulled away from the kerb, she slotted in four cars back, positioning herself so she could see his distinctive vehicle. He queued along the busy road, made narrow by more cars parking illegally to drop off children of all ages. If he behaved as expected, he'd follow the road around in a big loop before heading home again.

But he didn't. Instead, he pulled into a Co-op store and parked diagonally across both disabled parking bays. He was inside the shop for a while. Caro tapped her gloved fingers impatiently against her thigh. She could see him through the glass, talking to someone. Laughing. A woman, young and attractive. Her reservations receded completely, leaving her cold and calm.

He emerged from the shop with a bulging plastic bag and a bunch of cut flowers, looking so smug she growled behind her dark visor. He didn't even glance her way.

She followed at a distance — the traffic was thinner now, and she'd be more noticeable. As he approached the turn-off to the modern development he lived in, she closed the gap, gunning the powerful engine, but he didn't turn. Instead, he pulled up on the side of the road and stopped.

Caught unawares, she had no choice but to fly past him. There were too many witnesses on this stretch of road. She couldn't even stop and turn the bike here, because she'd be in his line of sight on the long straight stretch, and he couldn't fail to notice her this time.

Swearing under her breath, she drove on up the hill until she reached a junction that enabled her to make a U-turn. She rode back at a sedate speed, just in time to see him indicate, pull back onto the road, and complete his journey into the rabbit warren of houses he called home.

Caro pulled up at the next junction, a road that led to a car dealership, and realised her palms were sweating inside her leather gauntlets.

What had she been thinking? She'd been going to shoot him from the bike at close range. It would have been madness. Maybe this was madness, this bloodlust that had been building in her since the day Pieter told her about her natural father, about the way he'd raped her mother when she was barely more than a child and then murdered Grace's parents and burned down their farm.

Her hands shook as she pulled off the gloves. She hadn't even tried to fire the gun before with these on. Now, she realised that it would have been a challenge to pull the trigger.

This was ridiculous. Her earlier killings had been well planned, well thought-out. The latest one had been efficient in its way, despite the lack of time for planning, but thinking back, the man's wife could have seen her in the light from the open upstairs bedroom door and given her description to the police. And now this fiasco. Was she beginning to unravel?

She needed time to think, to plan, to decide where to go from here. Parking the bike next to a hedge, she walked up and down, swinging her arms. Exercise always helped her think clearly.

A bright yellow Porsche with dealer's plates drew her attention as it drove into the car dealership. A slick young man in a suit got out from the passenger door and went round to open the door for the driver, a young blonde woman with expensive-looking clothing and a designer handbag. Must have been for a test drive.

Caro slid the backpack from her shoulders and reached inside, pushing the original Irish plates from the borrowed Ford Fiesta out of the way. She waited for the dealer to lock the car using the key fob, and caught the transmission on her relay device, sending it onto a spare fob she kept for emergencies. She'd learned the trick from her colleagues who'd spent a happy few hours last summer hacking each other's keyless entry cars for the craic. Once they'd grown bored of the activity, and everyone in the building had learned to keep their car keys inside a Faraday pouch, she'd acquired the kit and kept it, thinking it would come in useful someday.

Unless the dealer sold the Porsche today, it would be there for the taking if she needed a fast car anytime soon. Always worth planning ahead.

She tested the new fob by unlocking and then relocking the Porsche while the dealer was busy chatting, then pocketed it. Maybe she'd never need it, but maybe she would.

Her successful little diversion had cleared her head. She retrieved the bike and thought about her next move. About how to separate Peter Birch from his wife. While she waited for him to reappear, she allowed her mind to drift back to the corridor in the hospital outside Grace's private room, where she'd faced up to Pieter with her accusation.

"Of course I knew about him," he'd said as she stood poised on her toes, ready to run. "They called themselves The Three Musketeers." His voice, always filled with authority, had kept her pinned to the spot, as paralysed as if she'd been bitten by a black mamba. "Your mother, your *father*—" he spat that word at her —"and that brainless South African politician friend of theirs. If anyone knows how to find the man who fucked your mother and planted you in her belly, it's him." His lips twisted in hatred. "He's a spineless coward, your father, a rapist, but Willem de Beer thinks the sun shines out of his arse. Even helped him fake his own death."

That's when the notion first entered her head. That she should try to find her real father, the man who abused her mother then left her and his own child to be beaten by a man she'd learned to hate and fear.

It hadn't been hard to track down Willem de Beer. He was at that time a prominent member of the government, hanging onto de Klerk's coat-tails from the time of Botha. His squeaky-clean reputation had earned him the trust of both sides, and photos of him shaking hands with Nelson Mandela on his release from prison had made the front pages of several papers a few years ago. Finding him would be easy: getting close to him, not so much.

So Caro had begun to plan. It had been ridiculously easy to meet the man in the end. She simply sent him a letter mentioning her mother's name and he replied immediately, inviting her to visit him at his luxurious home in the suburbs of Joburg.

She'd worn her best dress for the occasion, cut low in a sweetheart neckline, and arranged her hair in the style her mother had worn when she was young, all big curls that accentuated her elfin features and eyes that she'd been told were too large for her face.

The compound was guarded by uniformed men with guns at their hips and Rottweiler dogs on chain leashes. She'd had her rented car searched before she was allowed to drive between the striped, green lawns up to the front of the white stuccoed mansion he called home.

A peacock gave its mournful cry as she stepped into the house, the door opened by a black butler wearing white gloves and livery. Flashes of colour in the thick bushes hinted of tropical blooms and rare birds, but she was whisked into the cool interior before she could see more.

Willem de Beer greeted her as if she was an old friend, his eyes raking her from top to toe, taking in the soft, body-clinging silk of her dress and her bare legs. He licked his lips. "You're the image of your poor mother, my dear. How wonderful to meet you at last."

His hands were cool and damp and he had prominent eyes, reminding her of a frog. Caro forced a smile and endured a handshake that went on too long for comfort.

"Come, come," he said. "I have some refreshments laid out. We have much to talk about. And I can show you some photographs of the farm your mother grew up on too. Would you like that?"

"Very much," she said in a small, polite voice. "You're very kind."

He was openly admiring, almost salivating over her. He may have adored Grace, but his was an unconsummated passion, she was certain. He showed her the photos while they drank iced lemonade —"from lemons that grow in my garden, my dear" — and nibbled canapés. She wondered how her mother could ever have been friends with this effete man.

As soon as she saw the three of them together, she recognised her father. She might have her mother's mouth and face shape, but her athleticism was all his. And her eyes.

"Those were wonderful times," de Beer said, shaking his head. He couldn't be more than mid-fifties in age, this pale, flabby man, but he looked far older. "I'd go out to their farm

220

every school holiday, and we had such freedom then, you know. We'd ride all day and camp out at night beneath the stars. I remember lying awake, hearing a lion give his coughing roar, and shaking in my camp bed, but Harry always laughed at me for being afraid." He smiled ruefully. "He had the heart of a lion, did Harry, and your dear mother and I followed him everywhere, even into danger." A gusty sigh flooded her senses with the stench of stale alcohol and something garlicky.

"You call him Harry," she said, fishing.

"Harold Cavendish. His mother preferred us to use his full name, but Harry suited him better. It's a devil-may-care sort of name. I'm sure your mother must have spoken of him."

Gradually she teased out the history of The Three Musketeers. The man was lost in the past, words tumbling from his lips, encouraged by her obvious interest. How the two cousins had felt about each other — his jealousy came through clearly — and the tragedy of Harold's parents' death in a car crash.

"When Harold didn't reply to her letters, Grace turned to me, used me as a confidante. She was devastated when the farm was burned down and her parents killed, but even more so when she realised she wasn't going to inherit anything. Her father had dabbled in the stock market, and the farm was heavily mortgaged. She didn't have a dollar to her name, only her pretty face and her youth."

Caro tried to imagine the fear Grace had experienced. Her mother had never been brave or strong. She'd have turned to the first person she thought could keep her safe: Pieter.

"I wish I could have known you sooner," de Beer said. "In fact, I only wish Harry could have been here. What stories he could have told. Would have curled your toes, my dear." He heaved another sigh. "But Pieter would never have allowed us to meet while Grace was still alive." He glanced furtively at her. "Jealous, you know. Of the past we all shared. He hated Harry. Wouldn't have his name mentioned."

Caro smiled dutifully. "Where is Harry now, I wonder?"

He shook his head sorrowfully. "Dead, I'm afraid. Died a few years ago, but he was a true hero, my dear. He was the terror of Rhodesia when he was in the BSAP, sent on all the most dangerous missions, and then he was recruited by the British Army and went on to do heroic feats for them."

His bleary eyes shifted to the display of weapons he kept on his walls. "Harry knew of my penchant for collecting native weapons. It was he who brought me that set of spears, and the Indian knife." He pointed to a long blade with an ornate handle that took pride of place behind him in the centre of the wall.

"It used to belong to a Hindu rajah, I'm told. Harry won it in a game of cards, knowing how much I would appreciate it. There was once a jewel on the end of its hilt that was reputedly worth the price of a small country, but it was long ago removed. I replaced it with glass." The fake jewel gleamed in the low evening light as if it were a real diamond, but Caro wasn't interested in the old man's weapons collection. "How did he die, this Harry?"

"Killed in action, sadly, somewhere remote. Always knew he'd come to a sticky end, even when we were children together. Heart of a lion," he repeated. "No fear whatsoever."

But Caro noticed how his eyes gleamed as he spoke, and not with grief. No. More of a pent-up amusement at a secret only he knew and was not prepared to share.

She went back to visit Willem several more times over the next few months. He was harmless enough in his infatuation with her mother, reignited by her resemblance to Grace. She could put up with his soft white hands pawing at hers as long as he repaid her with idle chatter about his youth, and his knowledge of her father.

And then it came, the words she'd been waiting for, dreading, hoping to hear. They were eating pomegranates and he was using the rajah's knife to slice the fruit into segments so they could suck the cool juices. The drops that spilled on the white napkins reminded her of blood.

"My dear," de Beer said, leaning close to her so she could feel his body heat and smell the sweat on his skin, "there's a secret I feel I must share with you. I can't tell anyone else, but you deserve to know."

Her heart had stuttered, then beat more powerfully than before, adrenaline preparing her for action. "Are you sure you should tell me, if it's such an important secret?" she breathed, knowing that was what he needed to tempt him beyond discretion.

He wrapped a chubby arm around her shoulders and put his lips to her ear. "He's still alive. Your father, Harry Cavendish. I helped him fake his death."

She drew back, hoping he'd mistake the fury in her eyes for excitement. "No! Tell me!"

So he did. Harry had enemies who wanted him dead, so he, Willem de Beer, had given them what they wanted. He'd called in favours in high places. Each favour was but a tiny piece in the jigsaw of his well-laid plans. No one person had enough information to give them a clue to the final result: a burning vehicle at the bottom of a cliff, not discovered until predators had torn apart the driver, leaving only a dog tag to identify him.

And a new identity. An inspired idea, helped by Harry himself, who happened to have the driving licence of an old colleague in his pocket. A man who had died a couple of years previously and bore enough of a resemblance to Harry to be a believable substitute.

"It was fairly easy for a man in my position," he said. "I applied for a copy of the dead man's birth certificate, then applied for a new driving licence in his name. One of my contacts sorted the passport." He touched the side of his nose again and winked. "No one looked twice at it."

But when she asked him the name on the passport, and where Harry was now living, she drew a blank. He wouldn't tell her the name, and he claimed not to know the place.

"If anyone knew, and the information got back to certain parties, it would be his death warrant, my dear. So I told him not to tell me where he was going. I didn't want to know. As far as the world is concerned, he died in 1992, and that's the way it must remain if your dear father is to stay safe."

It was those last words that twisted the knife. He'd hinted and insinuated, but that was the first time he'd said it in so many words. And the last.

Caro left him bleeding on the pale marble tiles, his hand reaching out towards her in supplication. She kept the knife, wrapped in a linen napkin to stop his blood staining her dress.

* * *

With an effort, she dragged herself back to the present and the cars that were passing by with a repetitive hum of engines and gear changes. Had she missed the big jeep? Her hands tightened on the throttle controls. But fifteen minutes later, the dark blue four-wheel drive passed her heading towards the town centre.

Sunlight lit up the woman in the front passenger seat next to Peter Birch. Her cheeks were flushed, eyes shining, and she was laughing. He was grinning too, and looking about as smug and fat as could be, just like Caro's stepfather.

Caro dropped in a few cars behind them and followed.

CHAPTER 31

Aaron looked at his watch. He hadn't slept well the night before, his dreams troubled by a woman in a blue car.

He picked up the phone in McBride's office.

"DS Birch," the ACC said when she heard his voice. "What can I do for you?"

That was a good start. She sounded friendly, if a little distracted. "Thank you for taking my call, ma'am. I'm a little concerned about a woman who seems to have been following my brother's wife, and I was wondering if you know of anyone who could contact the Garda HQ in Dublin to ask for a name for her." He'd thought long and hard about his approach. He'd been tempted to pass his request off as a part of their current investigation, but in the end his conscience had forced him into the truth.

"This sounds intriguing." She paused, and Aaron imagined her frowning into the distance, that razor-sharp brain of hers racing through the possibilities. "Asha speaks very highly of you," she said. "Can I assume that you wouldn't be asking unless you felt someone was in danger?"

"Yes, ma'am. The woman I'm concerned about met my brother's wife, Ellie Birch, in Phoenix Park in Dublin a couple of days ago. She scraped an acquaintance, then followed Ellie and the children all the way home. She's been seen since, outside their house."

"Is it Ellie you're concerned about or the children?"

"I'm not sure, ma'am," he said miserably. "I only have my instincts to go on, and to be absolutely open with you, the word of a seven-year-old boy, my nephew. But Simon is mature for his age, and very observant."

She asked for details, and he told her what had happened, keeping it impersonal as if he was reporting events concerning a stranger, not his own family.

"I see." Another long pause. This was it. She'd either tell him to wise up and not waste police resources, or she'd help him. "What you'd like is to know if the woman really does work for the Garda Síochána or if she was making it up."

"Yes, ma'am."

"But you have no photo, only a vague description?"

His heart sank. "Yes, ma'am. Simon said she had red hair, long, tied back in a ponytail, and that she was bigger than his mummy. Ellie is a slightly built five foot three or four. Oh, and he said she had green eyes. And we have a description and registration for the car, but I've already run that, and it came up blank. There's no car with that registration number, and none of that make and colour listed as stolen, so she must be using false plates, which is suspicious in itself. The ANPR cameras on the motorway did pick up the car a couple of times, so the story hangs true."

"You will need to persuade your sister-in-law to file a formal complaint through the normal channels, to prevent us from falling foul of Data Protection laws, but I can possibly begin making some discreet enquiries of my own. Leave it with me."

The surge of relief came as a shock to him. He felt lightheaded, as if he'd forgotten to breathe. "Thank you, ma'am. I hope I'm not wasting your time."

"So do I," she snapped, and rang off. He grinned, and was still grinning when Asha walked into the room.

226

"Everyone's ready for the morning briefing," she said, then raised her eyebrows. "What's made you so happy?"

"I'll explain later," he said and followed her into the incident room.

Everyone in his small team was there, all looking alert and interested except Nic, who looked as if she'd slept in her clothes. Which she probably had, if the pile of printouts next to her laptop were any guide.

"Where are we with the case so far?" he asked the room in general, slightly ashamed that he needed to ask. He'd allowed himself to become side-tracked by Peter and Ellie's problems just when he most needed his wits about him. "DI Harvey, have you anything new for us?"

Asha nodded towards Nic. "I think you're all aware of the photos Gerren Penrose found and turned over to PC Stanley yesterday afternoon?"

Aaron wasn't. "Photos?"

Chris O'Neill slid a folder across to him, and he emptied the contents onto the desk.

"They're copies," Asha said. "The originals are bagged up as evidence. There are letters too. We can go over them later."

He went through the photographs, slowing at the worst images. He couldn't look up. He kept seeing Simon or Lizzie in this situation: frightened and covered in bruises. Without hope. He swallowed hard.

Asha seemed to read his mood, because she went on in her calm, even voice.

"Because of these photos, we've been looking into Caroline van Rooyen's family, specifically her father, Pieter van Rooyen. Nic, can you take up the story, please?"

Nic shuffled her papers nervously, then handed out stapled piles to the team. Aaron skimmed through his, seeing reports from South African tax authorities, news reports about stocks and shares, and other financial documents that put his brain into freefall. "Can we have a summary?"

She cleared her throat. "Yes. Basically, what I've discovered is that Pieter van Rooyen inherited a fortune from his father in the form of successful companies and capital. He worked hard to increase his holdings, but his reputation was unsavoury. He would buy up loans and then foreclose in order to acquire businesses he wanted, sometimes without even making the company an open offer first. He was known as a hard-headed businessman who skated close to the edge legally. There are rumours that he had the local police in his pocket, but I'm not sure that could ever be proved or disproved."

Chris O'Neill made a disgusted noise. "If there's one thing I hate, it's bent coppers."

Aaron and Asha both snorted. O'Neill looked embarrassed as his memory kicked in. "Well, I suppose you both have reason to hate them even more."

"Go on, Nic," Aaron said.

"His organisation thrived until about ten years after he met and married Grace Craig, Caroline's mother. Caroline was around ten years old when the businesses began to fail. Companies banded together to resist his aggressive tactics, and several of his assets were lost or damaged in some way."

Aaron's ears pricked up. "Damaged?"

"It's hard to be sure, but looking at an overview with the benefit of hindsight, it looks to me as if he could have been a victim of sabotage." She went on to describe the cargo ships lost at sea due to navigation failures that had caused them to run aground on reefs; factory fires; a virus that had infected the company's mainframe, resulting in huge losses of data that cost the company a fortune.

"He must have had plenty of enemies though," Dave Stanley said. "I mean the fella's a right bastard, isn't he? I'm surprised no one's put an end to him."

Aaron put the photos back in the folder and closed it. "What are you thinking, Nic?"

"His wife, Caroline's mother, was admitted to hospital more than once with injuries from falls in the house. Everything from black eyes to broken bones. There's a summary on the last page of the notes."

Aaron turned to the page and winced as he read on down. "My God. If we saw a pattern of abuse like this here, social services would be all over it."

"Maybe not, if the husband was as rich and powerful as Pieter van Rooyen," Asha said. "It's not unknown. It says here that she was suspected of self-harming and drug abuse. This was the eighties and nineties. It wouldn't have taken more than a hint to have everyone blaming the poor woman, but I don't suppose anyone looked twice at the highly respectable husband."

"What are we saying?" Aaron asked. "That someone was sabotaging van Rooyen's businesses as revenge for his abuse? Who are we looking at? The wife? The daughter? A victim of his rogue trading?"

"Or the daughter's real father," Nic said. She passed him a photocopy of a letter. He read it through quickly, then again more slowly.

"Someone took these photographs," Dave Stanley said. "Gerren Penrose thinks it was Rob Harris, or Harold Cavendish as he was then."

"You think he was behind the sabotage?" Aaron shook his head. "I'd have thought he'd be too busy carrying out his military duties."

"Military duties that included infiltration and sabotage?" Dave said. "I wonder if Harold Cavendish and his little gang of friends were behind Pieter van Rooyen's troubles."

Chris O'Neill tapped the obituary for Grace van Rooyen. "Do we know who wrote this?"

"The third musketeer," Nic said with a hint of impatience. "Willem de Beer."

"Willem de Beer who was stabbed in his own home with an ornate knife?" He pulled a photo from the set and turned it over to read the spindly writing on the reverse side: *Athos, Porthos and Aramis, June 1980.*

"They really did think of themselves as The Three Musketeers, didn't they?" Nic said. "William de Beer was a prominent politician by the time he wrote the obit. I wonder what the knife looked like. The one that killed him but was never recovered from the scene."

Aaron smiled at her. "Okay. Look into our politician and see where that gets us, Nic. If we're thinking that Harold and his mates had it in for van Rooyen's business interests, maybe the politician was involved too. Anyone else?"

Chris had a fresh report from forensics: the DNA results were in and Rob Harris's — Harold Cavendish's — blood was confirmed on the knife from the Newry scene, so that meant it had almost certainly been the same killer.

"And not only that, sir, but the DNA from the saliva samples confirmed it: the killer was a woman."

No other DNA or trace evidence had been found at the scene, any more than they'd found at the farm. It was confusing — it was as if this person knew about modern police techniques, but had forgotten all about it in the frenzy of the kill.

That set something buzzing at the back of Aaron's mind, but as soon as he tried to focus on it, it evaporated. He knew from experience that it was best to leave such ephemeral memories alone. Once he stopped worrying about it, hopefully it would come back to him.

He went on to hand out jobs for the day, but his mind was only partly in this windowless room with the constant hum of traffic outside and the tapping of keys at computer terminals. The other half was winging its way to Lisburn, worrying about Ellie and the children.

CHAPTER 32

Nic sat up, straightening her neck. Her shoulders and lower back ached, and her mouth was dry, but she had the scent now and everything else could wait.

Willem de Beer, politician, had been heavily involved in the early stages of power sharing between blacks and white people in South Africa, so he'd been in the public eye most of his career and his brutal murder had made front-page news.

Nic trawled through sensational stories from the gutter press and read serious speculation in the columns of the broadsheets that amounted to the same thing but with less drama and better grammar.

All agreed that de Beer may well have been killed for his political beliefs. Some suggested he'd been killed by a black gang member who wasn't happy about sharing power with the still-dominant whites; others hinted at a conspiracy within the white supremacist ranks that had led to his death as one of the assassins of apartheid. They dared not take on F. W. de Klerk, one paper claimed, with his powerful friends on both sides of the divide. Instead, they'd taken out his right-hand man.

The text was beginning to swim in front of her eyes until a phrase leaped out of the page at her.

Was Willem de Beer killed by one of his many girlfriends?

The police believe this to have been an impulse killing. Perhaps Mr de Beer came home and disturbed a burglar who had managed to get past his impressive security? Or so says the official version.

But there are whispers of a young woman, a frequent guest at the villa. Who she was and why she visited remain mysteries that Mr de Beer's close-lipped staff are not prepared to shed any light on, but there's no doubt that he liked young women and was frequently surrounded by crowds of fashion models and actresses at his expensive parties.

The murder weapon may have been an antique knife with origins in the Indian Raj. Mr de Beer was a known collector of weapons, and a source from within the household informed this reporter that such a knife is missing from the collection. It had previously hung on the wall of the room where Mr de Beer's body was found, but there is no trace of it so far. Without the murder weapon, it seems unlikely that the police will track down the murderer.

And it seems that the wealthy white community has closed ranks, with no one talking about the events that may have led to this fatal stabbing of a man in his own home. All attempts to identify his young female guest have met with blank stares.

Who are they protecting?

Does a savage murderess stalk the streets of Johannesburg?

She tracked down the post-mortem results for Willem de Beer. It had indeed been a brutal killing. He'd been slashed several times across the abdomen, resulting in evisceration. The attack was described as frenetic and disorganised. No killing blow had been delivered. The man had crawled a considerable distance towards the door, leaving a trail of blood behind him before finally expiring. Servants hadn't discovered him for some time.

Nic speculated that he may have given the servants orders not to disturb him, which would fit with the slightly sleazy impression she'd got of him from the newspaper reports. He'd wanted time alone with his young female guest. Privacy.

So, if Caroline van Rooyen had been visiting her mother's old friend, had he told her who her real father was?

Nic's tiredness melted away. She looked around the room, but only Dave Stanley was still there, and he was shrugging himself into his coat ready to leave. Lunchtime already?

"Dave?" she said.

"No, I won't get you another bacon butty. It's bad for you."

She laughed out of politeness. "No. It's not that. Can I run an idea past you, please?"

He sighed, glanced longingly at the door, then took his coat off and slung it over the back of his chair. "Okay. Shoot."

She showed him the article, but he just frowned at it uncomprehendingly. "So, the third musketeer is dead too. Does that make it a hat-trick? We already knew this."

"Read it all. The female visitor. The knife. The post-mortem describes it as a frenzied attack. Ring any bells?"

Comprehension dawned. "You think it's the same killer!"

"Well," she said defensively. "Bit of a coincidence, don't you think?"

"You think some woman from South Africa killed him, that she got away with it, and then several years later she turns up here and kills an old farmer in the middle of nowhere in County Antrim? And a cabinetmaker in Newry? Don't you think that's stretching belief a bit far?"

Nic deflated like a punctured balloon. "Well, don't you think it's possible?"

"Bit of a coincidence," he said. "Still, you could run it past DS Birch, I suppose. He likes you."

He left Nic a seething mess of indecision and self-doubt. Even those parting words about Aaron liking her had stung. It implied that she'd have his ear for all the wrong reasons, not because she was an officer with sound instincts.

Damn it. She pulled on her own light jacket. She needed a drink, something to eat, and the loo, not necessarily in that order.

* * *

When Nic returned from lunch, Asha and Aaron were alone in the incident room, talking quietly together. They both looked up when she came in and Asha smiled.

"Ma'am. I think the third musketeer might have been killed by the same person we're hunting for."

"All right, show us." But the disbelief was stark in Asha's voice, like it had been in Dave's.

Nic talked them through her thought processes and showed them the news articles.

"But Nic, this murder happened nearly ten years ago."

"What if it wasn't the only murder?" Aaron said slowly. "What if she's been killing in the years between?"

Asha's face paled. "The rest of Cavendish's team?"

"Well, I don't *think* she can have killed the first one, Major Bailey, because she'd only have been in her late teens, and she was at uni then, but she could have killed the last one, Beecher."

"But the only person to benefit from those killings, assuming you're right about Cavendish's squad helping him sabotage van Rooyen's business, is Pieter van Rooyen himself. Why would his stepdaughter do anything for him, never mind killing his enemies?"

Nic shrugged. "We know he was manipulative and unscrupulous. Maybe he tricked Caroline into doing his dirty work for him. He could have seen it as a neat bit of revenge: getting Cavendish's daughter to kill off his team."

"That poor woman," Asha said. Nic stared at her in shock. "I mean, she hardly had a great childhood, beaten repeatedly by a man who turns out not to even be her real father, then she's sent out by him to kill his enemies. It's possible he created such a habit of obedience in her that she did it without question."

"She'd known nothing but violence her whole life," Aaron said in a tight voice. "It's hardly surprising that she turned to violence as an answer for herself."

He looked awful, Nic thought. Haggard, and years older than he had that morning. Something was eating away at him.

CHAPTER 33

"Have you a moment, ma'am?" Aaron said. He looked tense and preoccupied, and he was calling her ma'am.

"Okay." Asha followed him to McBride's office and closed the door behind her. "What are you thinking?"

"I'm thinking that Nic's instincts might be right again. And if they are, I'm worried that Peter and Ellie might have been caught up in all this."

"What? How?"

He told her a story about an argument between his brother and sister-in-law that had blown up over nothing, then described the events that had taken place in Dublin when Ellie had taken the two children there on her own.

"It just keeps on nagging away at the back of my mind, this worry. This woman, assuming it's all the same killer, has targeted a lascivious old man in South Africa, followed by another man of similar age, who almost certainly grew up with the first victim. Then a man who abused his wife and daughter, and that's not even including the two soldiers from Cavendish's squad. If this is Caroline van Rooyen, she had a terrible childhood, abused by her father, or perhaps her stepfather. It fits the forensic psychologist's write-up on the killer in Newry, doesn't it?"

"Sandy's notes, yes. It does. But what are her triggers?"

"Maybe she's killing men who remind her of Pieter van Rooyen? Abusive types?"

"That could apply to Jibreel Khan, and maybe to Willem de Beer, but not to Captain Beecher, and not really to Cavendish, unless there's something about him we haven't discovered yet. And what has this to do with Peter and Ellie?"

"At first, I thought the woman they met in Dublin was interested in the children, but it seems she might have been more interested in the bruise on Ellie's arm. Apparently, she kept on going back to it, and asking the kids questions about their dad. I think she assumes Ellie is in an abusive relationship, and I think that might be the common factor here." He swallowed and licked his lips. "I know it's not a lot to go on, but I can't get the idea out of my head now I've thought about it."

"What about her reason for killing Cavendish?"

"He abandoned Grace pregnant and alone. He left his daughter, if Nic's suspicions are true, to be raised by an abusive father. Wouldn't that be enough of a trigger to make her want to kill him, if she was already suffering from an antisocial personality disorder?"

"Surely she'd have killed Pieter van Rooyen, not Harold Cavendish?"

Aaron shook his head. "I know. It doesn't make sense. Maybe Nic will turn up more cases, and that might help us work this out."

"But you're still worried about Peter?"

"Yes, I am. I just have a bad feeling, and it won't go away. I called in a favour from Lisburn station, and they've got a car doing a drive-by a couple of times a day, but if Caroline really intends Peter harm, that won't be anywhere near enough. She's shown us how clever she is, and she's not left us much to go on so far. Not a strand of hair, not a single print, nothing."

"There's the saliva on Rob Harris's wounds," Asha said quietly, not wanting to remind Aaron of that gory scene when he was worrying his own brother might be next.

"Yes, except for that. At least we have some DNA for comparison if we ever catch her."

Asha nodded. "We should ask the Prof if he can check for a familial relationship between the saliva and the victim. It should be easy to do since he now has results for both of them."

"I'll get onto that," he said, looking relieved to have something constructive to do.

Asha left him dialling the mortuary in Belfast and went back to the incident room.

Nic looked up as she came in.

"Anything?"

"I found photos of the knife used to stab Willem de Beer. It could be the same one, but I'm not an expert." She clicked the mouse and two photos appeared side by side on the monitor.

The photo from South Africa showed a blown-up area of a bigger image with a curved dagger slightly out of focus. The second was a PSNI evidence photo, and certainly the two looked identical to her eyes, but she knew what Nic meant. The different lighting in the two images made the South African knife look yellowy, whereas it had a blueish tinge in the recent photo. She sighed. "Good work, Nic. Maybe we need to find an expert on weapons from the Indian subcontinent."

Aaron came back in, but he appeared restless, unable to settle. He kept glancing at the open laptop on the desk as if expecting it to do something. "I asked ACC Miller to contact the Garda HQ in Dublin to find out if they employed a civilian tech who matched the description Ellie gave me, and she's just called me back."

"And?"

"They have a financial crime expert in their cybercrime division called Carol Clancy who matches the description. ACC Miller has asked for a photo to be sent over but warned them to keep it under the radar for now."

Asha's mouth dried. "You think you've found Caroline van Rooyen. Do the Gardaí keep a DNA database of their employees?"

238

"Apparently they do, but it's not complete because it's a voluntary sample. ACC Miller hasn't requested access to it just yet, because she says she'll need substantial evidence to support such a request, but it's there should we need it."

The laptop pinged and Aaron slid into the chair behind the desk, his face intent. Asha moved to a better position as he opened the email attachment, and a colour image filled the screen.

A pair of green eyes smiled out at them, set wide in a heart-shaped face framed by dark auburn hair. There were laughter lines around the eyes and mouth, and Asha thought for a fleeting moment that she'd probably like this woman if she met her. Then she remembered who it might be.

"Nic?" Asha called. "Bring up Caroline van Rooyen's university photo, the one you aged."

Aaron brought his laptop across to compare the two images side by side. The resemblance was undeniable. Asha tried to swallow, but her mouth was dry. "Get this to Ellie and ask her if she recognises the woman," she said. "Can you send it electronically?"

"I can try. We have a family message group, but neither Ellie nor Peter are that good at picking up messages." His long fingers flew across the keyboard as he spoke. "I'll send it using a few methods. Hopefully one will get through."

"Phone one of them to tell them to check."

He lifted his mobile to call, but his face darkened as no one answered first one and then the second number. He left terse voice messages both times, telling them to ring him and to check the message app.

"I'll try the house," he said. "They must be in an area with poor signal. At least I can leave voicemails on the landline."

"Maybe you should head over there," Asha said, trying to sound calm. "Just to reassure yourself that they're okay."

But then his mobile rang. He fumbled with it, almost dropping it on the floor before he managed to swipe across to answer it. "Peter?"

His face fell. It was clearly not his brother.

"So they're a match?" he said. He met Asha's eyes with a bleak look and mouthed, "*DNA.*" If the DNA was a match, then their killer really was Harold Cavendish's daughter.

He ended the call. "The dead man was the father of the killer. We're looking for Caroline van Rooyen."

Nic cleared her throat and Asha jumped. She'd almost forgotten the young constable was present.

"Ma'am? I might have found something else."

Her heart sank. "Another knife murder?"

"Not exactly," Nic said. "There was a case a few months ago of an attack in Dublin. It was the early hours of a Sunday morning and there'd been a fight outside a popular restaurant. Some sort of domestic, by the sound of it. Husband and wife decided to have a very loud slanging match inside the posh restaurant. They were politely asked to leave, but they continued the argument outside on the pavement. Then the fella took a swing at the woman and knocked her down. Next thing, some complete stranger just went for him with fists and nails, screaming blue murder. She had the fella down on the ground, punching and kicking him, then she ran off. It wasn't until she'd gone that he realised he'd been stabbed."

Asha's mouth went dry. "Did he survive? Do we have any CCTV or an artist's impression of the attacker?"

"Yes, he did survive. And we have better than an artist's impression. Someone filmed it on their phone and put it on social media."

"Let's see," Asha said.

"It's poor-quality footage. It was dark, and everything happened very fast, but . . ." Nic brought up the short video footage.

The quality was awful, and the owner of the phone had evidently imbibed freely themselves during the evening because the hand that held it was unsteady enough that Asha felt the first roils of nausea from the tilting image.

A man and woman were screaming at each other with thick Dublin accents and language ripe enough to make Asha wince. Then the man threw a punch. It didn't look as if it really made contact, but the woman tried to dodge and seemed to go over on her high heels, landing in an untidy heap in the gutter.

Before she could even try to get to her feet, someone from the crowd darted at the man, fists flying. Asha leaned in to see better, but the photographer had been taken by surprise and the view was mostly of the woman's feet. She wore smart black trousers and leather boots with a heel.

Then the man fell to the ground, and his attacker followed him down, the flash of metal in her hand as it rose and fell once, twice, and a third time. She straightened, not before Asha caught a glimpse of a mane of hair glinting in the flash of phone cameras, landed a couple of kicks in the fallen man's kidneys, then ran off. The photographer tried to follow her with his camera, but she had already pushed through the crowd and disappeared.

Asha let out a breath. "Is that her, do you think?"

"Well, according to the hospital report, the knife could be a match. A similar shape and size of weapon, anyway." Nic drew breath. "If it is the same woman, she seems to be targeting men who beat up women."

Aaron was tapping at his mobile again, still trying to reach his brother. The strain in his face melted her. "Put out an alert for Peter and Ellie's cars," she said.

CHAPTER 34

Ellie was having a wonderful morning. They'd sat outside in the sunshine, sipping coffee and nibbling tray bakes, but more importantly, they were talking again. They meandered between the rows of plants, queued to pay for the potted rose Peter had insisted on buying for her, and held hands as they walked through the car park.

And then she saw the motorbike.

The rider had her visor raised as she drove the powerful machine slowly along behind a heavily laden estate car. As if aware of Ellie's gaze, she turned her head and in that moment their eyes met.

A gauntleted hand lowered the visor, the bike accelerated and was soon out of sight among the rows of parked cars, but it was too late. Ellie had recognised her. She stopped dead, the pulse pounding in her ears.

"What is it?" Peter asked. "Are you okay? You're as white as a sheet."

She blinked, trying to clear the panic that was fogging her brain. Was it the woman she had met in Phoenix Park or was her imagination playing tricks? But then why had the woman accelerated away? She'd swerved around the car in front, almost hitting a shopping trolley in her haste to escape.

242

Peter was standing in front of her, shaking her gently with his free hand. "Darling? Ellie? What's happened?"

"She's here," Ellie managed through numbed lips. "The woman from Dublin. I just saw her. She's riding a motorbike." She pointed in the direction the motorcycle had headed.

"We should tell Aaron," he said. "But first, let's go back inside where there are more people about. And I'm getting you a cup of sweet tea." He chafed her hand as he shepherded her back inside, and she let herself be guided until a thought struck her.

"The children! We need to let the holiday club know. If she knows we're here, maybe she'll know they're there?"

His eyes widened as the implications dawned on him. "You think it's the children she's after?"

"Lizzie. Yes." She licked her lips. The memories were coming as flashbacks: Lizzie on the swing, giggling as the woman pushed her. Lizzie in the woman's arms, smiling down into her face. Lizzie was too young to be wary, and she'd seen the woman chatting to Mummy, so she'd assume it would be safe to go with her. And how sure was she that the holiday club would be as careful with safeguarding as the regular school was? Did they really remember all the parents' faces when the kids were being picked up?

She tugged at Peter's arm. "We have to get to them, Peter. Now!"

He caught some of her urgency. They ran out of the shop together and across the car park, dodging cars until Peter beeped the remote.

The drive back into town was a long, drawn-out nightmare. Peter slammed a fist against the steering wheel as yet another traffic light turned red two cars in front of them.

Ellie tried the school again, but she got the same recorded message asking her to leave her number and they'd call her back.

"Call Aaron," Peter said. "He'll know what to do."

She tried, but they were out of signal again. This whole area was patchy, but it had never seemed to matter before.

Finally, the gates of the school appeared in the distance, but a gas company was digging up the road just ahead of them, and the traffic light, predictably, glowed red.

Ellie released her seatbelt and fumbled for the door handle, but Peter grabbed her wrist. "No. The car will still be quicker." He glanced at her sideways. "And I'm not risking you. Stay put."

The lights changed and the cars in front slowly lumbered forward. Ellie wanted to scream at them to hurry, but that way lay madness. She closed her lips so tightly the muscles ached.

Parents weren't permitted to park in the car park, but Peter pulled the big jeep in nonetheless, and swung it into the space reserved for the school principal.

They were both out of the car and up the steps to the glass doors in a flash. Peter rang the doorbell, and Ellie fidgeted until a harassed-looking classroom assistant appeared at the door and buzzed them in.

"Mr and Mrs Birch. Whatever's wrong?"

They both spoke at once, but Ellie knew her voice had been drowned out by Peter's baritone.

"Where is Lizzie?"

The classroom assistant, never one of the school's brightest, blinked at them. "Lizzie? She's probably still with her age group doing art, unless they've already gone to the sports hall. If you wait here—?"

Ellie didn't wait for her to finish. She snatched at Peter's sleeve and dragged him along the corridor to the new extension where the Primary One class was housed. The classroom wall dividing it from the corridor had glass from waist height. She strained for a sight of blonde pigtails but couldn't see them among the groups of heads bent over their artwork. And she didn't recognise half the children present because the summer club was open to all children in the area.

Peter pushed the door open so hard that it banged back against the stopper. A dozen heads snapped up with startled expressions. She still couldn't see Lizzie, and surely her daughter would have called out to her if she'd been present?

244

"Lizzie?" Peter shouted, making the children closest to them jump. "Where's Lizzie?"

The teacher straightened up from where she'd been helping a little boy with his drawing. "Mr Birch!"

"Daddy?" The little voice came from behind them in the corridor. Ellie spun around to see her daughter, eyes like saucers, coming out of the toilets.

Peter swept her up in his arms and hugged her close until she tried to push him away.

"Daddy! You're hurting. Stop it."

He put her back down gently and dropped to a crouch, so he was her height. "I'm sorry if I scared you, darling."

Her bottom lip came out and the big blue eyes turned shiny, the prelude to a tantrum in Ellie's experience. Lizzie had always liked an audience for her mood swings.

She stepped in. "Hello, Lizzie. Are you enjoying holiday club?"

The lip returned to normal, and her eyes sparkled. "Yes, I'm going on the trampolines next!"

With normal service apparently resumed, Ellie tugged at Peter's arm. "Well, off you go then, darling!" As Lizzie raced off, Ellie turned to the teacher, who had come over to them. "Sorry for the interruption. Do you know where Simon is, Lizzie's brother?"

"Yes, he's with the music group — in the classroom just behind you. You can see him through the window from here." She pointed, and they saw Simon and a group of four other children all playing with musical instruments, everything from a kazoo to a tin whistle. Simon, predictably, was the one with the kazoo.

Once they'd explained why they were there, the teacher frowned and nodded in sympathy. "I can assure you we won't send the children home with anyone other than their parents or a nominated guardian, as per the form you filled in when you signed up for the classes." She thumbed through a set of files by her desk. "You've nominated Aaron Birch as guardian if you're unable to collect them. But if you'd feel more comfortable taking them home now . . . ?"

"Ellie, I'm sure they'll be safe here, now that we've explained the situation. And the school is like Fort Knox." Peter sounded as embarrassed as she felt. "At least let's report all this to Aaron before we start scaring the kids."

She could hear the excited chatter of the children as they began to make their way to the sports hall for trampolining. She couldn't tear Lizzie away from that on a whim. She'd never hear the end of it.

CHAPTER 35

Caro's pulse raced. That had been far too close. She'd had to act fast as soon as the wife recognised her. That woman was sharp, sharper than her slug of a husband.

She rode back through the town to the car dealership and rolled the bike out of sight behind the same hedge. She kept the helmet and gauntlets on in case of CCTV.

The bright yellow Porsche was still parked right next to the office, perhaps ready for another test drive. She retrieved the cloned key fob and opened the door, slipping in behind the wheel. Tinted windows helped to hide her, but there was no one in sight through the floor-to-ceiling windows of the showroom and she hadn't seen any CCTV cameras on this side of the building, so she shed the motorcycle helmet and gloves and shook her hair loose.

The tank, unusually, was almost half full. The dealer must have been using it as his own runabout because showroom cars rarely had enough fuel in them for more than the occasional test drive. As she pulled onto the road, she tapped her fingers on the wheel and smiled at the responsiveness of the vehicle. Now she just needed to locate the blue BMW, but that shouldn't be any trouble: she'd placed a tracker beneath the wheel arch at the garden centre.

The handheld scanner showed the jeep to be parked back at the school where she'd seen him drop the kids, so presumably the wife's knee-jerk reaction to seeing Caro at the garden centre had been to rush off to protect her children. Caro pursed her lips. People could be so stupid. What could she possibly want with a pair of mewling brats? Her interest in them had only been a means to earn the mother's trust, but she must have played her role too well.

After a while, Peter Birch's car was on the move again. If she'd been at her work desk, she'd have been able to hack into its telemetrics and get data about its speed and heading, but this basic device with its stop–go position locating would have to do.

She waited until the car was on the motorway before she started the engine and headed out in pursuit. The sky darkened, steel-grey and purple clouds massing over the town, and as she pulled out of the slipway to join the motorway city-bound, the first heavy drops of rain began to splatter on the sloping windscreen. When the wipers didn't start up by themselves, she snorted and hit the stalk. A car like this, and they'd skimped on automatic wipers?

Sitting low down as she was in the sports seat, the road spray was a real nuisance. She leaned back and concentrated on the task ahead — it would do no one any good if she crashed and killed herself. The car stuck to the road like a limpet, and she began to enjoy herself as she flashed past slower vehicles until she spotted the rear lights of a dark blue jeep just ahead.

Following with a few vehicles between them, Caro waited for her moment. Cars joining the carriageway from another slipway forced her across lanes, leaving her exposed, but Birch didn't change speed or lanes, just continued at around 65 mph in the middle lane.

Every so often, she'd slip across lanes to check on him, then drop back out of sight.

She knew this stretch of road from her research, and from her last trip into Belfast. There was an underpass not too far ahead, and she had an idea how she could use it.

She crossed two lanes and gunned the engine, her head pushed back against the headrest as the car accelerated. Glancing sideways, she saw Birch's startled face as she shot past him, then he was in her rear-view mirror.

The underpass closed over her, a momentary relief from the driving rain. As she'd anticipated, most of the cars were still travelling above the 50-mph speed limit.

She chose her moment, calculating angles and speeds, then flicked the handbrake on, spinning the wheel. She caught it before it completed the skid-turn and wrenched the wheel back to keep it from hitting the car on her left, but her sudden erratic partial handbrake turn had the desired effect.

Chaos reigned as drivers fought to stop, or to steer to miss her. The car she'd almost hit swerved to its left, colliding with a small hatchback and spinning it on the wet road surface. The next car had no time to stop and rammed it side on. She watched the fallout through her mirror until a bend took it out of sight.

CHAPTER 36

Back on the road, Ellie's head was beginning to throb with the after-effects of fear followed by embarrassment at causing such a fuss in their children's school. In her own car, she'd have had some ibuprofen tucked away in the glovebox, but she knew from experience that Peter wouldn't be carrying any in his. She rubbed her eyes with the heels of her hands, trying to massage the pain away.

"Call Aaron," Peter said. "We need to tell him that we've seen her again."

"What if I was imagining it?" Ellie asked, surprised at how tired and hopeless her voice sounded.

"You weren't," he said firmly. "I saw her too. She definitely matched Simon's description."

"Okay," Ellie agreed. "I'll phone him, shall I? Or text?"

"Phone," Peter said. "And tell him we're heading up his way now. I'm going to drive us straight up there."

Her phone buzzed with incoming messages as she picked it up.

She looked at the screen properly for the first time. "Hold on, I've a bunch of missed calls and texts. I'd better check them first."

Peter didn't answer. His eyes kept flicking to his rear-view mirror. The big car accelerated along the motorway.

The missed calls were all from Aaron. And there was an unread message showing on their family message group too. She tapped on it, and a face filled the screen.

The phone slid from her limp fingers and clattered on the floor in the footwell. She dived to retrieve it, but at the same moment the car swerved and she bumped her head on the passenger door handle as she was thrown sideways.

"What the hell are you doing?"

"Sorry," Peter said through gritted teeth. "There's some lunatic behind me. He's going to cause an accident if he goes on like this. I was too busy watching him and didn't keep my eyes on the road ahead."

She caught her phone and unlocked it again. The same face still stared out at her, but she was ready for it this time. She scrolled down and read the message beneath it.

Is this the woman you met in Dublin? If it is, call me straight away.

Her mouth had become dry. She found Aaron's mobile number and rang it. He picked up on the first ring. "Thank God, Ellie. Where have you been?"

"We've been checking on the kids. I saw her today, Aaron," she said. "She was on a motorbike, but it was definitely her. She realised I'd spotted her and raced off. We were worried she might be after the children, but they're fine and the summer club knows not to let them go home with anyone but us." She was babbling but couldn't seem to help it.

"Ellie, have you got Peter with you?"

"Yes, he's driving. We're on our way to you now."

"Where are you?"

Ellie looked out of the window at the familiar countryside flashing past as they flew up the motorway. "M1, not far from the Westlink."

"Keep going. I'm sending a car out to intercept you and escort you in. Tell Peter not to stop for anything. Do you hear me? Just keep driving and stay on the line."

"Okay," she said in a wobbly voice. "Peter, Aaron says to keep driving and not stop for anything. He's sending an escort for us."

Peter's eyebrows shot up, but he still gripped the wheel, eyes locked on the road ahead. His foot maybe came down a little heavier on the pedal, but he didn't say anything.

He glanced back in the mirror again, and Ellie dropped her sun visor so she could use the vanity mirror to see behind. It wasn't a great view, but she could see some of the following traffic. "What is it, Peter?"

"That idiot is still back there somewhere," he said. "I just saw another vehicle swerve to get out of his way. He nearly ran them off the road."

Ellie turned around in her seat, straining against the seat-belt to see behind. A flash of yellow appeared a few cars back, something low and very sporty. It had started raining a while back, and the road spray made it hard to see details. "Yellow sports car?"

"That's the one. Fancies himself as Lewis Hamilton."

The yellow car pulled out into the overtaking lane and rocketed past the queues of cars all heading towards Belfast, dodging in and out of lanes to overtake on whichever side gave him the best advantage.

"He's coming past us," Ellie said unnecessarily.

She tried to catch a glimpse of the driver, but the windows were tinted and she couldn't even see a silhouette. He left a spume of water hanging in the air behind him, and Peter's wipers had to work at full speed to clear his view.

"Phew. Glad he's ahead of us," Peter said. He eased the speed just a little and his fingers relaxed on the wheel. "Now what was that you were saying, Aaron?"

Ellie put her brother-in-law on speaker.

"What was that about another driver?" Aaron asked.

"Just some boy racer in a Porsche. He's away now, thank God. What's the big panic about, Aaron? Do we need to phone the school, maybe have someone look after the children?"

There was a silence, as if Aaron had put his phone on mute, then a click as he came back again. "No. The children should be fine, but I can have a PC drive over to collect them later if we think it's necessary. It's you I'm worried about at the moment." His voice sounded strained. "An unmarked car should be with you in about five minutes. He's coming out from Lisburn Road station. He'll drop in front of you and flash his hazard lights a couple of times. Don't pull over, just follow him here, okay?"

A thousand questions fought for priority in Ellie's head, but she didn't get the chance to voice any of them. "Look out!"

Through the road spray ahead of them, a kaleidoscope of red and flashing orange was emerging. Peter hit the brakes and the car juddered as the automatic braking system kicked in, trying to stop the skid on tarmac slick with water.

But there was no stopping at this speed. The rear end spun and Ellie grabbed at anything she could reach to stop herself being thrown around.

The sound of rending metal would haunt her nightmares. Even before they made impact, it was all around them. Car after car, skidding out of control. Then the jeep hit something big, and the airbags exploded, peppering Ellie's face with what felt like shotgun pellets. Her head hit the bag and rebounded, thumping the headrest. Pain lanced through her neck and shoulders.

For the longest time, everything was a swirl of powder and suffocation, noise and impact as more cars joined the pile-up.

She tried to fight free, lashing out all around her. The airbag subsided and she blinked the tears from her eyes, coughing. She was still alive. She could see and hear. The car shook again as another vehicle hit them, or more likely one of the other vehicles behind them.

For a moment, she just took deep breaths, glad to be alive, but then she remembered Peter.

CHAPTER 37

Aaron heard Ellie scream followed by the screech of tortured metal, and he almost threw up.

"Peter! Ellie!" he shouted, but there was no way they'd hear him over that noise. Then the line went dead.

He stared at the phone in his hand, mind racing. Asha gripped his shoulder, the warmth of her touch grounding him. "We need to see what's happening," she said. "I'll see if I can get a chopper up there."

She disappeared, and he was left alone in the office that didn't belong to him. He was out of his depth. He'd been in charge of this case from the beginning, and he'd done everything wrong.

His mind refused to focus. All he could think of was scenes of twisted wreckage and flames licking at car bodywork as the occupants screamed for help that couldn't possibly reach them in time.

As a rookie officer, he'd attended a multi-car pile-up. It had been a scene from hell. The fire service had been kept busy cutting people from their cars, and ambulances had queued up to carry away the injured, but the part that remained with him and haunted his dreams was the sound of a woman screaming

254

for her child. The child who hadn't been wearing a seatbelt. The child who had been fired like a projectile through the windscreen, past her mother, and into the vehicle in front of them. The poor kid hadn't stood a chance.

Aaron had thrown up on the grass verge, then Sergeant Lonnie Jacob had appeared as if from nowhere and taken his arm.

"Probationary Constable Birch, snap out of it. There are people here who need us."

And he'd been shamed into going back there to help. He'd been the one who held the woman's hand while she was cut from the wreckage. He'd seen the frantic fear and hope fade from her eyes as she was lifted clear and saw the tiny, crumpled shape on the side of the road, covered by a sheet.

And this was his brother, and Ellie. He could not freeze again. They needed him.

It took more effort than he'd believed himself capable of to rise and walk into the incident room. Asha was directing operations, with Nic and Dave and Chris all busy calling up help.

He automatically veered towards Nic's workstation. She had the ANPR camera image on her screen, and it told a tale that made the bile rise up again in his throat.

"Talk to me," he said.

She shot him a startled glance then swapped the view to a different camera. This one showed a more distant vantage point. The helicopter? That had been fast work.

"There was already a helicopter in the air, sir," she said. "We just redirected it."

The crash site was spread along the road, extending into the underpass at the western end of the Westlink. The road the other side of the tunnel was clear city-bound, suggesting the original accident had occurred inside the underpass. For more than a hundred yards in a south-westerly direction, crashed vehicles littered the road, obscured by smoke. The traffic on the opposite carriageway was backed up as people

255

slowed to rubberneck, but the officers on the ground would soon sort that out and get everyone moving again.

"Are you in touch with the helicopter?" he asked.

Nic nodded.

"Can you ask them to look for a dark blue BMW X7?" He gave Peter's registration number.

Nic spoke to the pilot and the camera view changed, becoming closer until Aaron could see tiny figures moving around in between the vehicles. He strained to pick out the shape of his brother's car, but from above it was impossible. They all looked much the same.

He tried Ellie's phone, but it went straight to voicemail, as did Peter's. Aaron drummed his fingers on the desk, hating the feeling of impotence. He wanted to get down there on the ground, to find them himself and help them even though he knew that was stupid. He was at least half an hour away and he'd get nowhere near the crash site.

Then he saw her.

Ellie was trying to open the door of a vehicle that was partially obscured by the back of an articulated lorry. It looked as if the front of the car might have run underneath it, slewing it around so the passenger door was clear but the driver's side partially crushed.

Ellie was trying to open the rear door on the driver's side, throwing her weight against it.

"There," he said, pointing to the screen. "Can they zoom in on that car?"

The camera took them closer. It was definitely Ellie. Her long hair was plastered to her head by the rain, and there was a dark stain on her shoulder, possibly blood.

"Are there any units close by?" he asked. "It looks as if Peter's trapped inside the car and Ellie's trying to get him out."

Nic looked up at him, anguish in her face. "There are units at both ends, trying to reach all the vehicles, but Peter and Ellie are right in the middle."

He wasn't sure what she saw in his face, but she spoke again to the pilot, then switched the view to the cameras above

256

the road on the overhead signs. She selected an image and resized it to full screen. From this angle, the lorry obscured most of their view, but Aaron could see Ellie tugging at the car door still, her mouth open as she shouted.

Someone got out of another car and went to help her, a man in a suit with a paunch hanging over his trouser belt. He pushed Ellie aside and took over from her, trying the door handle.

His superior strength succeeded. The door swung open, and he climbed into the back seat out of sight. Ellie leaned in after him, still shouting something.

Nic flicked back to the view from the helicopter, but neither view gave enough detail for Aaron. He needed to see inside that car. How badly was Peter injured?

Asha touched his arm. "I'm through to the officer coordinating the operation on the ground," she said, and handed him a radio.

Aaron introduced himself and explained the situation briefly. "The driver of the car is in danger," he said, working hard to keep his voice even as if it were a stranger he was talking about. "We have a suspect we believe is responsible for several murders, and evidence that the driver of the car is her next target. It's vital that he is protected." He didn't mention that Peter might also be trapped inside his car. The emergency services were working at full stretch already, and his gut was telling him that Caroline van Rooyen was the more urgent threat.

CHAPTER 38

Humming a tune under her breath, Caro continued on for another couple of junctions before indicating to leave the carriageway. She was in no rush to return. The more confusion and fear developed, the easier her task would be.

By the time she'd rejoined the A12 heading southwest, traffic was already backing up. She stayed in the outside lane, shuffling along with the flow, until she reached the underpass again. Blue flashing lights strobed their message, and sirens raced past her. She pulled over courteously to allow the emergency services through like a good, law-abiding motorist.

Scanning the stationary vehicles on the other side of the road, she recognised the truck Birch had been following. She stopped the Porsche, not even bothering to pull to the side of the road, and jumped out, leaving the engine running.

No one paid her much attention when she vaulted the crash barrier, her spare knife held out of sight along her wrist. Birch's wife was at the rear door of their jeep, tugging at something, or someone. The front end of the car had wedged itself beneath the back end of the truck in front, the impact guard underneath the rear of the truck crushing the bonnet of the car.

Caro took in the picture with a glance. Birch must still be inside the jeep, no doubt struggling to get his fat bulk out if the driver's door was jammed, as it must be, judging by the way the car's metal body had been deformed by the collision.

She dodged between the vehicles and pulled Ellie Birch out of the way, hardly registering as the woman fell to the ground. The knife slid into Caro's hand in one, smooth, practised motion, and its warm grip gave her the strength she needed.

Birch was wedged between the seats. He must have tried to get out backwards, but now his legs just waved around in the air like a dying housefly while his upper body refused to fit through the narrow gap.

She knelt on the rear seat and brought her arm up in a restricted swing, driving the knife into his torso, again and again, imagining it was Pieter. In that moment of bloodlust, she made her decision.

Ellie Birch screamed at her, trying to drag her out of the car, but Caro was in a strong position, wedged into the back seat. The overweight body convulsed, a gurgling scream filling the air, high-pitched and almost feminine.

Her mouth filled with bile at the sound. Just what she'd expect from a man who hurt women. He was screaming like a little girl. She managed several more blows before the body collapsed and the legs stopped thrashing.

She shoved past the screaming woman. Why couldn't Ellie see that she'd done her a favour? No more beatings. No more fear. She shook her head, disgusted, and turned away.

No one else seemed to have realised what was happening. People were milling around in shocked groups, exchanging insurance details. It didn't look as if anyone in any of the nearby vehicles had been hurt too badly, not that she really cared. She'd known, when she pulled the handbrake, that there'd be collateral damage. It was worth it, if it took just one sadistic man off the streets.

Then a sound that had been nudging at her consciousness for a while forced its attention on her. The *whump-whump* of helicopter blades. She looked up into the wind and rain to see a black helicopter hovering, so low that the downdraught was sending up spumes of foam from the wet road.

She shoved the knife in the pocket of her hoodie and turned on the spot, deciding which way to run. No point going back to the Porsche, as she'd originally intended. It would be far too easy to follow, and the police would be able to track it with its telemetrics.

The helicopter couldn't follow her if she stayed out of sight, and in these conditions even their infrared cameras might struggle. She needed to reach somewhere with crowds where she could blend in and disappear. To the south of the motorway was a tall brick wall that hid whatever was behind it, but to the north only a mesh fence, separating the road and slipway from what looked like rough, boggy ground. In the distance, trees loomed through the rain.

Caro darted between the cars and threw herself at the fence. She caught her hoodie on the top and heard the fabric rip as she dropped down into squelchy bog that soaked her instantly halfway up her right calf. She staggered for balance as she pulled herself free with a sucking noise.

There was a path not twenty feet away. She squelched across to it, then shook the excess mud from her shoes and ran, heading towards the nearest clump of trees.

They weren't as promising as she'd hoped, and the helicopter still shadowed her, whipping the upper branches into a storm of flying leaves. She ran off the edge of the track to gain better cover, because there weren't enough trees to hide the track itself.

The rain was easing a little, so she wiped her face with a muddy sleeve and ran on with a lengthened stride, glad of all the years of training that she'd forced on herself. The adrenaline was fading from her bloodstream now, leaving her feeling flat and defeated. She'd made a cardinal error, and not planned her escape. She'd become so focused on killing Peter Birch that she hadn't thought beyond the knife sinking into his fat flesh.

A chill rippled across her wet skin, trailing goosebumps behind it. She upped her pace, cold air searing her lungs with every breath. Her brain began to focus again. Had she left anything in the car to identify her? Her rucksack had nothing personal in it, only the equipment she'd used to steal the car, and the tracker, but by now they'd have worked out that this hadn't been a random killing. She didn't carry a wallet or ID of any sort, just cash in her pocket. No mobile phone either. Her own department used them to track fugitives, so she was hardly going to hand the authorities such lovely evidence. There were the original number plates from the Fiesta, but as she'd stolen that, it shouldn't get them any further.

She'd worn gloves, so there'd be no prints. Hadn't she? She glanced down as she ran at the long, bare fingers and slim wrists projecting from her dripping cuffs. Where were her gloves?

She'd left them in the car with the helmet. Shit! The inside of the gloves would hold prints, wouldn't they? And her prints might be on file from her work with the Garda Síochána. If they thought to look there. Sharing of databases was a little sketchy between North and South, so perhaps she'd strike lucky.

That thought almost stopped her in her tracks. She really was unravelling. Luck had never played a part in her activities. She'd always had a clear mind and excellent judgement, which was why she was not only a free woman, but employed by the Irish police force, even while she killed on her own doorstep.

Okay, at least she had recognised the signs. All she needed to do was to discipline herself again, to regain that hard, well-trained persona that had brought her this far. She'd done it before; she could do it again.

And still the sound of rotors drummed, making it hard to think clearly. Ahead, the trees thickened where the path branched, but first there was an open section she'd have to cover. She paused, catching her breath, and squinted up between the trees. The helicopter was a long way behind her, still hovering over the bogland park. She must have moved faster than they'd expected.

CHAPTER 39

Nic tugged at Aaron's arm and pointed to the screen, which she'd split between the views from the helicopter and the on-site camera. A bright yellow vehicle had stopped on the westbound carriageway, immediately opposite Peter's car. For a moment, Aaron thought it must be someone wanting to take photos of the pile-up to sell to the papers, then a figure emerged from the driver's side, fiery hair blowing in the storm, and ran at the crash barrier separating the carriageways.

"Stop her!" Aaron shouted, as if the officer on the end of the radio connection could do anything about it. As if anyone could.

It was like watching a horror movie with the volume muted. He saw Ellie turn, then throw herself in between the woman and Peter's car.

The flame-haired woman cast her aside and reached into the car through the open back door.

Time slowed.

All he could see was a pair of legs clad in dark leather and the bottom part of her torso. Ellie picked herself up and dived at the woman, trying to drag her back, away from Peter.

Caroline van Rooyen ducked back out of the car and straightened up. Ellie went for her with fists flailing. Aaron couldn't hear, but he could imagine her screams of grief. A sob welled up in his own throat.

Asha put her arm around him and squeezed. Everyone in the incident room crowded around the monitor, but no one spoke. The only sound in the room was his own rasping breath, as close to hysteria as he'd ever been.

His eyes filled with tears, and the screen blurred. Dashing them away didn't help, because he was sobbing now, unable to draw breath past the pain in his chest. Was this what a broken heart felt like?

By the time he'd managed to gain some control, the flame-haired woman had gone. Nic was talking urgently to the helicopter pilot and to the man on the ground in turns, directing them to follow her.

"What happened?" he said. His voice was hoarse from the effort it took to control his emotions. "Where did she go?"

The traffic camera showed paramedics and police officers pushing in between the wrecked vehicles, reaching the scene. Someone had Ellie wrapped in their arms, holding her, draping a silver blanket around her.

Green-uniformed paramedics climbed into the jeep through the open rear door, but Aaron couldn't allow himself to believe there'd be anything they could do for Peter. Caroline van Rooyen had shown herself to be a ruthless killer, and she'd yet to make a mistake.

The children. Another cramping pain struck. He'd have to take Peter's place in their lives. Help Ellie to manage, both financially and with more practical care. He could leave the force. It was what Peter would have wanted.

He was hauled back to the present by Asha's voice.

"Fuck! She can't have just disappeared. We need feet on the ground. Now." He'd never heard Asha swear before.

The helicopter was circling above a patch of trees, but there was no sign of a running figure.

"Sir?" Chris O'Neill was at his elbow. "I have a patrol car ready to take you to the scene."

Aaron walked like an automaton behind him. Dave pushed a raincoat into his hands as he passed, and he mumbled his thanks. Then he was inside the car, and it was moving off, the blue lights reflecting on the wet tarmac as it pulled through the gates and onto the road.

Only then did he notice Asha at his side in the back seat and Chris O'Neill in the front passenger seat. He reached for Asha's hand, and she returned his grip, her fingers strong and warm, giving him strength to face what lay ahead.

The journey passed in a miserable blur of red rear lights, cars pulling over in response to the siren, and rain streaking down the side window. Even the sky was crying, but there were no tears wetting Aaron's cheeks now. His mind kept trying to replay those minutes of camera footage, but he refused to allow it. He couldn't bear the pain. Instead, he focused on what he'd say to Ellie. How he'd help her break the news to Simon and Lizzie.

The driver brought them across the edge of the city rather than along the main roads, so they came to the site of the accident by passing the wrong way along a slipway that brought them out onto the city-bound M1 just after it became the A12, or Westlink as it was usually called, waved through by officers in yellow vests.

The scene that met them was far worse than it had appeared on the overhead cameras. Some vehicles had managed to stop in time, but there was a series of minor pile-ups that spread westwards as far as Aaron could see.

He spotted the truck that Peter had crashed into, conspicuous with its bright green livery and red-and-yellow writing. He was out of the car door and running, aware that Asha was just behind him.

Blue lights flashed. Somehow, they'd managed to get an ambulance down here in between the cars and it stood with its back door open, stretcher ramp down. The inside lights cast a warm glow in the rain-induced twilight, but there was no one inside it. He ran past, dreading what he'd see.

A cluster of uniforms were gathered around, and he began to push his way through. Rain streamed down his face, plastering his hair and half blinding him, but then he was through, where Ellie huddled inside a tinfoil blanket, her face pinched and white. On the soaking ground lay a body bag, zipped up. Peter was beyond his help now, but Ellie still needed him. He wrapped her in his arms and held her, and she sobbed into his shoulder, her whole body shivering as if she had a fever.

"Ellie, I'm sorry." It wasn't what he'd planned to say, but it was all he could manage. "I'm so sorry."

CHAPTER 40

A sprint brought Caro back under cover, but now she had a stream on her left, fast flowing and noisy after the torrential rain, and a high fence to her right. She couldn't see what was beyond the fence, but it seemed to be built up. Maybe a factory, or offices?

The way grew rough, brambles and nettles twisting around her legs and slowing her down. She regretted leaving the path, but at least she was well undercover here. Even if the helicopter came this way, she'd simply have to drop down into the undergrowth to disappear, as long as the infrared didn't work in this weather. She was pretty sure her icy skin and wet clothes would obscure her outline even then.

But the beat of rotors sounded even further behind her and off to her left, as if they were looking for her among the waterways and ponds of the boggy marshland. Maybe they thought she'd gone full-on Rambo, painting her face with mud as camouflage.

The thought made her smile for a moment, until the reality of her predicament closed back over her again.

Ahead, she could hear the steady hum of traffic, and to her right, children's voices. A glance that way showed her girls in Gaelic football kit, with a smattering of boys among them. They were moving in the same direction as her, but not one looked her way.

The road was close now, but she'd be safer as part of a crowd. The green fence was high and spiked at the top, but she managed to scale it without further damage to her hoody. The top had started out bottle green but was mottled with stains and soaked until it was dark enough to match the foliage of the trees. She raised the hood, stuck her hands deep in her pockets, and slouched along in the wake of a group of older children.

One boy lagged behind the others, his attention focused on his mobile phone. Despite the rain, he'd taken his jersey off and draped it over the top of his kit bag, leaving him wearing just his team T-shirt.

Caro lengthened her stride to catch up with him then slid the jersey off the rucksack, shrugging herself into it in one smooth movement. She mimicked his way of walking as she tagged onto the group in front of him.

They turned left out of the school gates, so she stuck with them. A mobile phone would have been a good prop right now, in case any of the teenagers turned around and noticed an older woman behind them wearing a GAA jersey, but she'd have to hope that wouldn't happen. At least the hoodie mostly obscured her face as well as hiding her hair.

Caro was beginning to shiver. If only they'd walk a little faster. These children had all the time in the world. Didn't they know she needed to cover ground quickly? As she walked, she noticed something stuck in the sleeve of the jumper. She pulled it out and inspected the contents of the card wallet. She'd struck lucky. He had a prepaid credit card and a Translink iLink card.

A police car approached slowly on the opposite side of the road, two uniformed officers in the front scanning the pavements. Caro held her hands up as if she was holding a phone and pretended to be fascinated by it. It was hard not to stare at the car or look back after it had passed to see if it was turning around. She needed to trust her instincts now and keep going.

She didn't know this part of Belfast, but there were murals in Irish depicting images of hunger strikers, so she guessed she must be in a nationalist part of the city. Maybe that was for the best — her Irish was pretty good, and after years in Dublin she'd long since lost her South African accent and was able to pass as a local there. The accent was different here, sure, but a visitor from Dublin wouldn't be seen as unusual.

A couple of the kids in front of her climbed into black taxis, joining others inside. One taxi had a pram jammed in its boot, so the boot wouldn't close over it, and all the taxis seemed crowded, as if the local folk preferred to use the taxis like buses, getting on and off whenever they reached their destination.

The crowd in front had thinned to a handful, and the last few turned left into the car park of a biggish shopping centre. That wouldn't do at all, because there'd be CCTV everywhere. So far, she was pretty sure she'd been invisible to the cameras, just one footballer among many, but on her own, she'd stand out like a sore thumb.

Then, as she was dithering at the entrance to the shopping centre, a pink bus pulled up alongside her. She hadn't seen the destination, but anywhere away from here had to be good. The bus would have CCTV too, but she kept her hood tugged forward to hide her face from above, and swiped the iLink card. She had a handful of change ready in case it didn't work, but the machine beeped and lit up green.

The driver didn't ask her where she was bound, didn't even seem to look at her at all as she sank into the first vacant seat and sat with her head down trying to appear bored and half asleep while she remained watchful.

Another police car passed, going the same way as the bus this time, but she was on the left-hand side, so it would be hard to see her as the car overtook. Up ahead she could see a bridge with cars whizzing across it. That would be the motorway she'd driven down, what felt like hours ago.

The bus edged far too slowly beneath the bridge and onto another road that went off at right angles to the motorway. Caro risked a look out of the windows, to see if there were any landmarks she recognised. Nothing. Then, after what felt like hours, a sign loomed out of the watery sunlight: Balmoral Station in blue and white, with a stylised image of a train.

As soon as the bus cleared the junction, she got up and walked forward. The surly driver seemed to take the hint and pulled over at the next bus stop. She got out without looking back and walked the way they'd come, crossing at the traffic lights. The last thing her pursuers would expect was for her to take public transport.

She walked up the ramp to the Belfast-bound platform, assuming her travel card might not take her very far in the other direction, and waited for the next train alongside groups of schoolchildren and women with toddlers and prams.

Only when she was seated on the train with no one beside her and no one showing any interest in the fact that a middle-aged woman, wet and bedraggled, was wearing a football jersey, did she take a deep breath and begin to relax. Once she was in the city, she could pick up a change of clothes and alter her appearance. Then, when she was sure she was safe, she could make a last phone call to set her trap.

She'd spent her whole life under Pieter van Rooyen's control, too scared to defy him or even defend herself, never mind her mother. And then Pieter had become a means to an end for her. He'd been the catalyst, the reason she'd begun to train and attend martial arts classes even before he gave her the clue about her natural father. She'd joined a firing range, managing to keep it secret from everyone by using one of her fake IDs; London was an easy place to pick up such items if you were good at tech, and she'd always been very good at tech.

Yes, Pieter had been useful, even though he'd probably never know it. He'd given her the initial clues she needed to track down the man who'd raped her mother, and his price had been the men she'd killed first in India, travelling under a fake passport, and later in other parts of the world.

If her grandparents had still been alive, she'd have hunted them down too, for forcing Grace out of her own home and driving her into Pieter's open arms. If her mother had stayed on the farm, she'd have died in the fire and then she, Caro, would never have had to endure a lifetime of suffering.

Pieter had thought she was his pawn when he sent her to hunt down the men who'd worked with Harold Cavendish. He'd thought she had no idea what his real agenda was, but she had. When she'd hacked into his company's databases, she'd followed the money, just the same way she did now in her day job. She'd traced the source of the destruction that had been wreaked on his wealth. It had been Cavendish and his friends who'd sabotaged his ships' navigation systems. They'd set fire to his factories, and they and their sleazy politician friends had been behind the rumours of illegal activities that had put the authorities on Pieter's trail.

But she'd killed them for him happily enough. Not the first one: that had been down to one of Pieter's hirelings, but she'd known all about it, read it in the computer systems that her stepfather had been so certain were secure. He'd thought he was so clever, spinning her tales, reasons the men needed to die. It hadn't taken him long to work out that she hated violence to women, and he'd used that to fire her up, to send her off like an avenging angel after his enemies.

It had been child's play to pretend she'd fallen for his lies. He probably thought he'd trained up a pretty little weapon he could use whenever he wanted, but he was the one being played. The other killings had all been training, as far as Caro was concerned. Now it was time for the real challenge.

She'd been someone else's chess piece far too long, and it was time she played her own game. It had felt good, helping other women to escape from the same sticky web that she'd been unable to break, like her mother before her. It was time to end it, to take the battle to him. Put an end to his bullying existence. He'd trained her well, and now it was time to pit her wits against his. *Let's see who's clever now, shall we?*

CHAPTER 41

Ellie followed Aaron's gaze to the body bag, taking in his defeated posture, the despair in his eyes. "That's not Peter," she said flatly. "That woman killed a total stranger, Aaron, and I couldn't stop her." Hysteria was surging within her, and it was getting harder to maintain her carefully controlled calm.

"Peter's not dead?" There was stark disbelief in the question. He was as close to the edge as she.

"No. He's trapped, and the fire service are on their way to get him out, but he's alive and well." She turned him gently around to face the wreck of Peter's jeep. "Look."

A paramedic was in the back seat of the car, talking to the driver. She watched Aaron's face change, still not quite believing but with a sliver of hope in those grey eyes. He strode over to the car and peered through the driver's window. Then a broad grin broke out. He said something she didn't catch, but it was in a voice filled with relief and happiness.

A hand inside the car came up and made a rude gesture, and Aaron turned away, laughing. This was the time when hysteria might take hold of him, and if he lost control, what chance had she?

But she should have known him better. The old Aaron had returned — calm, competent, eager to get the job done.

He started throwing around orders with an authority that didn't quite fit with his youth, but no one argued. Within minutes, it seemed, a fire crew was on the scene, cutting Peter free from the wreckage.

Then a hand touched her arm, and she turned to see Asha behind her, a smile lurking in those dark eyes. "I'm glad he's okay," she said.

Ellie had always seen Asha as cool, self-contained, and a little bit distant, but there was no mistaking her warmth now. Ellie leaned into her, and Asha embraced her, holding her tight as a mother might with a child. A sob made its painful way up from deep inside her, and she buried her face in the tailored jacket, breathing in the scent of her skin that smelled faintly of peppermint.

It was over quickly. Slightly embarrassed, she eased herself back, head down, but Asha didn't seem to mind the tear-stains and suspicious silvery streak on the lapels of her jacket. She continued to steady Ellie with a gentle grip on her fore-arms while Ellie dug around in her pocket for a tissue and blew her nose.

"Sorry," she said. "I don't know what came over me." After all, she barely knew the elegant Indian woman.

"I do," Asha said softly. "He's safe now, and we're going to make sure he stays that way. Release of tension after a period of prolonged fear can be more draining than the fear itself. But it's all going to be okay now, I promise. Aaron's going to collect the kids soon and bring them home."

Ellie nodded, then raised her chin, anger beginning to rise in the wake of her weakness and embarrassment. "Do you know who this woman is? Why she's doing this to us?"

Asha sighed. "Yes, we do know who she is, and we know, or think we know, why she's doing this. Peter isn't the first man she's targeted, Ellie."

Comprehension swept over her. "The murder Aaron's been working on. Please tell me this isn't the same woman?" Shock began to take hold. She'd read of the murders in the newspapers. Of the brutality of the killings. And the bitch had had Peter in her sights. "But why Peter?"

Before Asha could answer, there came the screech of tortured metal as the fire service forced the driver's door from its hinges, revealing Peter sitting there as if he was perfectly relaxed — until she saw how pale he was, and the way his hands grasped the steering wheel.

She forgot Asha and ran over to her husband, but she was held back by Aaron.

"Sorry, Ellie, but it's not safe. Leave it to the professionals, okay? You can stay back here with me and watch, if you like."

The impact of the crash must have forced the engine backwards into the driver's footwell, because it looked as if Peter's feet were trapped beneath the dashboard.

"Is he injured?" Ellie asked.

"The paramedic says they won't really know until they get him out, but his vitals are all good, so he's not bleeding catastrophically or anything." He took a deep breath. "He says he can't feel his feet, but that doesn't necessarily mean anything at this stage."

The tension in Aaron's voice alerted her that all might not be as well as it seemed, but now she could actually see Peter, she was feeling a little better. She was so focused on the rescue operation that she didn't notice when Aaron and Asha both slipped away.

There was some cursing from Peter as the weight of the engine block shifted, then a flurry of activity that blocked her view completely. She edged closer in time to see him being lifted out, a neck brace pushing his chin up, and gently placed onto a solid board stretcher.

To her dismay, the paramedics started to tie him down with webbing straps. She pushed forwards to his side and took his hand, tears blurring her view of his face until she swiped them away. He was squinting up at her through broken glasses, and his skin was peppered with fine cuts and dried blood. He squeezed her fingers, but it was a weak movement, and then she was pushed aside again as people crowded around him, carrying the stretcher towards the back of an ambulance that stood nearby with open door.

"I'm going with him," she said breathlessly. When someone tried to stop her, she drew herself up, her fear for Peter giving her the courage to speak. "I'm his wife, and I'm travelling to the hospital with him."

Then they let her through, and a lovely, elderly paramedic helped her to a seat and handed her the seatbelt. Within moments, the ambulance was on the move, siren blaring out for the short journey to the Royal.

Peter's lips moved, but she couldn't hear what he said. The paramedic bent over him, and he repeated it. She turned to Ellie. "He says it's a good thing he crashed the car so close to a hospital."

* * *

Ellie was sent to a relative's room to twiddle her thumbs while Peter was assessed by the medical team. She tried hard to keep her thoughts positive, and even went as far as checking out the coffee-making facilities, but one glance inside the mugs set out for visitor use was enough to turn her stomach. Why couldn't they have disposable cups?

"Mrs Birch?" A young woman in scrubs was at the door, smiling at her. A lanyard hung around her neck, but Ellie couldn't read whether she was a doctor, nurse, or orderly. "You can come and be with your husband now."

"Is he going to be okay?"

"I'll let you speak to the doctor," she said, swiping her card to get them through a swing door and into a busy emergency ward labelled *Majors* where people in various states of undress lay on beds in curtained cubicles, some on stretcher beds in the main floor area, and a few in chairs. The place looked frantic, with staff moving quickly and professionally between patients.

Ellie searched for Peter, but it wasn't until the nurse drew back a curtain that she saw him, eyes closed, face pale against a white folded blanket that was doing the job of a pillow. Someone had removed his shoes and socks; his poor feet looked so vulnerable, swollen, and mottled with bruises.

"He's going down to X-ray in a minute," the nurse said.

As always in hospitals, it took forever for the doctors to decide that Peter had suffered no lasting effects from the accident. He'd be sore, and probably unable to bear weight on his legs for a while until the soft tissue damage to his lower extremities had healed. He wouldn't like that much, but he'd enjoy the pampering he'd get from her and the children, and at least he could dispense with the neck brace.

"You're getting home," she told him.

"Probably need my bed for someone else," he said in a weak attempt at humour. She laughed out of habit but suspected he was right. While they'd been in here, the ward had filled up with trolleys parked in every available corner, many with patients she assumed must be from the same pile-up they had been in. And if this was just Majors, what were the other parts of A&E like?

By the time they'd received the blue plastic bag with Peter's medicines in it, it was dark outside. As she followed the orderly pushing Peter's wheelchair along the corridors, Ellie wondered how they were to get home, but when they reached the main foyer and she took over pushing his chair, she saw a familiar lanky figure leaning against the wall. Aaron pushed himself upright, lines of fatigue around his eyes.

"Hey, Pete. Making Ellie do all the work as usual?"

Peter laughed. "She has such an easy time of it, it'll do her good to slave over me for a change."

She gave him a push at the back of his head, and he turned to look up at her, a smile in his eyes. How had they ever argued? They'd always been so close.

Aaron was quiet on the drive back to Lisburn, which she was grateful for because exhaustion was dragging at her.

She just wanted to see her children again, and kick off her shoes, letting the fear melt away in the comfort of familiar surroundings.

As he turned into the quiet cul de sac, she strained her eyes to see their house. The lights were on, and Simon must have been watching out for them because the door was flung open before they reached it. The aroma of something warm and savoury wafted from inside as she hugged her son, then Lizzie, who had climbed onto Peter's knee in the front of Aaron's car.

She helped Aaron unfold the wheelchair, and between them they helped Peter into it while Simon and Lizzie watched with wide eyes.

"Who's been looking after them?" she asked in a low voice. Earlier, when she'd been frantic with worry, Aaron had just said that he'd organised someone to stay with them for as long as needed. Still anxiously waiting to hear about Peter's X-rays, she hadn't asked who.

An unfamiliar voice sang out from the kitchen. "Come on in and eat this brown stew before it gets cold. We've been doing cookery school, haven't we, kids?"

Aaron laughed aloud. "I hope you've cooked enough for me too, Lonnie! I'm starving." Then, as an aside to Ellie, "Don't be fooled by Sergeant Jacob's easy-going nature; there's no one I'd trust more to protect you and the children."

An elderly police officer appeared from the kitchen, one of Ellie's aprons struggling to meet around her ample middle section, and a tea towel slung over her shoulder.

Simon took Ellie's hand and started to drag her into the house. "Yes, Mummy. Come and see what we've been making. It's—" he took a deep breath —"traditional Jamaican food."

The kitchen looked as if a bomb had hit it, with so many used bowls and pans stacked by the sink that she was sure Lonnie had used up her entire stock of cooking implements. On the hotplate, something bubbled and spat, leaving reddish brown stains all over her pristine range. She nosed inside to see chunks of skin-on chicken floating around in a sea of spicy

276

vegetables and sauce. If Lonnie thought she'd get Lizzie to eat this, she'd be sorely disappointed. Her little drama queen was dedicated to her bland diet.

But when they all sat down at the table, Peter still in his wheelchair, both children wolfed down the spicy food, making noises of appreciation.

Ellie met Peter's eye across the table. He winked and mouthed something that looked a bit like "*magic*".

CHAPTER 42

Aaron picked at his food. He'd spent a fruitless afternoon trying to work out where the hell Caroline van Rooyen had disappeared to. Even Nic had failed to find any sign of her on CCTV, and the helicopter had been redeployed to cover an armed robbery at the other end of the country.

He was drained, and had no idea where to go next with this awful case. But then he caught a glimpse of Ellie's face as she exchanged a wink with Peter across the table. At least today hadn't been a total write-off. His brother was alive, and he'd stay that way if Aaron had anything to do with it. A patrol car was stationed outside the house, and the two officers in it had instructions to walk around the place inspecting doors and windows at random times throughout the night.

Simon and Lizzie were proudly carrying through the dessert they'd made, something with sweet pudding rice and nutmeg that reminded him of school dinners. He needn't have worried: Lonnie hadn't failed them. It was melt-in-the-mouth delicious.

He swallowed the first spoonful and was preparing to take another when his phone vibrated on the table, where he'd placed it so he wouldn't miss a call.

He apologised and went through to the dining room to take the call. "Asha. Any news?"

"Not a trace, but the ACC has signed off on a publicity campaign, blitzing all forms of media and social media. With her face in every newspaper, on every TV screen and social media page, surely someone will be able to give us a lead."

Aaron tried to sound enthusiastic, but the campaign would probably just turn up the usual crackpots with sightings of the woman anywhere between here and Timbuktu. Still, it was worth a shot.

"How are your family coping?" she asked. "I heard that Peter's going to be okay, just off his feet for a while. Is Ellie all right? And the children?"

"Lonnie's had the kids all afternoon, so they're fine. I'm not sure about Ellie. She's the sort to blame herself, and she bottles up her emotions. But they seem to be managing fine so far."

"Good. Stay with them, Aaron. This case has been taken out of our hands now anyway, but even if it hadn't, you're better there with your family than racing around the country and worrying about them."

"You're the best, Asha. You know that, right?"

She laughed, then her voice went serious again. "We've identified the murdered man, by the way. He was over here from Eastern Europe, representing his company, a bachelor with no brothers or sisters, no children, and his only living parent is in a nursing home with severe dementia."

Aaron's shoulders sagged. It weighed heavily on him, that this man had died trying to help Peter. He wasn't sure how much Peter knew about the events that had unfolded while he was trapped, but Ellie had been right there, trying to tackle a knife-wielding murderer with her bare hands. He'd try to have a quiet word with her as soon as he could.

"Thank you, Ash. I wonder if we should move Peter, Ellie, and the kids to a safehouse. As soon as this goes live, Caroline van Rooyen will realise she's killed the wrong man, and she might just try to come back and finish the job."

279

"We've got that covered. The station in Lisburn is all over it, and they're not alone. Every officer in the province wants to be the one to capture her. She made it personal when she went after your brother."

Aaron stayed in the spare room that night, after he'd brought Lonnie up to date with the investigation so far. She was a great listener, was Sergeant Jacob. Once she'd gone home, accepting a lift from a patrol car that was finishing a shift, he lay staring at the ceiling.

He tried to imagine what he'd do if he was on the run, wanted all over Northern Ireland. She might steal another car or bike, if the helmet they'd found was any clue. Then she could be over the border and away before they found a trace of her.

Caroline van Rooyen was a clever woman, but she'd started to make mistakes. Attacking Peter in full view of the public, under the camera of a police helicopter, had been rash and stupid, yet still she'd escaped. Could they count on her making another error of judgement that would allow them to get close to her?

He finally drifted into a restless sleep just before dawn, and was woken shortly after by the sound of his niece and nephew trying not to wake him.

He yawned, stretched, and dragged his numb body out of bed, putting on yesterday's dank clothes with their sweat stains and creases. He knew from previous stays at his brother's house over the holidays that there was no point in trying to access the bathroom while Simon and Lizzie were on the prowl. Privacy was not a word in Simon's vocabulary, and the lock on the bathroom door could be turned from the outside with a coin.

Ellie was making coffee and toast. Her hair was pulled back into a severe ponytail that left her cheeks looking sharp and drawn. The purple bags beneath her eyes mirrored his own.

She brightened when he appeared and poured a mug for him. "Sleep okay?"

"Yes," he lied, taking a sip of the rich, strong stuff. "You?"

"Like the dead." They stared at each other for a moment, deadpan, then Ellie gave a brittle laugh. "How on earth do you ever sleep after a day like yesterday? Seriously, Aaron. You

280

have no right to look as young as you do, if that's an example of a typical working day for you."

He shook his head ruefully. "That was not a typical day by anyone's standards. How's Peter this morning?"

"Sleeping like a baby," she said, and they both laughed this time. Then she sobered. "Where do we go from here?"

He blew out a breath. "Honestly? I don't know. Last time I checked, they'd found no sign of the woman, but Asha and the ACC have designed a PR campaign to try to flush her out. We've just got to hope that it works."

"Will she come back here?" Ellie asked in a small voice.

"She might try, but if she does, we'll catch her before she can get anywhere near you."

Aaron gulped down the rest of his coffee, snagged a slice of toast from the toaster as it popped, and started for the door. "There's a patrol outside, and they're going to do checks of the place at random intervals. If you're worried about anything at all, you have my mobile number." He gave her a brief hug, then left, scattering crumbs down his front.

He was halfway to Ballymena when his mobile went off.

"Hi, Ash. Any news?"

"The campaign is live. It's on breakfast TV, Radio Ulster, Cool FM, and BBC NI are putting up an article online. We've flooded social media too. Most forces have something on their Facebook, and it's all across X, Bluesky, and Instagram. We're already getting calls, apparently."

"What about down south?"

"The ACC is working on it, but there's a bulletin out for her arrest, and they're cooperating with us so far."

Aaron tried to imagine the tiny incident room in Ballymena handling thousands of calls, and failed. "Who's manning the phones?"

"HQ have a team on it," she said. "We're getting copied into anything that sounds promising, but so far it's just the usual smattering of crazies."

Aaron glanced at his satnav. "I'll be with you in about twenty minutes. What's the mood like there?"

"Furious," Asha said. "Everyone's angry that she got so close to Peter in the first place, and then that she got away. There's a strong determination to catch her here."

"Good," he said, and hung up.

The incident room was buzzing with energy and noise. Clearly something had happened just before he got here, because no one even noticed his arrival.

Nic's voice floated above the chatter. "I think he sounds genuine. He's certainly got the accent."

Aaron pushed through to where everyone crowded around Nic. "What have you got?"

Asha answered. "A credible sighting from someone who claims to know her."

"Work colleague?"

Asha shook her head. "No. Someone who says he knew her in South Africa. A family friend, apparently."

"Let's see what's been put out there," Aaron said. Nic opened the BBC local news page to show the photograph of Caroline van Rooyen from her personnel files in Dublin. As she scrolled down the page, there was another image of her from her university days in England. She hadn't changed that much apart from the hair colour, and both photos showed her serious expression and guarded eyes.

"This is the transcript of the phone call," Asha said, handing him a printout. "You can listen as well, if you like?"

He nodded and Nic hit play.

A gravelly male voice rang out clearly.

"I hear you're looking for Caro van Rooyen." The thick South African accent was unmistakeable.

The operator was quick-thinking enough not to show surprise at the contraction of the first name. "That's right, sir. Do you have any recent information that might lead us to her?"

The caller chuckled, and Aaron found himself clenching his fists. It wasn't a pleasant voice. "I saw her early this morning, and I know where she's heading to. Is that sufficient?"

"If your information leads directly to Ms van Rooyen, sir, there is a reward available." That hadn't been what the caller had asked, but perhaps the operator was hearing what he expected to hear.

"Check ANPR cameras on the N7 heading south out of Dublin at around six or seven this morning. You're looking for a motorcycle that will probably be on your register of stolen vehicles. She was next to me at a red traffic light, and I recognised her when she lifted her visor. I saw her face quite clearly."

"We can certainly look into those cameras, sir. And did you say you know where she's heading?"

There was a pause as if the caller had forgotten he'd made that claim and was now trying to think what to say.

"I believe she might be heading towards the house of a distant cousin on her mother's side. The name of the cousin is Sophia Craig and she lives just outside a town called Adair, south-west of Limerick, I believe, but I don't know the exact address. I'm sure you can find it for yourselves."

"Thank you, sir. Can I ask how you know Ms van Rooyen?"

"Certainly, my boy. I knew her when she was a child in South Africa. I used to be a friend of the family, and I recognised her instantly from the photos you've been putting up everywhere."

"He did well to recognise her when she was wearing a motorcycle helmet," Aaron muttered.

The operator must have been thinking the same thing. "How certain are you, sir, that the woman you saw on the motorcycle was Caroline van Rooyen?"

"One hundred per cent," came the reply. "Absolutely certain. I saw her turn into a service station a couple of hours later, and she took the helmet off. No mistaking that hair."

The caller ended the call shortly after that without giving his name. "Who does the phone belong to?" Aaron asked.

"Unregistered pay-as-you-go," Dave said glumly. "Burner phone. And it was switched off immediately after this call."

"Which cell towers did it bounce off?"

"Only the one, putting him south of Dublin. At least he seems to have been where he says he was," Nic said. "But he could still just be a crackpot caller."

"I don't know. He called her Caro, not Caroline. That sounds like someone who knew her well." Asha was biting the end of a biro, not something he'd seen her do before.

"If he's a family friend," Chris said, "why's he so keen to shop her?"

"The PR campaign made it clear she's wanted for several murders, and that she's dangerous and not to be approached. Wouldn't that be enough for any good citizen to call the helpline?" Asha seemed sure that the call had been genuine.

"We need the CCTV from the service station," Aaron said. "And that ANPR if we can. Maybe we can get the car registration of the caller as well. I'm a bit suspicious, the way he turns up all pat, happening to know her well, recognising her, knowing about her cousin. Far too neat. Let's see if we can either confirm or discard his evidence as soon as possible. Any other promising leads?"

"A couple, and we're following them up, but this one seemed the most promising so far to me," Asha said. "We've put in urgent requests already for the camera footage. The ACC is leaning on the Garda to help us out, and they're complying. I got the impression that they're a bit sickened that one of their own has turned out to be a serial killer working under a false identity."

"They've just sent up the CCTV for the Apple Green service station on the M7," Nic said. Aaron pulled up a chair and watched as she skimmed through the different camera views. Some were inside the building, but several were of the car park.

"ANPR in Dublin puts the bike there at just after six thirty," Chris said. "The car that's stopped next to the bike at the lights has a UK number plate and tinted windows, so I wonder if that's the vehicle our tipster was in. I'll try to trace it. It's a big, fancy white jeep."

Nic switched to a map and put in the distances. "That would put her at the Apple Green services maybe an hour and a half, two hours later, say eight-ish?" She selected the timestamp for the car park footage and set it playing. "There!" A powerful motorbike drove slowly into view. The rider was slightly built, the features completely disguised by the helmet, and the camera was above and behind. The bike drove around to the lorry park, disappearing behind a big articulated truck that didn't look as if it'd be going anywhere soon, judging by the closed blinds.

"That's a fella, isn't it, not a woman?" Dave said, watching the biker's long, masculine stride as they approached the building.

Nic shrugged. "Could be either. I'll follow them inside." Nic swapped cameras. The tall figure walked up to the coffee bar, keeping the helmet on, and ordered a drink, which they took to a table out of sight of the camera. Nic flicked between views, but the biker had found the perfect spot, right in a dead zone.

The next time they saw the figure, they were leaving the building. They dumped something in a bin by the door, then left in a hurry.

"What was that?" Aaron asked. "It looked like a briefcase, or maybe a laptop."

"I'll get the Garda to check it out," Asha said, and disappeared to make the call.

The figure disappeared around the side of the truck, and they waited for the bike to reappear, but it didn't. The occasional car drove around the parked trucks but no motorbikes.

"I've got an owner for the white jeep," Chris said. "It's registered to a company: South Africa Holdings. That explains the caller's accent."

"Hang on. I recognise the name of that company. Give me a minute . . ." He called across to Nic. "South Africa Holdings, Nic. Didn't you mention that name earlier?"

She typed fast, then sucked in a breath. "Yes. It belongs to Pieter van Rooyen."

285

"Shit!" Aaron tried to work through the repercussions. "So we have Caroline's stepfather sending in tips to track her down, yet she killed his enemies for him? What's going on?"

"I don't like it," Asha said. "Something's not right. The first killings could easily have been done on van Rooyen's orders, but the last one, and the attack on Peter? They don't match at all."

"Maybe she's gone off script," Dave said. He'd been so quiet Aaron had almost forgotten he was there. "When she was following her stepdaddy's orders, she was probably under his protection to a degree, but now she's freelancing, isn't she? Killing people for her own reasons and hitting the headlines. Making mistakes too. I reckon she's lost the plot."

"And Pieter's trying to stop her before she goes too far?" It didn't seem right. Why would Pieter care what she did, as long as he wasn't caught up in it?

What if he'd manipulated his daughter to kill his enemies for him? It might seem like twisted logic to a man like him: trick her into killing her father's friends so Cavendish would see his own death getting closer. It would ruin his life, force him into hiding, then came the perfect form of revenge: his own child wielding the knife that killed him.

But now she'd gone off on her own killing spree? She was nothing but a liability.

"We need to get someone out there fast," Aaron said.

CHAPTER 43

"You stopped calling me," Pieter said. The sound of that harsh voice still brought the hackles up on the back of her neck, even after all these years. "You know I don't like it when you go quiet on me, Caro."

Yes, she knew. Way back when she'd been young and optimistic, she'd really believed she might have a chance of escape, a way to leave her old life behind. She'd thought she'd managed it, once, but it had all been an illusion. You didn't escape from a man like him.

"Yes, Pappie. I'm sorry. Things have been busy. At work, you know?"

Silence. He would have been having her watched, for sure. She hoped his spies had reported back to him, showing him what she was capable of. What he'd turned her into. If only he'd respected her, treated her as an adult, not as a wayward child in need of discipline and guidance.

"Where are you?" he asked. "I want you to come home, now you've done what you set out to do. There's a place for you, here in the company, if you want it."

What as? An assassin? That was about the only job she was really qualified for. That or a cybersecurity adviser, but he already had an army of those, ever since his companies had been hacked.

"What sort of job?" she asked, feigning interest.

"One you're trained for," he said.

"You really want me back in South Africa? You can make all the bad things go away?" She hated the whine in her voice.

He laughed without humour. "Yes, I can make it all go away. A clean slate." Of course he could. He probably had the government in his pocket.

She allowed hope to sound in her voice, tinged with a little wistfulness. "I'd like to come home, Pappie." She glanced at the laptop screen. She needed to keep him talking for another few seconds for the trace to finish. He'd be tracing her call as well, no doubt, but she knew her skills to be exceptional, and she believed she could win that race. "When do you think I could travel? Soon?"

"Yes, Caro. Soon."

Her laptop pinged quietly. Got him. "I've gotta go now, Pappie. I'll call again, I promise." She ended the call, then took out the SIM card and battery from the burner phone. She slid the laptop into her backpack and slung it over her shoulders before climbing back on the motorbike. By the time he'd worked out where she'd called from, she'd be at the other end of the country, leaving phone, battery, and card scattered along the route.

As soon as she'd put enough miles behind her to feel safe, she pulled over at an Apple Green service station and went inside, keeping her helmet on. She ordered a coffee, paying with cash, then found a quiet seat in a booth that wasn't overlooked by any CCTV before removing the helmet. The laptop still showed the trace, so she clicked on the map icon as she sipped the coffee.

She choked, spluttering droplets of coffee over her laptop. Her stepfather's phone had pinged cell towers in the centre of Dublin.

Bastard! He'd known exactly where she was. Might even have been watching her, laughing at her from some safe vantage point. He'd been manipulating her again and she'd allowed her hatred to blind her. What a fool she'd been. She was as certain as she could be that no one had followed her here, but now doubt ran ice-cold fingers along her spine. He was rich enough to employ a dozen drivers in a dozen vehicles. She would never have been able to spot them all.

She stood up quickly and replaced the helmet, head whirling. Where could she run that he couldn't follow? Heart pounding, she made her way back outside, dumping the laptop in the green, frog-shaped trash can at the door on her way, making sure it slid well down out of sight.

She'd parked the bike away from the building, which she regretted now, skin crawling with fear as she crossed the open space where any one of the parked cars could hold an enemy.

Because Pieter van Rooyen would have no use for her now. All his talk about bringing her home had been as false as her interest in returning.

There was the bike, exactly where she'd left it. She quickened her pace, eyes roving the area, searching for danger, but still the blow took her by surprise when it came.

She'd been punched in the gut before, by Pieter, and that's what she thought had happened until the second blow came, driven upwards through her diaphragm and into her lungs.

She gasped, and her legs began to fail her. An arm came around her waist, supporting her, keeping her moving towards the bike. Her feet dragged, refusing to respond to commands from her brain, but she was borne inexorably forwards.

A white Range Rover slowed alongside them, and her captor swung her around to face it. The rear window opened. Pieter van Rooyen leaned forward, his eyes travelling up and down her body, naked contempt in his eyes.

"You really should have shown some restraint, Caro my dear," he said, as if he were referring to an excessive appetite for ice cream or chocolate, not murder. "You have become careless, and I can't have that. What if the trail were to lead to me?"

She tried to answer, to tell him how he'd ruined her life and turned her into a monster, but instead of words, scarlet blood frothed from her lips, spattering the pristine white paintwork. Her stepfather drew back in disgust.

"Take her away. Make sure there's nothing to identify her, then get rid of the body," he said. "She can burn in hell with her whore of a mother."

Somewhere nearby, children laughed, and adults answered with impatient voices. This was a public place. Why was no one intervening? Couldn't they see she was in trouble?

As the Range Rover pulled away, she was bundled into the back of a small box truck that had been partially hidden behind it. Strong arms pushed her down onto the hard metal floor then let her go. She writhed, trying to bounce to her feet, but the floor was slick with her blood and her strength was failing. Then the door slammed, leaving her in the dim light from a stained translucent roof. There was a plastic sheet over the floor and taped up to cover the walls and ceiling. This was no ordinary truck: it was a death space, kitted out to make sure she left no forensic traces behind.

Well, she could at least make sure that plan failed. She tried to get hold of a fold of the plastic sheet, but it was thick and slippery, and she couldn't get a grip to tear it. She used her teeth, shoving her face into the corner where the plastic curved upwards, leaving a void behind where the van wall met the floor at a right-angle.

She still couldn't get a grip. Her teeth slid across the sheeting, and she was bleeding out. The edges of her vision blurred. Then the engine started, and the truck moved off, sending her skidding across the floor as it made a sharp turn.

Spread-eagled on the cold, hard floor, she stared up at the roof. The plastic sheeting billowed like clouds in a grey sky. If she tried hard enough, maybe she could imagine she was lying in an open field, or on top of the hill above her father's cottage, listening to skylarks.

There they were, the sweet, high notes of their song all around her.

No. That was her own breath whistling, high-pitched as her lungs filled with blood. It was the last sound she heard.

CHAPTER 44

The incident room was quiet, but it was the silence of the calm before the storm. Aaron beat a rhythm on his desk with restless fingers, waiting for the call, but when it came, he jumped.

"Detective Sergeant Birch?" The accent was from the south of Ireland.

"Have you found her?"

"No, sir. The bike is here, and we've recovered a laptop from the bin, but it's heavily encrypted so it'll need an expert to get into the files. We're looking at the CCTV footage now, but there's nothing useful yet."

"Look for a white four-wheel drive with English plates," he offered, giving the licence number. "We think it might belong to the man behind all this."

"Wait a moment, sir." A hand came over the microphone and Aaron hissed in frustration. "Sorry. Apparently they've found bloodstains on the ground near the bike. We have forensic techs working the scene now."

Another muffled interlude.

"We have a witness that claims to have seen a woman in motorcycle leathers talking to someone in a white jeep. We're asking around in case anyone has any dashcam footage, because the blood looks fresh. I'll get back to you if we find anything else."

He ended the call, and Aaron met Asha's eyes across the small office. He shook his head. "Bloodstains near the bike."

She pulled a face. "You think we were too late?"

"I need to know for sure," he said.

The next call was from a more senior officer.

"We've confirmed the white car, a Range Rover, but it's disappeared after the last ANPR camera. A witness claims there was blood spatter on the driver's side door, but I'm not sure how reliable he is. It was a sleepy truck driver who was woken by voices below his window. He said there was a middle-aged white man in the car, and he was chatting to a couple, a man with his arm around the waist of a woman who looked drunk. He didn't notice what happened to the woman after the white car drove off, but we're still looking."

It was almost an hour before the final call.

"We got CCTV footage of a white box truck leaving the services at around the right time, and a mobile unit pulled it over as it left the main road, heading towards the coast. When they tried to apprehend the driver, he put a gun in his mouth and pulled the trigger before our officers realised what he intended. Nothing on the body to tell us who he was, which is suspicious in itself—"

Aaron fought for control. "Was there anyone else in the truck?"

"No. The driver was on his own." Aaron gripped the phone until his knuckles ached. "No sign of the woman we're looking for, then?"

"Well, I was just getting to that. We had to wait for the fire service to come along with bolt cutters, but we finally got the back door open."

Would the blasted man never come to the point?

"And in the back of the truck, we found the body of a woman in motorcycle leathers. She's lying in a pool of her own blood, but we haven't been able to discover the cause of her injuries yet."

Aaron tried to reply, but the words wouldn't come. Asha took the receiver from him.

"This is Detective Inspector Harvey. Is the woman still alive?"

"No, ma'am. No signs of life. Looks as if she bled out."

The next thing Aaron was aware of was Asha's arms around him, holding him tight and rocking him.

"It's over, Aaron. She's gone. Peter's safe now."

end the next time he . . .

EPILOGUE

Aaron was struggling to keep his eyes open on the long drive
back to his flat from Ballymena. Sergeant McBride had
returned to work after her maternity leave, and he'd spent the
day bringing her up to speed on both their ongoing cases of
theft from farms and the big murder case she'd been disappointed to miss out on.

The team had given him a great send off, with cake and
alcohol-free Guinness, overwhelming him with their kindness. The early days of trying to bring them together into a
functional unit seemed a long time ago now, and part of him
wished he could have stayed in the grey, utilitarian station that
had seemed so depressing at first.

And where next? No doubt the powers that be would find
another placement for him. He just hoped it wouldn't be so
far out in the sticks next time.

A traffic light at a crossing ahead stopped him, but he
didn't care —was in no rush to go home to the empty flat.
Dave Stanley's trademark bald patch reflecting the red light
caught his eye, and Aaron realised he wasn't alone. The old vet,
Gerren Penrose, with Jack trotting along at his heels, crossed
the road with him, Dave laughing at something Penrose said.

He opened the door to the pub, the Fairhill Bar, and waited for the old man to pass through first. He even bent to rub the collie's ears as the dog followed his new master inside.

Aaron shook his head, smiling. Who'd have thought chip-on-the-shoulder Dave would end up best mates with the man he'd had pegged as a brutal murderer when this all began?

An impatient toot of the horn from the car behind sent him forward with a jerk as he realised the lights had changed.

He left the town behind, easing himself deeper into the sports seat of the Golf as the motorway stretched out in front of him. The excellent sound system blasted out his favourite Celtic rock, and the stresses and strains of the day faded as he focused his mind on driving at speed.

A phone call cut through the strains of Thin Lizzie's *Whiskey in the Jar*, and he tapped the display to accept when he recognised Asha's number.

"On your way home?"

"Yeah. Are you still at the station?" By which he meant her home station of Bangor.

"Hmm. You're on speaker, by the way. I've got Superintendent Sewell here, and he has some news for you."

Oh great, what next?

The older man's voice was a bit too loud, as if he felt he had to shout to be heard over the distance. "Got a new posting for you, Aaron."

"Oh?" His fingers tightened on the steering wheel. Was it significant that this was coming from Asha's boss, or had he just been given the job because he'd worked with Aaron before.

"Tom Casey's been on sick leave, as you know, since that boatyard fiasco, and he's been enjoying time with his grand-kids, so his wife has persuaded him to retire. If you'd like the post, it's yours. I've already cleared it with the bigwigs."

He let out a breath and only just resisted the urge to punch the steering wheel. A post in Bangor, with Asha again and the old crowd. It took a moment to calm himself. "That would be really good, sir. Thank you. When do I start?"

"I tried to dissuade him," Asha said, "but for some reason he thinks you're an okay sergeant despite your inexperience." The subtext was clear: she'd fought for him to be offered the position. He'd take her out for a slap-up meal at the weekend, to say thank you.

The rest of the drive back to his apartment in Belfast seemed shorter than usual. The traffic flowed out of his way and he slotted neatly between lanes as he reached the edge of the city. There was even a parking space available close to the building he lived in with Marmaduke. Life was definitely being kind to him today.

That ended when he reached his door. It was open a tiny gap, and he was always thorough about security, like everyone in the PSNI. He wished he still carried a side arm, but he kept a cricket bat just inside the front door. That would have to do.

The door swung silently, and he peered through the gap at the hinge side. The hallway was in darkness, but a thin strip of light showed beneath the door into the sitting room. His hand closed around the handle of the cricket bat, its weight reassuring, and he trod silently forward.

Heart hammering, he gathered himself to shoulder-barge the inner door, but before he had time to react, it was opened from the inside and soft music flooded out.

"I thought I heard a car door slam," Faith said. She glanced down at the bat in his hands and a dimpled smile broke out on her face. "Bit late for a game of cricket, isn't it?"

THE END

ACKNOWLEDGEMENTS

I'd like to thank my wonderful early readers, especially Fraser Buchanan, Anne McMaster and Noreen Jeffers. I'd also like to say a huge thank you to all the indie bookstores that stock our books, providing such a personal service to both readers and writers, especially Lesley at Bridge Books, Dromore, and Jo and Chris at The Secret Bookshelf in Carrickfergus.

A huge thank you must go to the team at Joffe Books. You've all been incredible, especially my managing editor, Laura, who had to hit the ground running when she recently took over my books from Emma.

Last but far from least, thank you to all my readers, especially those who have gone to the trouble to leave reviews or to message me, telling me how much they enjoy my books and gently nagging for the next one in the series. Authors are delicate creatures, easily losing confidence in their own abilities, and these words of encouragement are wonderfully reassuring when a writer is feeling a bit down, and beginning to think that their writing is rubbish. We really do thrive on praise and flattery!

THE JOFFE BOOKS STORY

We began in 2014 when Jasper agreed to publish his mum's much-rejected romance novel and it became a bestseller.

Since then we've grown into the largest independent publisher in the UK. We're extremely proud to publish some of the very best writers in the world, including Joy Ellis, Faith Martin, Caro Ramsay, Helen Forrester, Simon Brett and Robert Goddard. Everyone at Joffe Books loves reading and we never forget that it all begins with the magic of an author telling a story.

We are proud to publish talented first-time authors, as well as established writers whose books we love introducing to a new generation of readers.

We won Trade Publisher of the Year at the Independent Publishing Awards in 2023. We have been shortlisted for Independent Publisher of the Year at the British Book Awards for the last four years, and were shortlisted for the Diversity and Inclusivity Award at the 2022 Independent Publishing Awards. In 2023 we were shortlisted for Publisher of the Year at the RNA Industry Awards.

We built this company with your help, and we love to hear from you, so please email us about absolutely anything bookish at feedback@joffebooks.com

If you want to receive free books every Friday and hear about all our new releases, join our mailing list: www.joffebooks. com/contact

And when you tell your friends about us, just remember: it's pronounced Joffe as in coffee or toffee!